MW01516521

Butler, Till the Final Bell

Michael Anthony

MCW

MACMILLAN CARIBBEAN WRITERS

MACMILLAN
CARIBBEAN

Macmillan Education
Between Towns Road, Oxford, OX4 3PP
A division of Macmillan Publishers Limited
Companies and representatives throughout the world

www.macmillan-caribbean.com

ISBN 1 4050 2269 8

Text © Michael Anthony 2004
Design and illustration © Macmillan Publishers Limited 2004

First published 2004

All rights reserved; no part of this publication may be
reproduced, stored in a retrieval system, transmitted in any
form or by any means, electronic, mechanical, photocopying,
recording, or otherwise, without the prior written permission
of the publishers.

Typeset by EXPO Holdings, Malaysia
Cover design by Gary Fielder at AC Design
Cover illustration by Angela Staples

Printed and bound in Malaysia

2008 2007 2006 2005 2004
10 9 8 7 6 5 4 3 2 1

Series Preface

Michael Anthony's early novels have been enjoyed by generations of readers. *Butler, Till the Final Bell* is a major work from a matured writer, and brings to life a major figure from the past. Set against a backdrop of Trinidad's oilfield riots of the thirties, and rooted firmly in historical fact, this fictitious recreation of Uriah Butler's fight for better conditions for his fellow workers is seen through the eyes of a young couple. Jonas, a hotheaded amateur boxer, and his wife Elsie, are loyal supporters of Butler. With help from such unlikely sources as a prominent lawyer, an obeah woman and even the Governor of the island, the trio manage to outwit the plots of the oilfield management, the oil cartel and the police, while the workers' movement builds to follow Butler into strike action.

The Macmillan Caribbean Writers Series (MCW) is an exciting new collection of fine Caribbean writing which treats the broad range of the Caribbean experience. As well as novels and short stories the series includes poetry anthologies and collections of plays particularly suitable for Arts and Drama Festivals. There are also works of non-fiction such as an eye-witness account of life under the volatile Soufriere volcano, and another of the removal of an entire village to make way for an American base in World War II.

The series introduces unknown work by newly discovered writers, and in addition showcases new writing and favourite classics by established authors such as Anthony, Jan Carew, Ian McDonald, G C H Thomas and Anthony Winkler. Writers on the list come from around the region, including Guyana, Trinidad, Tobago, Barbados, St Vincent, Bequia, Grenada, St Lucia, Dominica, Montserrat, Antigua, the Bahamas, Jamaica and Belize.

MCW was launched in 2003 at the Caribbean's premier literary event, the Calabash Festival in Jamaica. Macmillan Caribbean is also proud to be associated with the work of the Cropper Foundation in Trinidad, developing the talents of the region's most promising emerging writers, many of whom are contributors to MCW.

Judy Stone
Series Editor
Macmillan Caribbean Writers

The Macmillan Caribbean Writers Series

edited by Judy Stone

Novels:

Jeremiah, Devil of the Woods: *Martina Altmann*
Butler, Till the Final Bell: *Michael Anthony*
Such as I have: *Garfield Ellis*
The Boy from Willow Bend: *Joanne C Hillhouse*
Dancing Nude in the Moonlight: *Joanne C Hillhouse*
Ginger Lily: *Margaret Knight*
Exclusion Zone: *Graeme Knott*
The Humming-Bird Tree: *Ian McDonald*
There's No Place Like …: *Tessa McWatt*
Ruler in Hiroona: *G C H Thomas*

Plays:

Champions of the Gayelle: (*ed Judy Stone*)
　Plays by Alwin Bully, Zeno Constance & Pat Cumper
More Champions of the Gayelle: (*ed Judy Stone*)
　Plays by Winston Saunders, Dennis Scott & Godfrey Sealy

Stories:

Going Home, and other tales from Guyana: *Deryck M Bernard*
The Sisters, and Manco's stories: *Jan Carew*
The Annihilation of Fish and other stories: *Anthony Winkler*

To Sandra, my daughter, for whom this is a special year, and for Butler himself, of course

1

URIAH Butler came out of the office fuming. This was the end. He could take no more. The manager of Apex Oilfields just did not care, and if he would not listen then he would be made to feel. Hickling just did not know or did not want to know, and he did not care a damn. He just did not understand. He just did not know what pressure and poverty were.

He, Butler, was not going to beg any more.

As he came out onto the roadside he looked up and down, and at the moment he was a little confused. He was not sure where to go. Because he had not thought of the outcome of the meeting. Hickling had acted as though he was doing him a big favour just inviting him to talk, but even so Hickling never had any intention of listening. He just wanted to be able to say he spoke to the leading agitator.

Butler looked round at the rigs and at the numerous oil storage tanks painted in red. He was not going back to work today and he had already reported sick. He did not know if he should go to his own house in Vessigny, or whether he should go down to the railway station and take a train to San Fernando to see Cola Rienzi. But he was also thinking he needed to call a meeting at once to inform the workers that one more move had failed and he was going to try no more. And that now was the time for action. This was of crucial importance. So perhaps the best thing was to go down and see Elsie.

He looked up, and he looked all around him and he could not make up his mind. It was about eleven o'clock and the sun was hot, and in any case he was so hungry that now it should not be too difficult to make up his mind. He would decide what to do afterwards but he was going up the road first. He was walking up to Chee Fong's shop at the junction.

He set out to go up the road, and Lance-Corporal John, standing in the shade of the eaves of the Labour Office, watched him go. As the lance-corporal stood erect against the Labour Office, with a big lagnet tree in front of him, he noticed the little limp and he could not help but chuckle. He said in his mind, *You so looking for trouble. What they do you in the 1914 war ain't enough! They shoulda blow out yuh leg. You think you smart, you holding all these meeting and say you forming union, just let me get me hands on you. Ah wonder where you going now? Ah so glad Colonel Hickling did tell me about this meeting so now I could track you. But he didn't even give you five minutes of he time, you goat!*

The lance-corporal came out into the road and watched the now distant figure walking. He, too, proceeded to walk slowly up the road while trying not to take his eyes off Butler.

When Butler got to Chee Fong's shop there were two customers inside it. Chee Fong was behind the counter and Chee Fong's wife moved to the far side by the window. Nobody said anything.

Butler said, "Chee, you have mauby? Make a drink quick."

The mauby jar was just in front of him, by the glass case, and was there for everybody to see. Chee Fong moved to it and his wife went inside and stood up behind the curtain. Of the two people in the shop, one sneaked out, and the other, an old man, half-leaned up on his stick and pretended he was looking at the prices of the tinned goods on the shelf.

When Chee Fong poured out the glass of mauby he just put it down in front of Butler, and Butler, thirsty, could hardly wait to get the glass to his mouth. Chee Fong's shop was an ordinary shop but it also sold things like mauby and sweet-drinks, and buns, drops, rock cake and, on occasions, corncake; and there was often pan bread.

Butler said, "Chee Fong, you have cheese? How much for a bread and cheese?"

"Four cents."

"It gone up? It used to be three cents." Chee Fong did not answer but turned to look at his shelves as if to see whether they were in a straight line. Then turning to Butler he said, "You want?"

"Yes. Oh Christ man, make it quick, nah. Ah going up the road."

Chee Fong's wife, who was still standing behind the curtain, suddenly felt good, not only because Butler was soon going up the road, but also because, in the tiny space between the edge of the curtain and the edge of the door frame, she spotted the policeman walking towards the shop. He was still a little way but it made her happy nevertheless. As Chee Fong pushed the bread and cheese to

Butler, and took the money, Butler turned to the old man: "If we ent – " Then he said, "Ay ay, is you, Pa Jakes? And you there so quiet and easy? You know I didn't see it was you?"

The old man smiled: "How you going, Uriah?"

"Pa Jakes, it's not how ah going, is where ah going, and to tell yuh the truth, I meself don't know. You see Elsie? Elsie Francois?"

"She at home."

"Oh, she home?" He drank the mauby and ate the bread and cheese a little faster. Chee Fong had cut the cheese so thinly you could almost see through it. And now he was charging a cent more. Butler turned to Pa Jakes: "Ah was going to say if we ent look sharp they'll charge us for the air we breathing, man. Chee, not you. I ain't talking about you. You fighting to make a living just like me. That is why I always say, Pa Jakes – that is why I always say we have to unite."

The old man smiled approvingly, but one could see he was uneasy, and as he gripped his stick he was wondering what excuse to make to get out. But as he looked out into the road he saw Lance-Corporal John approaching the shop, and he relaxed his hold on the stick. He said, "Uriah, things tough, boy, but what we go do!"

"It's not what we go do, is what we *have* to do, Pa Jakes. Look, you wouldn't believe me, but – "

As he said this Lance-Corporal John walked into the shop. Lance-Corporal John said nothing, but he looked through the window, and now he looked back at the road, and he breathed out with the sound "whew!" as if he was so glad to escape the hot sun. Then he looked into the glass case to see what was inside it.

Chee Fong was right there before him looking up coldly, with his head sideways as if to hear what the lance-corporal wanted, pretending he did not know Lance-Corporal John well. Chee's wife had come out from behind the curtain. Lance-Corporal John seemed hardly aware of them. He pretended to look at the calendar on the wall behind Chee Fong's head, with the flap on May, 1937. Then he bent to see what was inside the glass case, but as he looked on each side he glanced slyly to see what Butler was doing. When he had entered the shop he had heard a snatch of revolutionary talk, and he was poised and on the alert.

He was on the alert because this was the man who at a meeting the other night had said he feared no man, not even the King. In fact,

Butler had said words that sounded like, "Even if the King ... ."
When Butler had seen him writing, taking a few notes, Butler had
said, "Let Lance-Corporal John write. I, Butler, say not even him, because Uriah Butler will not move."

Lance-Corporal John had been bristling to arrest him. He had
said to himself, *This arrogant, boastful beast!* He had felt as if his
blood was boiling up inside him and he had wanted to call on
Butler to repeat, "Even if the King"! In fact on that occasion he
had actually moved off to confront Butler, but Acting Corporal
Gilroy Price had held him back and said, "You can't take him yet.
Wait, let's hear what else he saying. It's only if he inciting or
something like that ... ." But in fact there was nothing else. Not
in that strain. Lance-Corporal John had been breathing as if he
had short breath. He stood listening and waiting, but Butler did
not repeat the words. But he felt sure he had grounds for arrest.
"Even if the King ... ." Wasn't that treason? He knew what a rash
and wild revolutionary Butler was and he had felt on edge to trap
him. To beat and arrest him. He had not got the chance the other
night and he badly wanted the chance now.

His heart raced. He had not thought of it before he came into the
shop, it was just to keep an eye on Butler that he had followed him.
When he had seen Lieutenant-Colonel Hickling last night he had
promised not to keep Butler out of his sight, but Hickling or not he
just had to throw this pig in jail. But not without a licking.

As he kept sneaking a glance while appearing to look at the glass
case, Chee Fong said, "Ah waiting, Corporal John, you likee – ?"

Lance-Corporal John was taken aback by Chee Fong's voice.
Although he knew he was in Chee Fong's shop he had been
hardly aware of Chee Fong standing right there before him, on
the other side of the glass case, and he did not even notice Chee
Fong's wife leaning against the inner door. As a matter of fact he
had seen the old man with the stick near the window and did not
even realise it was old Jacobs. He had had his mind on one man,
Uriah Butler.

The lance-corporal looked at Chee, then said aloud, as if to himself, "Boy, like I really forgetting me manners!" Then he said,
"Morning Mr Chee. No, I ain't want nothing. Ah just watching."

He might well have said, "Ah just watching Butler", because
Chee knew. Chee knew that this was all he was interested in.

In any case, although Lance-Corporal John was a little hungry there was nothing in the glass case that appealed to him. And although when he looked at the mauby he felt thirsty he never drank mauby in the shop. The reason for this was that he wanted full respect from Chee always, so he wasn't going to drink any mauby and eat any rock cake in his shop. And be chummy. Of course Chee Fong would like him to be chummy. But a police informer was a police informer. And Chee was getting paid for it. He turned to the side window now, and suddenly he said, "But! But! How you do, Pa Jacobs?"

Pa Jacobs simply said, "I there, yes, Corporal. I quiet."

Pa Jacobs had kept well within himself. He had been waiting tensely for a clash of words between Butler and the lance-corporal.

Lance-Corporal John said, "Pa Jacobs, what happen to you! You saying yuh quiet, but you always quiet. You don't give no trouble. I only ask how you do but I know you ain't do nothing."

Pa Jacobs turned his head away to look through the window.

Butler finished eating the bread and cheese and he gulped down the rest of the mauby. Then he went to old man Jacobs and took both his hands in his, letting the stick fall to the floor. He said, "Pa Jakes, the sun stinging but ah have to leave you. The mauby cool me down." Then he picked up the stick, and handed it to Pa Jacobs.

"Okay, Chee," he said, as he left.

Chee Fong did not answer, but instead, when Butler was far enough away, Chee Fong, his wife and the lance-corporal began to laugh, and Pa Jakes joined in the laughter too. They looked at Butler walk towards the junction, then turn right.

Lance-Corporal John said, "You fellers laughing? This is the most wickedest bastard in Fyzabad. Ha! The mauby cool 'im down! Eh heh! So what the france he mean? Now he cool down ah wonder which part he going to hot up now?"

Pa Jacobs looked at him.

The policeman said, "Ah really wonder where he heading for?"

Pa Jacobs said, "By Elsie."

"He tell you that?"

"Yes, he ask me if she home."

"Oh God! Ah better walk down the road then."

"She ain't home. Elsie in Siparee."

"What for? She's a busybody, you know." He looked towards Chee Fong. Chee Fong turned towards the southern window. He had known Elsie long enough to know she was conspiring with Uriah Butler. In any case that was not news because Lance-Corporal John had seen her on Butler's platform a few nights ago when Butler was addressing the workers. She did not speak from the platform, but she associated with the Butler people. Anyway, yesterday he, Chee Fong, had given the lance-corporal all the latest on Elsie, and so John knew very well she was not only a busybody but also what she had gone to Siparia for. But it was the big fish the lance-corporal was after. He always thought: *Once you hook the big fish and break the neck, the rest ain't nothing.*

Pa Jacobs said, "Is not Elsie so much but the feller she living with. That boxer boy. They calling him Kid Fearless," he chuckled. "I does call him Hothead. You know him, Corporal? He working ah think is Forest Reserve."

Lance-Corporal John was looking out into the road and his mind was flitting here and there. He was not bothering about small fry. He was just itching to arrest Butler. Even if he did not have a good enough reason, but could find an excuse, that would be all right. By God's grace he would find something. But the excuse had to be sound. Not to give cause to any magistrate to embarrass him by throwing out the case like the last time, and even saying things about him. Now focusing on the limping man he said to himself, *That Grenadian feel he smart but he'll find out smartness. At least before anything happen I'll make me baton talk this time!*

He came to the front door and then he looked up the road towards the Apex oilfields, then back towards the camp and offices, then he quickly looked in the direction in which Butler had gone. He saw no sign of him but he did not panic because he knew he would soon catch up with him because Elsie was not there.

As the lance-corporal looked he got all worked up because he was thinking of the trouble Butler was causing the oilfield employers and the supervisors of the various fields. What hurt him deeply was that these men were all Englishmen and not used to any backbiting and disloyalty. The lance-corporal's breath began to come fast again and his chest swelled with anger. This crazy Jezebel, he thought, this limping Lucifer was whipping up the workers and was beginning to draw massive support because the workers were like so many monkeys, aping their leader. Colonel Hickling himself was so worried, he wanted to have Butler behind bars immediately. But despite all the information Hickling was giving to the Legislative Council – information which he, John, supplied – despite all Hickling told these people they were still allowing Butler to incite and run free. And this was only because Governor Fletcher was fiddling and twisting and turning and getting on like a silly clown!

Of course he couldn't say that to Hickling. He could not refer to Fletcher as a silly clown. For as useless as Fletcher was, these Englishmen always closed ranks with each other. He knew that very well. But as he was thinking this he was also thinking that while he was bothering about Fletcher and Hickling, Butler must have already come back from Elsie's place and gone. Or perhaps finding that Elsie was not at home he was just sitting down on the steps there waiting. This thought got him a bit excited. He had the full picture in his head and if he was lucky enough to catch Butler on those steps that could be a charge of trespass or, better still, it could even be loitering for the purpose of committing a misde-meanor. In his head he quickly changed the word 'misdemeanor' to 'felony', because he was not sure he could spell misdemeanor, and some magistrates liked to go out of their way to embarrass the police. In any case 'felony' sounded more serious.

Now he had already stepped out of the shop and was out in the road. He was not sure if he had said any 'so long' or 'see you' to Chee Fong, but that was of no importance. He had forgotten Pa Jacobs completely. As he reached the road and turned towards the junction he was not sure what to do. He did not want to take that rugged track to go into Elsie's place because, on second thoughts, he felt sure Butler was not there. He glimpsed the informer, Gustav, and he snapped his fingers and called him to walk along with him. Just as a witness, he told Gustav. His mind was occupied with Butler. *That busybody could never sit down in one place so long waiting on anybody*, he told him-self. *Not when there was trouble to be made.* Yet when he reached the junction and looked along Vessigny Road and did not spot the man with the limp, he walked into the track.

When he reached Elsie's house and saw nobody on the steps he was just about to wheel round again, when he noticed the door ajar. He blurted out, "Ay, ay! What is this?" Then he cried, "Anybody home? Anybody living here?"

Gustav had stayed in the bushes out of sight.

Lance-Corporal John called again, "Anybody living here?"

Jonas came and opened the door, and he was taken aback to see the police uniform. His heart beat, voom boo-doom. He stood at the front door and said, "Constable John, you want to tell me you ain't know somebody living here?"

"Hay! That's the way you talking to me? If you ain't respect this face, please respect me uniform. They call you Hothead but if yuh head hot I could cool it, you know. Who you have in there with you?"

Hothead retorted, "This house is mine and I know the law and I could have anybody in me house if I want, because it's mine. And I could tell you, Constable, the magistrate just waiting for you this time, so what the blazes – ?"

"You using obscene language, Mr Hothead? You using obscene language at a police officer?"

Hothead said, "Since when 'blazes' is obscene language?"

He said this a little coolly because he himself was not sure how to assess 'blazes', and he did not want any policeman saying in court the accused was using obscene and violent language and that was why he had to do so and so.

Jonas said again, "Lance-Corporal, I know my rights. But in any case what I saying is this: so I have to have somebody in here with me because me door open?"

"Well listen – "

"No. You listen to me now. Even if I have somebody with me you have to know who it is? Why? You have a search warrant? Well come and search, ah have a jamette. That's against the law?"

Lance-Corporal John was stopped in his tracks. He always forgot that Hothead was what they called a bush lawyer. This brash, muscular young fellow had got the magistrate to insult a lot of policemen already, including he himself. From what Jonas was saying he felt Elsie was there. He toned down now and said, "Well, is not me who calling yuh wife a jamette. Is you. What she doing – she busy? Where she is? Ah want to see her."

"If is Elsie you talking 'bout she gone San Fernando."

"San Fernando? And how come you say ... ? Look, who is this other jamette?"

"How you mean 'other jamette'? So you want to call my wife – listen Constable, you could prove that to the magistrate?"

"I ain't call Elsie nothing. Let me see her."

"I tell you she went San Fernando."

"And you stay home? That's funny. I know you working Forest Reserve and – "

"But I ain't know any law against staying home."

"Well I'll tell you frank, Mr Hothead – "

"My name is Jonas Blyce."

"Otherwise known as Hothead."

"And otherwise known as Kid Fearless."

Lance-Corporal John could not stop chuckling. Then he gave a little mocking laugh. He said, "Sometimes I see you skipping when ah passing. Quite from the main road. But ah never see you in the ring yet." Then he chuckled and said, "Kid Fearless. I suppose that's why the other night yuh favourite boy said, 'Even if the King ... '."

Jonas just stood looking at him.

The lance-corporal scratched his head, "Both ah you fearless – you know what ah mean? You win any fights yet?"

Jonas said, "Come back to what you was saying. We was talking about how ah stay home. You want to tell me I ain't have no right to stay home? That was what we was talking about."

"But is the same thing Hot- ... ah mean, Jonas. It's the same thing because when you stay home you could be helping those communist boys, you see me point? It could well mean the fellers could be on strike, and yuh boy saying, 'To hell with the King! If the King want oil to help England, to hell with him!' Not so?"

Although Jonas was a hothead he did not rush to reply. Because Lance-Corporal John was clearly out to trap him. And he, Hothead, could have been well and truly trapped because the obvious answer to that was that if the King wanted oil to help England, let the King look in England for oil. But this was exactly what John wanted to hear. And he had even brought a witness. Jonas had long ago spotted Gustav by the bushes under the coconut tree. Anyway, that was exactly what John was waiting to hear: "... if the King want oil, let him look in England for oil." This was bound to be seditious.

Jonas said, "So, Lance-Corporal, because I staying home it could mean the fellers going home too – on strike?" He laughed.

"You could laugh. Hickling ain't laughing though. Because if oil stop pumping is King George bottom what in fire."

Hothead's mouth snapped to give him the answer, but he had to shut his mouth quickly and grind his teeth. He shook his head. He said, "Lance-Corporal John, if is Elsie you come to. Elsie Francois. If is Elsie, she ain't here. So you'll come back, eh? You could come back this evening to see if she come. Oh God, Lance-Corporal, you is a nice man because you standing up there but a little bit again you was carrying me down. Lance-Corporal – "

"But what the france you mean by saying a little bit again ah carrying you down? What you have up there?" The constable stared.

"Take it easy. I ain't have nothing up here. Nothing for you to carry me down for. Look, don't come up the steps, you know, Lance-Corporal!" His face suddenly changed as the policeman made a move. Hothead grew fierce, and he stepped back and picked up a beer bottle from the floor. "Don't come up the blinking steps because you ain't have no search warrant. You know the law. Don't come up, you know. I name Kid Fearless!"

Lance-Corporal John stopped, his heart thumping. He was on the fourth step. He did not blow his whistle because there would be no policemen around. He glanced round but Gustav had already gone. He stood up there, motionless. He said, "I just want to know who up there. Who you have up there?"

"Who up here is *my* business."

"While ago you talk about a jamette."

Hothead was keeping his eyes on him, expecting a sudden lunge. He was measuring exactly on what face bone he would smash the bottle. Maybe between the eyes. The lance-corporal said, "Well, I ain't doing you anything but if you had anybody up there like Butler, that's illegal and I'd have to come and take him, but I could see that you on yuh lonesome."

"*You* could come up here to take somebody? Without a search warrant? You want to try, Officer?" Hothead's eyes were red with determination. He was gripping the head of the bottle and swinging his arm from side to side.

Lance-Corporal John forced a smile. "Kid Fearless, yuh playing bad-john but you ain't no bad-john, you is only a boxer, and what you should have in yuh hand is a glove, not a gin bottle. Oh, that's a beer bottle. Gin expensive. I watch yuh first two fights at Emporium Hall, remember? And you was good, but you is a boxer, not a roughneck. Look, I could go now for a search warrant and come back. But is a waste of time because I know you on yuh lonely."

"While ago you said you never saw me in the ring and now you saying you watch me first two fights! Go and get yuh search warrant, you – "

"Why you checking yuhself? Use yuh obscene language!"

Jonas felt disgusted and furious. He felt like letting John come up, then suddenly jumping and releasing a flying-butt, only that both of them would be tumbling down the steps together. Thirteen steps. He would be risking getting badly hurt. He said in a forced calmness, "I want to know how the hell even if I was harbouring Butler here I doing something illegal. Butler is a fugitive?"

"We have a warrant for Butler. Inciting to riot."

"Well, arrest him. Go and arrest him and you'll see what Fyzabad will do to yuh backside!"

The lance-corporal was incensed and he actually thought of rushing Jonas and labouring blows on him. And he would have rushed him too. But to rush someone up some steps was virtually impossible, and in this case it would be stupid, for with the slightest movement Hothead would just smash the bottle on his head.

The lance-corporal was just looking up at Jonas and saying nothing. Jonas was blowing hard. He said, "Lance-Corporal John, go and get yuh warrant. Go, nah. If you think it have anything here to seize, go and get the warrant and come back. And you could bring reinforcement. I waiting right here for you."

Lance-Corporal John began to descend the stairs without turning his back. He knew the record of this hothead and he did not take his eyes off him, except to glance round fast to see that those boots of his trod on wood and not on air. He was keeping his eyes on the hand with the beer bottle and hoping his reflexes were fast enough for him to duck in time if the bottle was released. He was sweating with humiliation and anger. He kept descending the stairs backwards, his eyes riveted on that hand.

Then he felt the ground under his boots, and he glanced round quickly to see where the track was. When he got far enough away he turned fast and walked with haste. Then he broke into a run towards the road.

2

WHEN Jonas went back into the bedroom Butler said, "Where he gone?"

"He went down the Vessigny Road but I ain't sure if he going back to the station. I think we better move quick."

"You braver than ah thought. You have the right name: 'Kid Fearless'. He say he see yuh two fights in Emporium and yet he asking if you win any fight yet?"

"You worrying with that son of a so-and-so? He only trying to sweeten me to get at you."

"You think he feel I was here?"

"Yes, he thought perhaps you was here. At first. He mighta come up the stairs and rush you if I wasn't here."

"I would ah beat that beast to a pulp."

Jonas looked shocked. He said, "Uriah, please don't tangle with policemen. Try and avoid them. We don't want you for no roughneck. We want you to lead the workers. Lead us to victory. Lead us to the New Jerusalem. Squeeze those foreign bloodsuckers. Bring them to their knees. Look, Uriah, ah getting worked up, O God. You always say, 'don't let the infidel mislead you'. Please, Uriah, keep away from stooges like Lance-Corporal John. Look, you know something? John will kill you cold just to make Hickling feel nice. And the rest of the bloodsuckers will say: 'What a shame. It's their own people.' Look, let me say this – we have only one Uriah Butler. Don't tangle with police. Just lead us. *We'll* tangle for you."

Butler smiled but he felt scared. People had such faith in him!

Jonas glanced at the main road, then the track. He said, "You could smile, Uriah, but from what I could see, it wouldn't take much for Lance-Corporal John to wipe you off the face of Fyzabad."

Butler chuckled. "Wipe me off the face of what? Look, come on, forget John. What's happening? You ready or what? We going?"

"Yes, yes."

Jonas looked round him. "You have everything yuh taking? You forgetting anything?"

"I ain't have nothing to take. Just me Bible."

"No papers? Okay, let me tell you quick because we have to get outa here fast. By the way, don't latch that door. Leave that top part open for when Elsie come back. Okay, now I hope you know that back road." He pointed due north. "We'll have to cut through that way until we get well past Vessigny, and then we'll have to cross the main road then duck in again until we get near Godineau – "

"Yes, I realise that."

"Then by Godineau River it have a little trace. It's a short-cut to Cross Crossing. Ah don't think you know that one. You'll follow me."

Butler said in his mind, "No. *You'll* follow me."

Jonas looked outside carefully. He said, "Let's make a move." He checked to see if all windows were closed and if the top half of the kitchen door was left open for Elsie. Then he said, "You ready?"

Butler said, "You sure we'll see Rienzi?"

"It's *now* you asking that? We just have to. Why you say that?"

"Sometimes he's so busy and especially – "

"We just *have* to see Rienzi. For instance hear that stupid lance-corporal with, 'If Butler there we'll have to take him.' You ain't commit no crime. You ain't break no law. How the hell they could take you. You have to talk to Rienzi about that! After all, he's yuh legal adviser. What make you think you won't see him?"

"He always in court, man. He – "

"If he in court we wait! Uriah let's get to hell outa here. If that blasted lance-corporal come back with reinforcements – " Jonas hurriedly opened the window again to look in the direction of the main road. He closed it then peeped through a crack in order to see along the track. Then he said, "Come on. Let's go."

They got out of the room fast and, leaving the steps, instead of going towards the main road they walked along a little track that led to a patch of bamboo and lagnet trees. Were it not the dry season it would have been very waterlogged here. They walked past that and when the track wound towards the main road, they walked to the edge of the main road and suddenly ran over to the other side. Butler himself did not want to run. How could the police capture a man who had done nothing illegal? He would mention the matter to Rienzi but that was all. He committed no crime; he feared no foe. He always knew that the warrant for incitement was only a trap, anyway.

When they got to the Godineau River they walked beside the bridge railings on the other side and then along the two-mile stretch of Mosquito Creek. They didn't talk much but walked fast, and Jonas felt as if he had his heart in his hand. He was scared that at any moment a police van would pull up.

He was taking no chances, but when they got to La Romaine, and especially Cross Crossing, his tenseness was over. But he was still very nervous for Butler. They walked down Sutton Street to meet Broadway, then turned up to Harris Promenade.

From the Broadway end of Harris Promenade the row of law chambers was just within a stone's throw – literally – and the two calmly walked over.

3

WHEN Cola Rienzi spotted Butler he was excited. He said, "Come, come. Hurry up, man!"

Butler hurried up and went into Rienzi's chambers. Jonas's heart was racing. He sat in the waiting room, not too far from Rienzi's secretary, and he wondered what new move was there – if what had happened was in Butler's favour or not.

Butler sat down, and as Rienzi looked among his papers, Butler kept thinking, *I wonder what the hell Cola have to tell me.* For he had seen at once that something unsettling had happened that had made Rienzi nervous. Rienzi kept looking among his papers but he did not find any letter for the simple reason that there was no letter. Every time he sat in his chair to have discussions with anyone the first thing he did, by habit, was to get the previous correspondence. But there was nothing on the matter because Governor Fletcher was not such a fool as to put in writing what he had told Rienzi.

Rienzi said now, "Uriah, you are a hell of a man. Didn't Swithin tell you to come here at eight or earlier if you could make it? I have court this morning so I made a point of telling Swithin – "

"Which Swithin?"

"How many Swithins you know!"

"Swithin Paul?"

"Well, of course. I told him to tell you it's urgent, and I even gave him money to give you in case you had no money to travel, and I told him – "

"But wait. Cola, what really happening? You have me completely baffled. What happen?"

"Well I'll tell you, but first I want to know. You didn't see Swithin at all?"

"But who tell you to give Swithin money? You will give money to that man who can't see a bottle. And *you* in particular, eh! You forgetting what happened to Ralph Mentor some years ago when he gave Swithin money for you – in an envelope, mind you – remember how Swithin spent it out and it was you who had to save him from jail? I mean you is a regular fool or what, Cola. But tell me, what happen? Come on. I really dying to know."

"You touched on the right word there, boy. Dying. If you don't – " He checked himself. He did not want Butler to panic. He said, "Tell me first, Swithin didn't visit you? You didn't see him at all?"

"I saw Swithin Paul on Friday night but he didn't come to me. In fact, he was called to the bar – Crossroads Bar in Vessigny. When ah was passing ah heard his mouth and I had no idea he was coming to me and so ah didn't interrupt the good-for-nothing drunkard. But if I did know – that is good English, Cola? – If I did know?"

"The Queen's English. But for heaven's sake don't take this matter lightly. I want you to get out of this part of Trinidad tonight. This very night."

Butler straightened up: "What's this? What happen?"

"I don't know how I could explain, but I have to try. You know all these discussions passing between me and Governor Fletcher over your matter. And you know the entire Legislative Council up in arms against what they call the 'soft' way Fletcher and Nankivell dealing with you – you know all that."

"Aha."

"Anyway, this is off the record, but they planning – that's the British Parliament – they planning to crucify Fletcher. But anyway to come back. Some mad group in the British Parliament, in touch with the radicals in the Legislative Council here, decided that the oil has to flow and I don't know who said what, or who arranged with who, but Fletcher received some anonymous despatch from London saying – " He stopped and looked around him. He went and made sure the door was shut properly. He looked through the window, which was quite low, to make sure that nobody was outside. He said, "Some secret message Governor Fletcher received and he called me on his private line saying he had to see me immediately. He didn't tell me why, he didn't say what for. And he couldn't. I went up to Port of Spain yesterday, late, because I had to reach there in darkness, and I had to slip, quite secretly, into Government House. I had to disguise me identity because, as you know – "

Butler nodded.

Rienzi said, "Okay, hear what Fletcher told me. He said that from the coded message his information was that a frigate had already left England and was speeding down to Trinidad with – listen to me but don't panic – with a sharpshooter on board."

Butler was silent.

"You know what the sharpshooter is for?"

Butler did not answer.

Rienzi said, "You know? You must know. They said it is to remove the blockage, and let the oil flow."

Butler smiled.

"And you know who is the blockage."

"But I can't believe the British Parliament – "

"But you weren't listening? It's not the British Parliament. It's a faction. And Fletcher wasn't supposed to know about it. And maybe even the Police Chief, Mavrogordato, doesn't know, nor Inspector Power. Let's face it, the British don't do things like that. But it's a mad faction. But I haven't told you everything. You don't want to know when the frigate's due?"

"When?"

"Tonight!"

Butler sat up stiffly. Rienzi said, "And you know what port it's coming in to?"

"No."

"Brighton."

"Brighton? Just over there? That's the port for Apex."

"Say no more. But apparently even Hickling doesn't know. We may have our suspicion, but no evidence. When everything is over we may be able to investigate it, but even that will be hard. But Uriah, at this moment these matters aren't important. What's important is you. I want you to fly. You hear me? Sometimes at your meetings, people say things like, 'There's only one Butler.' What I know is, if you go – meaning, if you kick the damn bucket – nobody else I know could come forward like you. We'll have to look all over the place to find somebody to take up the mantle. I, for one, am a busy man and please save me the looking, and save the people of Fyzabad. So Uriah, I want you to fly, please. To prevent your kicking the bucket I want you to move the damn bucket."

Butler smiled.

Rienzi stood up and put a hand in his pocket.

"That's okay, Cola, I have some money."

"You refusing money?"

"Well, I got pay. I happen to have something."

"You sure, Uriah? You have enough?"

"Yes, yes. If I didn't have enough I'd tell you."

"Well go far, you know. Really far. I would think you should go to some place like Blanchisseuse, or Toco, or better still Mayaro. You know Mayaro?"

"Aha. Lovely place."

"They know you in Mayaro or not – that's the police. But in any case the police can't touch you, even if they know you. What I want you to do is this: when you arrive, just go to the police station there and ring me, just saying, 'Cola, this is Lerbut. I'm here in Mayaro.' Okay? This is only for three days. The frigate leaving Trinidad on Wednesday and you are back in Fyzabad on Thursday. That's what Fletcher said, the frigate's here till Wednesday. So on Wednesday night go to the police station. I have a nice Panama hat here for you to leave with, and you don't think you could do with a shave? Okay, okay – as you like. On Wednesday go to the station in Mayaro – I'll talk to them. They know me name. Go and ask to ring me. Here's me number." He scribbled on a piece of paper and handed the paper to Butler. "When you ring, just say: 'Cola, this is Lerbut, Mayaro's nice.' And I will say, 'Go on,' which will mean 'Gone' – just in case the operator's listening in. And of course that will mean the frigate's gone and you could come back home."

Butler chuckled. He said, "And what's this Lerbut about?"

"I just changed the syllables in your name: Butler to Lerbut."

Butler chuckled again.

But Rienzi went on to other things. He said, "Who is that feller with you? The feller you came with."

"You don't know Jonas, the boy we call Hothead? You met him in Fyzabad. He is me right-hand man, bodyguard and everything."

"You have a hothead for your right-hand man?"

"Well, he is a young feller and very enthusiastic, and he is no trouble. He and his wife say they love Uriah Butler. That's all. He's always with me."

"All right, but I want you to make me a promise. As nice and charming as Hothead is, even if he was Coolhead, don't tell him anything about this. Nothing. When you go out he'll be waiting?"

"Yes, he in the sitting room."

"Well, as soon as you go out there, ask him for an excuse. Say Cola Rienzi sent you on a mission. And look, Uriah, I don't want you to go back to Fyzabad. Because I don't know who is who, and who's in on this thing. Somebody could try something. They just intend to snuff your light out. Go directly to Mayaro – "

"But Cola, what about all those appointments I have?"

"And if they blow out your candle what about the dozens of appointments? Eh? The oil workers will fret with you, not so? After they put you in the burial ground! I suppose the candle will be on your grave then." Rienzi watched him, then he said, "Look, Uriah, when you leave this office you go directly to Mayaro for me, please? And don't converse with anybody on this matter."

He stood up and again put his hand in his pocket. Butler got up too. Rienzi said, "Take this extra money."

Butler took it and looked at it. He cried, "Good God, Cola, you tell me I spending three days but you give me money for a month."

"Nonsense. You just go. Waiting for your Mayaro phone call."

As soon as Butler and Jonas got out of Rienzi's chambers, Butler said, "Jonas, Rienzi sent me out on a mission. I can't talk about it. You catch a bus and go back to Fyzabad." Jonas stood up and watched Butler walk away. His heart felt heavy and he wondered what was this secret assignment.

He stood feeling a bit lost, and then he thought, *I'd better pass and see Sharkey about this boxing bout. I know he vex with me. Ah sure, sure. But since I already in San Fernando I'd better go.*

4

WHEN Sharkey saw Jonas he shrank back, surprised. He said, "Fearless, what happen, boy? You 'fraid?"

"Who me? I frighten? And you calling me Fearless?"

"Well, after I make you sign up the man I ain't see you again."

"But you ain't ask 'Why?', yet."

"Why?"

"Well that's what ah come here to tell you."

"Look, I hope you'll be still fighting, though. I hope you ain't cancelling nothing."

Sharkey half-stood, half-leaned against his front steps. He looked quite concerned now, and his eyes were fixed on Jonas. Jonas, with one glance, took in the neat little painted house with the curtains behind the glass windows.

He said, "No, that's all right. I in training, that's all. You signed me up to fight Young Tiger and I'll fight him. No matter the rest say that I 'fraid him. So I'm in training. You think I'll sign up to fight Young Tiger and I wouldn't be in training? It's Young Tiger, you know! Ah signed up just three weeks ago, it's not as if – "

Sharkey looked at him. The fact that Fearless had said: "It's Young Tiger you know!" made Sharkey believe he was truly scared. But he hoped not. But Sharkey himself was scared for Jonas.

"Okay, Fearless, it's all right. I really glad to see you, man. And to hear you in training. Because, I'll tell you what," and he lowered his voice, "I believe you'll floor him, you know. Yes, looking at yuh raw power I could see you'll put him down."

Kid Fearless smiled. He said, "I meself don't feel so. But the ring, that night, will have two boxers, and each ah them will have two legs and two hands, and two gloves. And may the better man win."

"Talk, boy. Talk yuh talk. I find you looking fit. You skipping?"

"Only yesterday – " He paused, and then he shut up. He looked around and then he scratched his head. He was going to say that only yesterday Lance-Corporal John saw him skipping. But he didn't want to mention anything about the police, for he remembered the fuss Sharkey made the last time. But he didn't see why he should let Sharkey interfere in his private life. He didn't interfere in Sharkey's. Yet to avoid the argument he said, "Well, you know, I was going to say – you know me. Only yesterday ah did some skipping – "

"But so what? You should skip every day. You training, not so?"

Sharkey was upset that Jonas should talk as if skipping was a big thing. He asked, "Who is yuh sparring partner?" The way Jonas had to stop and rub his head showed Jonas had no sparring partner.

Sharkey said, "And you done with politics, ah hope? That stupidness ain't going to lead you nowhere. You have a punch bag?"

Jonas mumbled something and Sharkey said, "What's that?"

Jonas said, "I'll tell you facts. You see, in the first place that's why I didn't come all the time. You is me boxing promoter, you trying to get fights for me, but I'll tell you the truth: I don't like to come here, you know. Because I have my life and you have yours. You telling me about politics, to keep off it. If I believe in Butler – if I feel to throw in me lot with Butler, and sacrifice for the future of this little country, that ain't have nothing to do with boxing – "

"There's where you wrong. Don't bother with that Butler talk! Like ah tell you the last time, you can't serve two masters."

"But why not? The Bible said man can't live by bread alone."

"Oh, you quoting scriptures now! Butler coaching you?"

"Not a matter of Butler coaching me. But when you say I can't bloody well serve two masters, that's scripture too! So what the hell!" He stiffened up and his face hardened.

Sharkey said, "Oh, you helling me. One of the little fellers from down there did well tell me yuh name was Hothead. I was only guiding you because you want to be a boxer and I talking for your own good – that is, if you don't want Young Tiger to eat you raw!"

At this point Jonas just didn't want to say anything. In fact he shouldn't have come here at all. He couldn't help wondering who was the little feller who told Sharkey he was a hothead. But he was angry with himself for "helling" Sharkey and even "bloodying" him. It wasn't Sharkey he needed to bloody, but Young Tiger. He said, "Look, Sharks, I just pass here to tell you what happening and to let you know I ain't cancel nothing, I getting ready for May 18th. It so easy to get in a little dispute. We don't have to quarrel."

Sharkey looked towards him and laughed. Then he looked up at the window. "Evelyn! You up there – "

Jonas said, "No, it's all right. Don't call her down. I going. Ah have to go." And his tongue nearly slipped again because he was going to say he came up early this morning with Butler.

But at this stage, Sharkey did not really care. He had already made up his mind. He simply thought, *You is a complete waste of time. I ain't going to tell you nothing about Butler no more. I just waiting for May 18th, and when Young Tiger done devour you and beat you bad, I just finish.*

But he retained a smile on his face. He said, "So you going back in the oil, boy, eh?" He grinned brightly. "You kids from the Deep South don't like San Fernando at all?"

Jonas smiled. He liked the line: "You kids from the Deep South."

He said, "Sharks, I think you's a great feller. I mean, you tidy. You have a nice tidy house. Painted up and thing. Evelyn is a pleasant person. Look, Sharks, the fact is, let me tell you this: is true, I is a hothead. I hate to quarrel with you when I come here. I just don't like to quarrel because me tongue say things ... I don't mean."

Sharkey was quiet. Then he said suddenly, "But who quarrelling? I ain't quarrelling with you. What we'll quarrel for?"

"No, just that I didn't like helling you. Think I better go now."

"But keep in training. You know what kinda right hand Tiger have? But you could do it. Because when you boxing you like to get up on yuh toes and bob and weave and dance, and when he get tired you could make him miss regular. I telling you that you could put him down. I have that kinda faith in you."

He was just a little older than Jonas, and his face, at the moment, was looking pleasant and nice. He and Jonas were standing up near the steps of his house just beside his gymnasium. He looked at Jonas on the side but although his face was nice and soft and pleasant he kept thinking: *You think I have patience with you fellers? I want three or four young boys, willing and who want to win. I could train them, and keep them in shape and keep them on the right track. If you want to follow Butler, then follow Butler. But if you think when 18th May come you'll beat Young Tiger, you wasting yuh blasted time. He'll eat you raw. He'll tear you in pieces.*

Jonas watched the smiling face, and felt sorry he had been so harsh. He said, "I know you worried, Shark. But hear this: I, Fearless, when that final bell ring, I wouldn't be the one on the canvas."

Sharkey had the urge to laugh. But he controlled it. He said, "Kiddy, you don't think I know that? Tiger can't eat you raw like how he does always boast. You keep in training for me and don't let me down. Only do that. You okay man, you think I 'fraid for you?"

Jonas took his hand, "Okay, boy. Have to make it down now." And he said, "I'd better go down to the wharf and catch a train."

"Take something to Cipero Street and get a bus for Fyzabad!"

"Oh, yes. Oh God. I forgetting how San Fernando is."

"So try and keep in touch, Jonas. Don't forget, we can't afford to fail. Take yuh training serious. Young Tiger ain't no walkover. Oh, just keep this in yuh head: you have Coronation Day and then Coronation Carnival to come. The Carnival is the 18th May. Keep that in mind because that same night is the date with the Tiger."

Sharkey was still sitting and he looked towards Jonas as if he, Sharkey, had passed on a very clever tip. Jonas had nodded quietly. He hurried out into Drayton Street in the hot sun, but just before him, over Mount Naparima, there was a huge patch of grey. He looked up at it. His mind was enraged. He was still hearing Sharkey's voice: 'Keep this in yuh head. You have Coronation Day to come. Keep that in mind because it's that same night that is the date with the Tiger.'

He said to himself, *Just fancy, Coronation Day and Coronation Carnival. Who cares about this stupid Coronation anyway? When Butler call that strike we'll show them Coronation Day!*

When he got to Coffee Street he was still vexed. He waited for a bus, not to take him to Cipero Street but to the wharf. In fact, he would have gone down to the wharf in any case. Sharkey did not know his plan. And of course Sharkey was not familiar with Fyzabad or with where he was living. He had only to get off from the train, cross the road, and he was right in front of the track leading to his house. He had not planned to go home directly, but now that he thought of it he would go straight home, see if Elsie was there and find out what happened in Siparee, tell her about Uriah, then eat, because he was already feeling hungry. And if possible he wanted to do some skipping and shadow-boxing tonight.

He said to himself, *I wonder what mission Rienzi have Butler on, boy? If I have to contact him he'll be home?* And then he thought, *Coronation Day! You could beat that? You think you could ever change yuh own people?*

When he got to the corner of Coffee Street his thoughts were flowing so much he did not even notice the junction, and now he had walked nearly a quarter of a mile and was not far from the corner of Medine Street. But he stopped there and waited for a bus.

There was not much waiting at the Medine Street corner, and in fact a few buses had passed while he was walking and daydreaming. He took one and went down to the railway station on the wharf.

He got more worried when he got down there because the railway clock showed it was ten minutes to three. He had been thinking it was only about two o'clock. The sun had gone in completely now and when he looked up the skies were slate grey. The clouds were heavy looking. He said to himself, *Rain will fall.* Then he wondered if Elsie was able to have a chat with Mamselle Marie Vidale and what did Mamselle Marie say. He did not want to think about that too much. He was too anxious. He bought his ticket and joined the little crowd on the platform because the train was near. In fact he could hear the distant rumble. He said to himself, *If rain fall I mightn't be able to do nothing. But ah have to train for Young Tiger. I have to take this fight very serious because I want to find out if Young Tiger will eat me raw. You think he'll need tooth-pick?* He smiled. And then he suddenly got bitter again. For he was hearing Sharkey's voice in spite of himself: 'The night of the Coronation Carnival.' *They brainwashed all of us,* he told himself. *He want me to win, and not just to put money in his pocket, although I ain't no damn fool. You think I is a damn fool? He said he know ah could beat Tiger and he have faith in me. But that's a lot of cash if ah win and that cash have to share with the promoter. But I don't mind. But I want to win for Elsie. And then when I win a few more fights I'll change Sharkey … .*

He had hardly realised that the train had come until he saw people getting inside.

5

WHEN Jonas reached Fyzabad he hurried to the main road, walked a little way until he came to the track which led to his house, then trotted towards the house. He hurried because Fyzabad was so wet and chilly. There must have been heavy rains here for water just streamed down the drains and the road was full of puddles.

When he reached the house he ran up the steps, and he had hardly got inside when he called out, "Elsie, you there?"

He already knew she was there from the things that were on the table, and he had noticed her wet felt hat on the box in the corner.

But she came out of the bedroom right away. She said, "Oh, Jonas you back? And I only just come back in the bedroom to light this candle. I was looking out for you all the time. Where you went?"

"I had to go San Fernando. Uriah was here, you know. He came this morning and he said he was under pressure and he had to see Rienzi. Remember last week when he had to meet Hickling, and we was feeling so good? It was the same sort of thing, a stupid waste of time. Hickling didn't intend to negotiate nothing. Hickling just wanted to get Uriah to shut up and was advising him that it was better for the people if he didn't make no trouble – "

Elsie said, "You know I had a mind so! Where's Mr Uriah? When Hickling called him everybody got excited. Me too. But I still had a mind Hickling wasn't going to negotiate nothing. Where Mr Uriah is?"

"I'll tell you in a minute. But what I want to say now is, we'll have to raise hell in Fyzabad. If we was only united, Elsie. Butler always calling for unity. If we was only united you think we'd have to go through all this hell? Oh God, girl, the whole ah Fyzabad should go up in fire and brimstone."

"Jonas, for Christ sake take it easy. You always so hothead! That's why they calling you so."

He was sitting at the table with his face buried in his hands.

Elsie said, "You rush in, you ain't even ask what happen in Siparee. You ain't even ask if ah get wet. I mean, I know the pain and the suffering we going through, but we is God's people, Jonas. We only poor. You'll let them break you down?"

She looked at him as he sat leaning right over on the table, his elbow on the table and his hands under his chin. She said, "And you ain't even tell me if he see Cola Rienzi or not, because I know Rienzi always so busy, and if he see Rienzi what Rienzi tell him?"

Jonas got up a little but he was still leaning on the table with his hands under his chin. He was in fact extremely anxious to know how Elsie had fared at Siparia. All the way coming on the train he had been wondering about this, and when he had run through the track from the road to the house it was mainly because he wanted to know what had happened at Siparee. But since Elsie mentioned Rienzi now, he sat down again. He said, "Uriah only wanted to see Cola Rienzi to tell him what happen because Rienzi was always telling Uriah he mustn't call the strike if Hickling offering to negotiate, and so he wanted to tell Rienzi it was really a trap, and a sham, and a damn trick, and that Hickling was just playing for time. And Uriah just wanted Rienzi to give him the all-clear because – "

"Rienzi gave him the all-clear?"

"Well, yes. I mean it look so. I ain't see Uriah since we left Cola's office. He went out on a mission. I don't know what it is, and when you see Uriah ain't tell *me*, water more than flour. For all you know it involve the Governor. You know how Fletcher like him. Oh God – I don't know what to say. I'm a little worried about Uriah. I don't know what is the mission. Jesus. I worried, oh me darling. About you, Elsie, you saw her? Marie Vidale. I mean Mamselle Marie."

"Oh, you want to know now?"

"Well is I who sent you."

"Mamselle Marie said from what she could see, we'll win."

Jonas lifted his head and looked at her.

"She said God don't like suffering. She said we only have to have patience and we'll win in the end."

His heart sank. He opened his eyes wide: "But, ah mean, patience? Patience? Same old story. Same old thing. Everybody saying we have to have patience. Hickling saying it all the time. His patience mean 'never'. Oh God, how long! We have to wait fifty years, Lord? We done wait fifty years orreedy."

"We didn't have oil fifty years aback. You yourself tell me that."

Jonas held his head. "Yes, I tell you that. I tell you that. But oil was always there in the ground. God put it there for us. But they taking it, Elsie, they taking it. Oh God, what is this? Have mercy on your people, Lord. These oppressors didn't have to wait fifty years. The rich always oppressing the poor. Oh rock of ages cleft for me!"

"Look, Jonas, you don't have to rave. You listening to me? I talking – " She stopped and went to the other side of the table and stood up facing him. "Look, why you always saying this kinda thing? I ain't against the rich, you know. I want to be rich. So I ain't bothering with scripture now. I bothering with justice."

"And what you think I crying out for?" He lifted his head.

"The point is Mamselle Marie damn right to call for patience. But she don't have to mean *fifty* years. You just have to be extreme. For example, as you say, the oil was always there in the ground. But these people come and drill for it. But listen, we'll get it. God put it there for us, as you say, and we'll get it. We just have to take time and make haste." She stopped and said in a softer tone: "You like that statement? About 'We just have to take time and make haste'?"

"Who said that? I believe in it. I bet is –"

"*You* said that."

"I? Oh shucks. I forget. When?"

"You said that in the public meeting in Aripero but you yourself ain't practising what you preaching. Everybody know you as Hothead."

There was silence. He again cupped his face in his hands and leaned on the table.

"Jonas, why you have to do that silly pose? Yuh head in yuh hands! I know you in agony but I in agony too. But you just can't collapse."

He sat up and that moved her. His face was drawn. She said, "Now listen. I'll tell you about Mamselle Marie. She is not an obeah woman. No witchcraft. She is what you call a seer woman. She told me so herself. But she said she doesn't like to say she's a fortune-teller because most times what she have to tell is misfortune. And she doesn't like to tell horoscope because it's mainly horrors. A pleasant lady. I had to laugh. But what was jokey for me was serious for her. So I got serious too, you know me! But I'll tell you, no black magic and all that nonsense. She just working with God – a woman who could see what in the future."

"That's why I sent you."

"Okay, okay. She took me in a room with a lot of balisier bush and rosemarie, and deetay payee, and mint. It had some candles lighting. It had some cojoroot and gullyroot in a basket and, I think, some cinnamon leaves, and zeb-a-pique and other herbs – gosh boy, I never know wild bush could smell so sweet. I even saw black sage and vert-y-vert. In the room she have a big table. She put a candle on the table, and she made me light it, and she have some flowers. She put the vase on the table, she tied her head with a red cloth, then she start to pray. And when I say pray, I mean pray, you know. Oh God, boy! I was feeling as if the house trembling. Afterwards she break out singing a 'sankey'. Then she sing 'Just as I am without one Plea', and then she prayed again – sincere you know, opening out her arms and calling Jesus to come. Then she burn incense to purify the place. Then she ring a bell and she break out singing 'Bread of Heaven, Bread of Heaven, Feed me till I want no more'. Jonas, I ain't shame to tell you, I cried like a child."

He was silent. She went over and shook him. "Ah talking to you."

"Ah listening," he said. Tears were in his eyes.

There was a little silence. Then he said, "She is Baptist? They say she is Baptist."

"Yes, Spiritual Baptist. A big impressive kinda woman. Like Jimmy Hughes's wife in Lagon Palmiste. That type. After she prayed the second time, she put her hand on me shoulder. She said, 'Ma Jonas, is a matter of time but you'll win.' "

Jonas was a little excited. He said, "She call you Ma Jonas? She know about me?"

"Well, I tell her. I tell her me name is Madame Jonas."

"Oh."

"She said it twice. 'Ma Jonas, the day will come.' Then after she prayed and she took up the vase and she made that Baptist sign, she said, 'Ma Jonas, patience and sacrifice.' Then she said, 'You say yuh husband is a hothead, but he working good. God is love.' "

"She said that?" Jonas looked at her excitedly.

"I wouldn't lie to you. You is me husband. She said, 'He working good so far, but when you rash, and you head hot, it's easy to spoil things.' And oh yes, I remember this: she said, 'God take six days to make the world. Six days. Madame Jonas, I want to ask you, he couldn't do it in any less? Eh? The Master couldn't do it quicker than that? It have anything the Lord can't do in the twinkling of an eye? But he took *six* days just to show us we have to have patience. We have to labour and to wait.' "

Jonas was staring at her. He said, "That Mamselle is deep!" He was trying to remember where he had heard that line: 'Learn to labour and to wait.' It wasn't scriptures. Probably poetry at school.

He looked at her, "So on the whole it was a good day, then."

"Very good day. A blessed day. Is only when I came back here I meet rain. And rain soak me. But me heart singing."

Jonas said, "You see this heart?" He rapped his finger on his chest. "This heart ain't singing yet because I ain't see nothing yet."

"Why you saying so?"

"Because everybody saying to wait and to have patience and I ain't going to feel glad just on any kinda promise. Because how much a promise cost? Nothing. Words is wind. I want to see action. This Mamselle remind me a little of Mona Miranda."

"Yes, but not so much, although Mona is yuh friend. But I think there's where you have straight obeah."

"That's what they say. But I meself ain't believe in that. You could call it obeah, you could call it witchcraft, as you well know I ain't no disciple of Mona. She's just a friend. But I'll tell you something, Elsie: If I could get somebody to work a deep obeah on Hickling just to sling him outa here – you think I wouldn't try it?"

She giggled. She knew he didn't believe in obeah. She asked: "You came down by train or by bus?"

"Train. I was walking straight down to the Railway Station from Coffee Street but at Medine Street ah took one of those pug-nose yellow bus. Oh, by the way, I went to Sharkey, you know."

"Oh yes?"

"Yes. And Sharkey kept on reminding me of me coming clash with young Tiger. He said he seal the deal and don't let him down."

Elsie looked at him. She had really never approved of boxing but she just had to support Jonas. She said, "Well, Sharkey want you to win. You told him you skipping?"

"Could be. I ain't sure. But that ain't going to cut no ice with Sharkey. He want to know that ah deep in training. Not only skipping but shadow-boxing, weights. Punch bag. I ain't even have a punch bag! He asked me, but I didn't answer. I passed it off. Let's face it, Elsie, Sharkey's right. The opponent is Young Tiger, you know. And Tiger's unbeaten so far. Take that! Put it in yuh pipe and smoke it. I is the out-and-out underdog."

She was going to the kitchen but she stopped to look at him. "Well, I just don't want to see you get licks. I always say either do it or don't do it. If you doing it you have to do it good. You have to train. Because if anybody have to deal out the licks it must be you."

He began some explanation as to why he couldn't do the things he should be doing because of the number of things he had to do and she knew it already and didn't listen too much and she was thinking maybe she should have asked Mamselle Marie if he'd win. She thought of this only for an instant and then she quickly dismissed it. Neither she nor Jonas put this matter in the same sort of class as the Butler issue. But in any case it would be a waste of time for Mamselle Marie to try to 'see' that, because everybody could see it already. Jonas did not have a chance. She just wanted him to acquit himself well, and not to take too many blows. She was in fact worried by something Mamselle Marie had said about Uriah Butler but she would not tell it to Jonas for that would only set him off – he had already been ranting and it wouldn't take much for him 'to go off his rockers'. That came from Hickling. Maybe the English talked like that. But back to the Mamselle – although the Mamselle had told her that in the end it would be all right, she wanted to see Uriah to tell him. That was why she was anxious to know where Uriah was. But Rienzi sent him somewhere – maybe to Fletcher. She didn't like Mr Uriah going through those gates of Government House but she did not let Jonas know this for fear of pushing him further off his rockers. Jonas had stopped talking. She said, "What you was saying? Me mind went on something else."

"Can't remember what ah was saying. Look, the only thing I don't like about Sharkey is this. Look, Elsie, we have to face facts. Sharkey ain't want me to follow Butler. He said sport and politics don't mix, and that I can't serve two masters and all that sort ah nonsense. I say to hell with that. He said he's talking to me for me own good."

"Oh, I see. Not for *his* good." She looked at Jonas and shook her head. She felt glad in a way that Jonas was disenchanted with Sharkey. If he gave up boxing no love would be lost for her.

She said again, "Not for his good, eh? If you win that fight with Tiger he wouldn't get anything?"

"He'd get more than me! What's wrong, girl, you dreaming?"

"More than you?" She was genuinely shocked and annoyed. She had known that as promoter Sharkey would have to share in the prize money, but it would be ridiculous for him to get more than the winner. And what was he doing to get that? He was all the way in San Fernando and Jonas was on his own. She said, "He have to get more than you when you is the one taking all the blows?"

"You see how you getting on now? That's why I didn't want to say anything. That's the way it is, Elsie. But I'm lucky. I didn't have to get that fight. Tiger's unbeaten you know. Speedy Collins backed out from the return bout, and rather than let the whole thing fall through Sharkey squeezed me in. The Boxing Board didn't want to approve, but they agreed only because of me last fight in Emporium Hall – "

"That was a lucky punch," she said, and went for the broom to sweep out the kitchen.

He was surprised to hear her talk boxing talk. He said, "I know it was a lucky punch because I said this meself. If Collins was making style and ah get in me uppercut, so what? That ain't cheating. The point I making is that if it wasn't for Sharkey I wouldn't be fighting Tiger. The Boxing Board nearly didn't sanction it."

"What is sanction?"

"Ah-h, oh-h. Oh well, to say it's all right. You know, the fight's okay. Aha. So if ah win you know what that would be? And then ah'll be getting two hundred dollars."

That was a lot of money and she stopped sweeping and watched him: "Jonas, you sure about that?"

"But how you mean? Signed and sealed, girl." He paused a little and then he said, "But you know, sometimes when I think about it, this is ridiculous. We oilfield workers working so hard and facing so much pressure to get eight cents a hour, nine hours a day, that is seventy-two cents; so for the whole fortnight we taking home – let me see – eight dollars and sixty-four cents. But you only have to jump in a ring and you making so much money. Two hundred. For just about one hour or so if you go the whole ten rounds. And that is after the promoter take his. You know, things ain't so bad for some people in this 1937."

"If you want to win you have to train."

"But how I could train with all this Butler business? This is a serious situation. Then, too, I ain't even have a punch bag."

"Once you ain't take me for yuh punch bag."

He smiled, and she saw him and smiled too.

She felt tender towards him, she didn't know why. In fact, she *did* know why. He was a hothead and rough and ready in many ways, but he loved justice and fair play and he was prepared to fight for those things, and sometimes it seemed as if he didn't mind dying for them. But one thing was certain, he was prepared to sacrifice boxing for Butler. For the changes Butler could bring. The amount of money boxers were getting did not touch the problem. How many boxers were working for Apex? And in fact she hated boxing. But although she wanted him to stop, since he was so staunch she would stand by him. And it was true that although she could do with two hundred dollars, she would not want it if he had to take licks for it.

She looked at him as he still sat at the table there. His face was not cupped in his hands now but he was so tense and nervous, he could not relax. She wanted to laugh at him but she could not. They were fighting this battle together. They were fighting this battle and sometimes it seemed as though they were alone. The four thousand or so people in Fyzabad never really seemed to care very much. Didn't the oil-workers care? Yes, they cared. They cared very much about their pay! She tried to push this out of her mind now. Jonas appeared so hard and rigid, yet he was so soft inside. With all the 'hothead' he was, he never lifted his hands to hit her, unlike so many of those men who beat up their wives. Even some of the top men in the movement supporting Butler did that sort of thing. The very men crying aloud for justice and equality. They weren't training for the ring but their wives were their sparring partners and punch bags. Instantly, she became vexed and worked up, but she calmed herself. She said, "Anyway, boy, if you training, train good. It's not only a matter of letting down Sharkey. What about me? What about yourself and Mr Uriah? So you better train to win."

"Well, of course."

"And the main thing is that we have to support Mr Uriah and, well, we have to fight the good fight."

"Till the final bell."

She hardly heard that. She was astonished to hear herself saying, 'fight the good fight', because that was exactly the name of the last hymn Mamselle Marie had sung when she went there.

She sat on the edge of the bed and leaned back against the head-rail, thinking. Jonas said, "I could see that you real tired. You had a long day, girl."

"You saying that so easy! You could say that again. I dead tired. But I feeling content." In her mind the melodies of the hymns were spilling over and beating like quiet breakers on a shore.

After a little while she heard the voice of Jonas as if from far away. "You want to rest, girl. I so glad you went Siparee. You really believe what she say? About Butler? You ain't fooling me up?"

"Eh? Oh crackers, Jonas. I was dozing off orready. What you said? Fooling you up? How I could fool you up? You is me husband. Boy, I feeling sleepy orready, yes? I had a full day. Leave me now, nah." She stretched out on the bed and turned her back.

After a few minutes he bent over her. She was already in a different land. He whispered, "I ain't Jesus, I is just Jonas. But I have to say this: 'Well done, thou good and faithful servant.'"

He got up quietly and went for his skipping rope and then he went downstairs.

6

THE space under the house was high enough to allow Jonas to skip and he skipped until sweat was running from him like a river. As he skipped he counted, and when a nearby clock struck nine, he skipped up to the next hundred and stopped. Then he began shadow-boxing, bobbing and weaving and ducking, and rolling imaginary punches; sliding from left to right, backward and forward, feinting, speeding up his footwork, using the whole space as if he were in a huge ring. There was a gaslight hanging from the centre of the ceiling, and this was so powerful it brightened the entire floor, and in that light his footwork and his bobbing and weaving had the illusion of magic.

The light attracted Felix as he was coming through the track. As it happened he was coming straight to the house, but when he saw the bright light he stopped short and he said, "Ay, ay!" And when his eyes got used to the light and he saw Jonas feinting and bobbing and weaving he said knowingly, "Oho. I see."

He stood up and watched for a while and then he decided that the best thing to do was to go and sit down by one of the pillars and wait. When Jonas finished in a flurry of punches and uppercuts and straight jabs, Felix cried, "Punches, boy! That is workout! When you start out again?"

Jonas jumped, then put his hand on his heart. He said, "Boy, is you? Well, you could ah kill me cold. With all me punches you could ah knock me out without a blow. Good thing me heart strong. I didn't see you. How you get here?"

Felix grinned, "How I get here? I was passing on the main road, going up by me uncle. You know old Braddy? No? He over there. Between here and Vessigny. And I was just thinking to meself, boy you ain't see Jonas for so long, I wonder how he going. So I stop and turn in the track, cause ah tell meself, at least, Felix boy, you could say how-dee-do to Jonas. So long we ain't see. When you start back – I mean, when you start back to train?"

Jonas was still surprised. He grinned back and said, "Tonight."

"Tonight? That's what you said? Tonight? The first night? And you moving so?"

Jonas felt thrilled. Not only because his performance was impressive but because this was the man he had floored with the lucky punch, and whose career seemed to have ended that very night. And he had always felt Felix was bitter and angry with him.

He said, "Yes, I only start back tonight. And that was only because me promoter, I mean, you know how Sharkey is – Sharkey was vexed ah wasn't training. I was there this afternoon. Yes, in San Fernando. He said he didn't see me for a long time, he only hope that ah was training. Had to admit I was only skipping. He turned blue. He said Tiger will eat me raw. He said ah like too much damn politics. Leave Butler alone. That's what he said. The man make me feel so shame I had to start back training from tonight."

"He said leave Butler alone? Butler? That man is a saviour."

"You feel so too? Ah never knew you was a Butler man."

"But how you mean?" Felix looked as if shocked. "Every man jack round Fyzabad have to be a Butler man. Not only in Fyzabad, in all Trinidad. People should be marching for Butler, too. You think without Butler we could stand up to Hickling and this bleddy colonial government? Thank God for Fletcher though."

Jonas forgot all he was doing and all he had intended to do. He had intended to rush to the shower as soon as he was finished so that his body wouldn't get cold before he finished sweating. He knew this was the key for keeping the muscles in trim and it was a golden rule which he never broke. But now he forgot all about it.

He said, "You saying thank God for Fletcher and I so glad and so grateful for him too. I so glad he's Governor, but Felix why it have to be like that? We only asking for justice. We shouldn't have to beg for nothing. Oh God, man."

"Well, Butler will fix them up. This morning I was down in Point Fortin because they had this march down there – "

"A march?"

"The oil workers. U.B.O.T. boys. Sometimes I think United British Oilfields worse than Apex. I'll tell you about it afterwards. But I saw this boy you'll be fighting. Well, when I looked at him I say to meself, 'Kid Fearless done win. He don't even have to train –' "

Jonas stared at him as if wanting to know what he meant.

Felix said, "You see him lately? He looking so haggard."

"But how come? Fellers telling me that this Tiger acting like if he let loose from the wilds, how every morning he running from Erin to Point Fortin – that must be thirty miles if it ain't nothing. They telling me how he cutting timber – "

Felix, who was laughing all the time, now said, "Well, they trying to frighten you, and they succeed. Look," his face got serious. "Don't make nobody make a monkey outa you. Tiger's in a bad way and he trying to hide it. He know he can't win that fight so he sending out friends to try to scare you. I was in Point Fortin and I talk to Tiger. But I couldn't stay long because I had to be in the march. But Tiger tell me, 'Kiddy, you is me bosom friend and I'll tell you because ah know you wouldn't tell nobody. I fighting to make this training but I can't make it. I can't even skip. And I can't back out of the fight in case Kid Fearless say it's fear, but between you and me he don't even have to train. But please, please don't tell him nothing.' " Kid Felix looked up as if to heaven: "And now just look at me, Lord! I doing exactly what Tiger tell me not to do." He turned to Jonas. "It's only because I feel so close to you, because of the nice way you deal with people. You never realised that, eh?"

Jonas was shocked. He simply said, "No. I never realised that."

"Tiger is not a bad feller but I ain't shame to say I'll feel let down if you don't win."

"I could only say thanks, Felix. Felix, me boy." He turned his head away. He was embarrassed to remember that lucky punch. It was only six months ago.

Felix said, "Look, and I'll tell you something else Tiger tell me, but keep it under your hat. It's a little little feller who flooring him. A little tiny feller. You know what the truth is? Tiger have malaria."

"Oh Jesu. Malaria?"

"Mosquito bite. But he can't talk, after all the build-up. It have so much build-up all over the place, as you know. Gosh, you'll be really famous when you win that fight."

"Yes, but the man ain't at his best!"

"But what we going to do about that? And then nobody don't know. But anyway, life is like that. I ain't saying Tiger's arrogant but sometimes life set a trap for you."

Jonas was pensive. Why was he training so hard to beat a sick man? He said, "I feel as if ah cheating."

"Cheating? Nobody can't say you cheating nobody. You sign to fight a man, you fight him, and you win – that's all."

Felix looked at him as he sat down there thinking. Then Felix got up. He said, "Boy, I so glad to see you. You looking in tip top shape. I always like yuh style, the way you move, and yuh – well, yuh ways in general. But ah better go over by Uncle Braddy now. He living just down the road by the other side."

"Well, in that case one day I must come over."

"Yes. Sure. Uncle Braddy'll be glad to meet you. He'll like yuh footworks."

Jonas himself got up. He thought, "Christ, I shivering?" His perspiration had dried up on him and it was only now he realised how coldly the breeze was blowing. At least he was feeling chilly.

Felix took to the little track and he stopped and said, "You keep it up, Fearless. I have to come to see that fight. Mind you, you wasting time training so hard. But ah like the way you moving."

Although Jonas was feeling cold he didn't hurry upstairs. Neither did he hurry to the shower. He did not know what to do, as his body seemed stiff. He wondered if he should warm up again.

But his head was filled with Felix. He thought, *What's this, really!* Six months had passed and the fight between them had been sensational. He had been on the point of being knocked out when it happened. His unexpected uppercut had made all the difference. Felix had fallen as heavily as a log of wood, and the surprising defeat was the biggest news in County St. Patrick. At the count of seven Felix, bleeding and not knowing where he was, had tried to get up on his rubbery legs, and now as Jonas remembered how the handlers at the other end pelted in the towel he decided to go upstairs for a towel to have a shower.

Felix had long reached the main road, but rather than walk in the direction of where he had shown that his Uncle Braddy lived, he turned the next way towards the junction. It was not that he had decided that he was not going over to his Uncle Braddy any more. It was simply that there was no Uncle Braddy.

When he reached the junction he walked towards the shop at the corner to wait for one of the brown buses. He had timed it well. He knew that the last bus was at ten p.m. and he wasn't there five minutes when the bus pulled up. He merely looked at the bus to make sure it was a Siparia bus, and when it stopped he went inside.

It was just on the outskirts of Siparia that he was going, near the Mora forest. When the bus reached, although it was nearly half-past ten, he went to the house and passed on the side of it towards the back, because he knew his friend so well he expected him to be in his gymnasium. When he got round to the back the light blinded him for a moment and then he went and sat in the easy chair.

As soon as he sat down Tiger left his sparring partner and came to him. "What happen – you went as you said? You saw him?"

"The man in training. They told you he wasn't doing nothing of the sort but when I reached there the man was shadow-boxing. And he moving good. I saw him with me own eyes."

"You didn't tell him nothing about me, though."

Kid Felix laughed. "I only tell him you sick. You have malaria."

"Oh, God!" Tiger burst out laughing. The fellow he was sparring with remained leaning over the ropes of the ring and watching.

Felix said, "You better go back. I'll wait till you finish."

"Listen," Tiger said. "I wanted to find out a few things – "

"It ain't really have nothing to find out. Kid Fearless ain't even a real boxer. And you know when he started to train? Tonight."

"Tonight? This very night! And you say he looking good?"

"Yes, he looking good. But not good enough to beat you. I mean, after all. You know Fearless ain't belong in the same ring with you."

"The Boxing Board didn't say so. The Board didn't say so at all."

"But if they didn't put him who you woulda fight with?"

"I ain't saying he shouldn't get the bout. In fact I want a bout. It only make it easier for me, that's all."

"If it's easier it's better. But you prefer Speedy Collins, not so?"

"I didn't say that."

"But I could see that."

"But you know Speedy have more class. And a better punch."

Felix couldn't help laughing out, "Hay! Hay!" Then he said, "Well hear that. A better punch. I used to say so, too. Tell me, how you prefer to go down? A better punch or a lucky punch?"

"You talking about you! Fearless put you down because you was careless. This Tiger will never go down. Look, I ain't underrating

Fearless. I training hard. You know for yourself I cutting down Mora trees, I running to Erin. I skipping something like two, three hours. That's far too much work to fight Fearless, but I doing it. Don't say I ain't appreciate Fearless, but this time Fearless stepping outa his class. He could ever put me down?"

"Okay. Okay. But he looking good. The only thing is that he have so much 'Butler' talk! Can't stand it. I can't say I like the guy."

Tiger thought, *Of course not. I wouldn't like nobody who put me down.* He said aloud, "I hear he is a nice feller."

"But only talking politics."

"Yes, but still a nice feller. I hear he's a hothead but only in the Butler business. I ain't have nothing against that. Only that for me, if it ain't boxing it's nothing. You see where I living, in the bush? I is a real tiger when ah get in the ring. So I can't be like that Jonas – "

"That Judas!"

"You can't forget how he put you down, eh? But that's what a boxer climb in the ring for – to put down the other man. That's his job, else he's a blinking clown." He saw Felix starting to speak, but he said, "Let me finish. I know you want me to beat him to a pulp. You always tell me so. But fool him to make him stop training hard. No, no. Can't take that. Let him come with all he has, man. When I'm in the ring, it ain't have no tiger more wild than me. Doesn't matter who come in front of me, me duty is to put him on the canvas. But for God sake let Fearless train, because the harder the wood, the quicker ah cut down the tree."

"Fearless should spare you the trouble and follow Butler in full. Two madmen. I don't know why the hothead take up boxing."

"Well, because he could win a fight here and there. Didn't he put you down? I ain't laughing at you, but you was a promising feller. So if he could go for politics and go for that too, why not? Look, Felix, since then you don't box no more."

Kid Felix just looked away in anguish.

Tiger said quickly, "Let's not talk about that. I going back and spar. But before I go, this is one thing that I ain't going to let no blasted boxer do to me. Put me down. I fighting Fearless on the 18th May, the same day with the Coronation Carnival, and it will be Carnival in that ring, whether he train or didn't train. I'll make masquerade with him. But when you go and encourage the man not to train, first of all you know I ain't have no pity in any ring, and when I start to butcher the man and bring blood, and mess up the man and mess up the place that will make ah outcry. So if you is me friend don't do that to me. Not only that, but if after two, three rounds all Hothead's eyes and nose start to bleed and they throw in the towel or the referee stop the fight, how I will feel? All these months of training, running to Erin, cutting down poui trees, and mora, and mahogany, and after all that, after I get in the ring, they stop the fight, and I ain't even raise a sweat yet! Eh? And I ain't even show me ring craft because all I get is three rounds? And then you say you is me friend?"

Then he looked again towards his sparring partner who was waiting on him and he said, "Oh my God, look how I keeping Ackbar so long." He lowered his voice. "Why I wanted to see you was this. Ackbar is a good boy. He badly want a bout, but it's like hell to get him on a promoter's card. But I was talking to this same promoter, Sharkey, and Sharkey said he'll match him up with somebody for the Christmas Boxing Festival but he don't know with who. I want to talk to you about that. He is your weight, and you suddenly stop because Hothead put you on the canvas. No, man, not so. God forbid. We have to get you in the ring again. Ah mean a man of your talents playing the ass! Boxers don't come through the window you know. We'll have to get you in the bloody ring again."

"To have blood all over the place?"

Tiger turned away and laughed. He said, "That's the spirit. You'll come back? Eh, Kiddy? What you say – you'll consider it?"

Kid Felix sat there watching the two boxers sparring. Tiger was throwing out jabs, and grunting with each thrust. He was standing close up to Ackbar, moving his head about as if looking to choose which part of the ribs he wanted, then throwing out lightning-fast jabs. Of the two, it was Ackbar he wanted to watch, just to see his style. But Ackbar was so new he hardly had any of that.

Nevertheless, Kid Felix felt very nostalgic for the ring. For a long time now he had been silently wondering if he should return, and he wanted to ask a question or two at the right time. And now, look who should take it in hand. The reigning middleweight champion, Young Tiger. And Tiger was even matching him up already, and with an apprentice, to help him return in style. He began to dream of what he could do with Ackbar. Because he felt sure he could put him to lie wherever he wanted to on the canvas. And then in his mind's eye the crowd was erupting with applause, and people were fawning on him and just wanting to touch him.

But the feeling surging in him was the joy of having befriended Kid Fearless, and the chance that Fearless would give him a return fight. His mind lit up brightly, thinking of this, and he began to feel there was nothing better than being in the ring again.

7

URIAH Butler left Vessigny very early and came up to Fyzabad Junction, then he went across to Jonas's house. It was early but not too early to go to the house of someone like Jonas Blyce. He hoped to meet Jonas at home, or even Elsie, but knowing how the Fyzabad women were quick on the move he didn't expect she would be there.

As he crossed the road to go into the track, he was sure he spotted a policeman on a bicycle turning the corner into the Fyzabad main road. His heart thumped. He had left early to avoid the Fyzabad policemen, and he nearly walked into one of them.

Not that he was afraid of them, but he did not want to meet them in this season. Especially Lance-Corporal John. Gilroy Price was all right. Price never bothered him too much, but the lance-corporal was always looking out for him, and he did not want to be held up at all this morning and asked foolish questions. Not today. He had heard Charlie King was in Fyzabad but he had not seen Charlie King yet, and he was sure Charlie King had not seen him yet either, for Charlie King was sure to know who he was, and sure to follow him. Anyway, when he crossed the main road into the little track he felt much better. He walked up to Jonas's house, and even before he called, the door opened, and at the top of the steps was Elsie.

He said, "Oh, you there. That's great. Morning, Elsie. Jonas home? Something a little urgent. Me boy there? I have to talk to him. And then ah going down Siparee. I want to see the lady."

As he spoke Elsie was just standing there and watching as if it was an apparition before her. Her body was trembling. She said in her mind, *Thank you, Father. He safe.*

Butler said, "Oh God, Elsie. I here talking to you, I asking you something and you ain't answering me?"

"You asked for Jonas? He went in the shop. When he come – "

"Something happen? What happen?"

She didn't want to talk yet, nor to be pressed into talking, so she just said, "Nothing ain't happen. Not really."

"You sure?"

"But we want to know where you was. We was so worried. We trying to find you and we off our rockers."

He started to walk up the steps. "Off what? I was in the countryside. I had to go in a hurry."

"But Mr Uriah you know how Jonas is. He crazy when it comes to you. You'll go to the countryside and not say nothing?"

He stood up before her. "I couldn't say anything. I just couldn't. I shouldn't even tell you, but when yuh husband come you'll hear."

"Something happen, Mr Uriah? Oh God, what it is?"

"Nothing. Nothing really. When you husband come."

"Well, Mr Uriah, something have to happen if you say you have to see Mamselle Marie today."

Butler laughed. He went and sat on the chair in the landing. He said, "Elsie's just like her husband. She ain't have no patience."

She said, "You'll want Jonas to go Siparee with you?"

"If it's okay. That is if he able to go."

"If he able to go? Mr Uriah you know he'll drop everything and go. Nothing will stop him as long as you want him to go."

"You really touch me and I thank God for you two."

"No. Is we who thank God for you."

As she was talking, every few seconds she kept looking outside and along the little track to see if Jonas was coming. Now she looked towards Butler sitting on the chair.

She did not ask anything but her heart was beating fast. Why did Butler want to see Mamselle Marie so urgently? If he knew what she and Jonas were going to tell him then she would have thought him wise to want to hear what Mamselle Marie could see for him, but she was really flabbergasted when, just like that, he should say he had to see her. And urgent. She was really anxious to know what went on and she began feeling quite concerned. Especially so as now, when she began to think about it, it did seem a coincidence that she had a certain experience only on Saturday, and now here was the usually calm and confident Uriah Butler saying he had to see Mamselle Marie urgently. She couldn't help wondering whether the two things were connected. She looked along the track again, but she did not see Jonas, and she took the matches and went to light the fireplace. Every now and again she peeped along the track.

When Hothead came and saw Butler he was astonished. He said, "Uriah! Good Christ, what happen? You ain't living in yuh house no more? No, something did have to happen. You looking so haggard. I wanted to see you urgent and I went down to Vessigny, twice, but you wasn't there. I didn't know what happen. I nearly come down to Vessigny this morning – "

Elsie interrupted, "Well, I guess it was Vessigny you went because you left to go in the shop and you stay so long and I mean I know Chee Fong shop's only just up the road."

"I don't go to Chee Fong again."

"Oh, no?" After what happened she was not going back either. She waited anxiously to see if he would tell Butler why he wasn't going back there, or if he would just start the subject. Jonas looked at her, then it seemed he wanted to ask her a question. As Butler was looking away she nodded her head. Then Butler went to the window looking up at the greyish skies through the trees and he turned back in and said, "You ain't find it looking a bit dark and heavyish?"

Jonas said, "Yes, it have some water up there. Rain will come."

"I thought it was a little chillyish this morning," Butler said.

"Me, too." Then he said, "Uriah, we have to talk."

"Sure we have to talk. That's why ah come."

"You come to talk to me?"

"So I can't talk to you now? Since you in training? You think I don't know?"

"Yes, ah start back. Only since Monday. They tell you orready?"

"They don't have to tell me nothing. I can't see yuh chest? You could put a lot of people on the canvas." He chuckled. Elsie listened and she brightened up. There couldn't be anything wrong, really.

Jonas had the Rienzi mission on his mind but to all appearances it was successful. He felt relieved and wanted to keep Butler in this light-hearted frame of mind. He said, "Oh, you saying I could put a lot of people on the canvas? It's only one man I have to put on the canvas. I mean, you done know ah signed up for Kid Tiger. But you have yuh own list: Hickling is number one – let me see, not John because this lance-corporal is really small fry; let's see: Inspector Power, Mavrogordato – Mavro is the chief contender; Judge Gilchrist, Charlie King – Charlie King is a real heavyweight, a Joe Louis. You have all o' them to put on the canvas some day soon."

Butler chuckled again. "But I ain't training. Not even skipping."

"But you orready have the footworks!"

Elsie was standing at the table looking at them. She had put breakfast on the table and she was ready. But she did not want to interrupt them. She felt overjoyed that Uriah Butler was in her house, because while he was there he was safe. Funny, she had had no idea he was coming this morning and it must have been the spirit of the Lord that made her send Jonas to buy smoke herring and milkbread. And she had been grating chocolate when Mr Uriah appeared. She felt very happy to see he was not tense but calm and relaxed – but of course he didn't know of the new danger. She glanced at the bake on the table. She had made a nice, brown coconut bake which was smelling so good the aroma pervaded the whole house. And she had made this without even knowing Butler was coming, nor even if he was around. The truth was that they were wondering whether he was alive! She stood there, and as she saw Butler glancing towards the table, she said, "Jonas, you coming? You and Mr Uriah could come and have yuh breakfast, you know."

From the time she said that Butler got up and walked to the table. He said to Jonas, "I don't know about you but I could knock out that bake right now."

Elsie laughed.

After they ate, Jonas called Butler into the back room. As they sat down Elsie walked in timidly. She said, "I could sit down here?"

"You'll ask that, Elsie? Tell Uriah what happened Saturday."

She came round the table and sat down. She put her hand on Butler's shoulder and said, "Mr Uriah, I'll just talk plain. That Chee Fong shop, that's a dangerous shop. Don't find yourself in it again. Else you is a dead man."

"How? What happen?" Butler was alarmed.

"I went in there last Saturday. When I was climbing up the steps I hear whispering. So I stand up there because the door was half closed. I was just about to call out 'Mr Chee' when, peeping in the crack by the hinge, there in the corner by where Pa Jakes always sit down, who is there but Charlie King, Pa Jakes and Chee Fong, and they talking about how to trap him and then what to do."

Butler asked, "How to trap who?"

"You!"

He chuckled, but he was very disturbed.

Jonas looked at him. Butler said, "Pa Jakes was in that?"

"In the middle of it."

He looked as if he couldn't believe it. He smiled with pain.

Elsie said, "We want to tell you, please not to go back there."

Jonas said, "That's why I was going down Vessigny this morning. Avoid these places Uriah. Keep in the open. If you in the open they can't touch you. They wouldn't be so brave to touch you in Fyzabad."

Butler was thoughtful. After a moment he said, "Elsie, you said this happened Saturday evening?"

"Yes, around seven so. But where you was for these past few days? You tell me in the 'countryside', but where? 'Countryside' sound like holiday business! Jonas was down Vessigny twice and the neighbour said you wasn't there for the whole day. What happening? We know something going on but what?"

"I meself ain't sure."

Jonas said, "From the time you left Rienzi and you said you was on a mission I tell meself if it's something you could talk about you wouldn't leave me out. I ain't even tell Elsie much. Believe me."

Butler said, "Well what really happening is a military secret, but ah talking to you two and I feel sure it will stay right here." He lowered his voice. "You know when we went to see Cola that day, Hothead, Cola was sending to call me! He orready sent a feller. I don't even want to call any name but it was Swithin Paul. But let's leave that. I didn't see Swithin. Leave it. I was dealing with Fletcher through Cola and that's a tight secret. Fletcher got word of a plot in Fyzabad to kill – " he stopped.

Elsie said, "To kill who?"

"To kill Butler."

Elsie trembled and buried her face in her hand.

Jonas said, "But Uriah, how you knew all that?"

"Cola Rienzi."

"And how Rienzi know?"

Butler laughed. "Guess."

"Can't guess," Jonas said nervously. His head was already hot. "Governor Fletcher."

Jonas whistled short and shrill. Elsie uncovered her red eyes.

Butler said, "Rienzi told me don't tell nobody nothing. Just disappear. Go deep in the country. Go Mayaro or Toco or Blanchisseuse or something. Somewhere far. Just for three days."

"Oh yes? How come? Why three days? And how come the Governor know about this? It was a Government plot?"

"Just Colonial Office. The man was a sharpshooter. Came down by the packet boat. Special confidential instructions to Fletcher, but Fletcher is a real friend. Fletcher *had* to know because he was supposed to protect this man in case the man got caught. Caught? Hm! The man came quite Fyzabad. He drew a complete blank. The packet boat was on a special mission. It went back last night."

Jonas was dumbstruck. He asked, "Mavrogordato, and Power, and Hickling, they knew about it?"

"Cola Rienzi didn't know if they knew about it. But the man was staying at Government House. This was official business. Official business but undercover. Look like the Secretary of State for the Colonies wasn't even in on it. Was some radical faction inside the Colonial Office. Yesterday the Governor got in touch with Rienzi to give him the all clear. Rienzi got me through the Mayaro police station. I reached back down last night."

"Oh, is Mayaro you went to? How Rienzi knew where you was?"

"When I reach Mayaro I went there and telephone him."

"You went in the police station? But Uriah you is a brave man!"

Elsie was looking at them. She had her hand to her mouth. Butler said, "Nobody there know me. I had on a big panama hat."

Both Jonas and Elsie laughed.

Elsie said, "But why you chose Mayaro?"

"It have any better place – any more peaceful hide-away?"

Jonas said to himself, *He taking this whole damn thing as a joke. But look at that. Look what the so-called democracy come to, eh? They saying, 'Children of the Empire you are brothers all', and at the same time they sending sharpshooter in yuh backyard. This Uriah said some time ago he's on the edge of darkness. Hm. In fact he was almost in the blooming precipice. Look what woulda happen to Fyzabad if that killer did find him! Blast it. And Butler still love the*

British. And sometimes the way he talk make me believe in the British too. Jonas looked up at the ceiling and with his arms out-stretched he said softly, "Oh Saviour, put a hand! Mash up their plans, oh Jesus!" He bit his lips.

Butler was looking at him. Elsie got up from where she was sit-ting and said, "You know what is the only thing to do now, Jonas? Take Mr Uriah to Siparia now to see Mamselle Marie. Take him right away – you hear me? Good Lord, ay! Put a hand!"

As they got up, Butler said, "Miss Elsie?"

"You calling me *Miss* Elsie?"

"You call me Mr Uriah all the time."

"Out of respect. But just call me Elsie, please."

"And please call me Uriah. Okay? As I was saying, Elsie, you are calm and will understand quicker than a lot of people. That British plot upset you, but that's not like the British. They don't do things that way. Well, look, we have this case right here. Fletcher saved me life. And he is Governor. And he let out their big secret. Mind you, if the Secretary of State get to hear Fletcher siding with a guerrilla they'll hang him by the ... by the big toe. But Fletcher saved me life. Look at that. Maybe the sharpshooter was right here in Fyzabad. Maybe the sharpshooter was right there at Chee Fong."

Elsie said, "I sure that day he was right inside the shop."

They were all silent. Then Butler said, "Another thing I wanted to say: I ain't superstitious. I only half believe in Mamselle Marie. But me second night in Mayaro, I was sleeping under a shop and – "

"Under a shop!" Jonas stood up.

"No, it was nothing. It was in a quiet part called Radix. Near a family called the Goulds. A young man passed riding a bike, and he stopped and talk to me so nice. Just about fifteen years old, you know. He said he was some Arthur Julien or something. Pleasant people. It was about five in the afternoon and the breeze blowing cool. The coconut trees, the zecack patch right in front of you. And the sea just whispering. You bound to sleep! And right away I had this dream. A little girl dressed in a sort of pur-ple, like zecack. She came up to me and said, 'You is the Uriah Butler?' So ah say, 'Well, yes.' She said, 'As soon as you go back to Siparee, go to Marie Vidale. Ma Marie want to see you.' That's why – " He looked at Elsie.

"Oh yes, I see. Oh, is so? Oh yes. That is a sure sign. Okay, Jonas taking you there right away. Jonas, get ready to take Mr Uriah to Mamselle. I have to run downstairs to wash some clothes."

8

BUTLER did not go down to Mamselle Marie right away. When Elsie went downstairs to wash the clothes, Jonas went into the kitchen to make a drink for Butler. He cut up the green limes Elsie had placed in the kitchen and quickly made some lime-punch, and it was when he was taking it to Butler that he met Butler snoring away in the chair. He tiptoed back and went down the steps and told Elsie.

She said, "Sleeping? He dead tired from that Mayaro what-you-call-it? That ain't joke, you know. Mayaro's how far – about eighty miles so? And the strain! I couldn't take that."

Jonas was sure Mayaro was more than ninety miles away, and he felt Uriah should get a medal for fleeing there, surviving, and arriving back – all in three days. Uriah had been on the run for the whole weekend, thanks to the Colonial Office. He breathed out hard and shook his head. He did not want to think about it. He sat down in his little gym and watched Elsie washing the clothes over a tub and scrubbing-board. Right now she was washing his oilfield clothes, mostly khaki, and he never found out how she managed to get out all those heavy stains of oil and tar. She did not spare the bar of blue soap and as she pushed the khaki over the sharp ridges of the scrubbing-board he could see her hands so white with foam it was as if she were wearing white gloves. He got up and drew nearer to her.

She saw his move from the side of her eyes and she said, "Suppose Uriah wake up and ain't see nobody?"

"He might think he still in Mayaro."

She laughed. She said, "That's joke for you. You mustn't laugh at that."

"He really having a hard time. I sorry for him."

"You sorry for him but I 'fraid for him." She stopped, straightened her back and turned round. "I'm scared, because anything could happen. What I don't want to think of is what woulda happen if Fletcher didn't phone Cola Rienzi and that sharp-shooter did come and meet Uriah in Fyzabad."

"Oh, Elsie, please. Please don't talk about that. You know how much I try not to think about it? You know how bitter I feel? I try to push this outa me mind but just hearing that nearly make me faint."

"If the British only know Fletcher let out their secret – "

"They'd shoot him! They'll court-martial him and shoot him. But of course that wasn't the British Parliament – that was a crazy faction. But even so, if they found out Fletcher was in touch with the agitator at all they woulda blast him to bits."

"You think they'd do that? Wouldn't people want to know why?"

"They ain't so brass face to make *that* public – that scandal about the sharpshooter – but I know what they woulda do. They'd bloody well recall Fletcher and clamp him in confinement. They might even trump up charges like treachery. You think the British making joke? You never hear about the Tower of London?"

"No."

"No? One day I'll tell you."

She settled down to washing again and he settled down to watching her. Watching her gave him a much heavier heart to think of Butler. There it was: Elsie just cooked and washed and cleaned out like dozens of Fyzabad women, and these women did these heavy tasks cheerfully and never complained. In homes where there were children these women washed and cooked and did all their chores sometimes with the babies on their arms. They tidied the bigger ones and sent them off to school. What did the men do?

He went on thinking and he remembered how Butler often talked of these scrubbing-board women. And he himself, Jonas, never called to mind he had one in the house. And *he* himself did nothing in the house either. He drew nearer to her and she saw him from the side of her eyes but she went on scrubbing, pressing and pushing the heavy-duty khaki against the scrubbing-board. He didn't know where she got the strength from. He did not feel –

Her voice startled him, "Ay ay. Why you looking at me so?"

"Hm. Looking at you? Just thinking, girl."

"I hope you thinking the right things."

"Life so funny. I was thinking about Butler again. As you know Butler always talking about scrubbing-board women. Those women who always over the tub and scrubbing oily khaki and blue dock overalls and who still always do everything in the house, and who don't even get appreciation. Looking at you I was remembering that. Is all those things Butler fighting for. He always say the men don't realise the women is the power behind the home. It's true."

She gave him a harsh sidelong glance, and then she seemed to get calm again. Then she said, "Power behind the home? Yes, I agree. Power to take blows."

He said nothing.

She said, "Not you though."

"But Butler want to change that, Elsie. You remember the last time he talk in Emporium yard he said he want to ease the lot of these ladies, and he was hoping the men folk would recognise their contribution and give them – what he said again? – yes, he said the men folk should give them 'a better and brighter day'. That's how he put it."

She said, "Yes, a better and brighter day on the scrubbing board. Yes, sisters, and a longer day, too."

"Oh, Elsie, why you turn so caustic?"

"Me? It ain't have no caustic soda here. It only have blue soap. But you right. A little caustic soda could take off those stains from the overalls." She turned and stared at him for a few moments. Then she said, "Look, boy, go up and see if Butler still sleeping, eh. And if he still sleeping go and buy some split peas and some pigtail for me. I have rice here and I'll make a quick cook so you two could get something to eat and then you could go Siparee. Go up now."

9

JONAS had to be quick. Since he no longer dealt with Chee Fong, he had to go all the way to the other side just past the police station where old Bowgee had his little shop. As he hurried to the shop, sweating, Lance-Corporal John called him over.

The lance-corporal had a big smile on his face. He said, "Mr Jonas, man, long time I ain't see you, man."

"You was wanting to see me?"

"Yes, I was only thinking about a short chat with you. It's because I ain't seeing you."

"Okay, nice of you, Lance-Corporal, but I'm in a great hurry. I just hurrying to the shop over here. I have – er – I just have a good old friend he just passing through – "

"But you coming all the way here to find a shop? I mean, I ain't saying Bowgee ain't good, but Chee just next door to you and – "

"Lance-Corporal, I just have to go." He gave a forced smile. "I ain't have much time. Ah hearing a rumbling. That is the Siparee train for San Fernando? I might have to go San Fernando."

"To meet Butler? We ain't seeing him these few days."

Jonas felt his heart begin to race. He said, "Constable, you will excuse me – I ain't see Butler for a few days meself. I have to go San Fernando to see about me boxing affairs."

"Oh I see. I just wanted to ask a few questions. Let me call the acting corporal."

Jonas was so irritated he could have gone berserk. He said to himself, *This stupid fool of a lance-corporal's only trying to detain me. Through wickedness. But if I leave he'll want to arrest me.* He said, "Lance-Corporal John, I have a visitor home waiting for me and we going San Fernando. Look, I could just go off?"

Lance-Corporal John had already called Gilroy Price and now Gilroy Price rushed into the Charge Room.

"You call me?" he asked the lance-corporal, and suddenly seeing Jonas, he said, "Oh, is you? What's the trouble now?"

"I was just going on me business but this wicked policeman call me in here and detaining me."

The acting corporal was suddenly fuming, "How you mean wicked? – Look, watch yuh words eh! You calling him wicked? You inside the police station and you insulting the officer?"

"Corporal Price, you ain't know. I have somebody waiting on me in me house for us to go San Fernando and I tell Lance-Corporal John that and he still wouldn't let me go."

The acting corporal asked, "He holding you?"

Lance-Corporal John seized on this. "You calling me wicked. I holding you?"

"Sorry. Okay, then." He moved off.

The lance-corporal said, "Wait a minute, the corporal talking to you and you moving off?"

The acting corporal whispered, "Let him go, let him go."

The lance-corporal said, "The young feller came in here and was asking me if that is the train from Siparee going to San Fernando."

"You come here to ask the lance-corporal that?"

"I didn't come here for that but when I hear the noise I ask him because I was thinking of going San Fernando. And I'll tell you why, Corporal. A few days ago this constable was at me house and I hear him say if Butler was by me he would have to come upstairs and arrest him. Corporal, that bound to be crazy. I ain't see Butler for about three days but so far as I know Butler ain't tried and convicted yet so how he could be a criminal? And even so he ain't running away from no police so anybody could have him in his house, why not? Well I going San Fernando to see Cola Rienzi to find out."

The voice of the lance-corporal said, "You sure is Rienzi you going to? And not to see about your boxing affairs?"

Jonas felt as if blood rushed to his head. "Lance-Corporal John, that is my business!"

The acting corporal was so taken aback that he pulled his cap off to dust it. Jonas said, "Corporal Price, I ain't railing against you, you know."

"But you taking up Butler fire-rage!"

"Fire-rage? So what? I can't go San Fernando to see who I want? That is the lance-corporal business?"

"Didn't you ask the lance-corporal if the Siparee train came in yet – or something like that?"

"I ain't breaking no law if I ask a question."

"True, but whether the train came in or not is not the officer's business. So don't insult him."

Jonas stood there speechless. Acting Corporal Gilroy Price put back on his police cap. He said, "You said your name is Jonas. I'll save you a train fare. What you said is true – you could talk to anybody in your house and you could have anybody in your house once the person is not a fugitive from justice. Now whether the Siparia train is in or no, I don't know. It's not my business."

Lance-Corporal John who had felt small to hear the acting corporal contradict him and say, 'you could have anybody in your house', recovered sufficiently to laugh when he heard this last part. The acting corporal went on, "This sun so hot. Lance-Corporal, let the young man go and see about his train."

Butler and Elsie had been waiting for Jonas until Elsie was frantic. And now it was well past half past eleven when Elsie suggested that if Butler did not go alone he wouldn't be able to go at all. This was because after the twelve noon train left there was no other train for Siparia before five. And that would be too late. She explained to Butler in detail how to get to Mamselle Marie after the train reached Siparia, and she hurried out to look all over Fyzabad for Jonas, starting with the police station.

Butler had to hurry to the railway station – in fact he nearly missed the train. But when he arrived at Siparia he walked straight to the house and knocked.

After a few moments a lady with a dotted head-tie and a full, brightly-flowered dress came to the door.

"Ma Marie?"

She knew the voice. She was amused that he was so heavily disguised. She said, "Oh, you come?"

She opened the door for him to enter and the strange sweetness of what seemed to him like wild flowers and incense all but overcame him. Up to this moment he was not sure he believed in Mamselle Marie, but he had felt so persecuted and uncertain, and yes, he was afraid. And he wanted to know why she sent to call him.

She took him into the deep recesses of the house. There were lots of strange pictures on the wall, and bouquets of different types of wild blooms and sweet grass, and there was a cluster of balisier in the corner. He could smell the sweet scent of metivier, and he breathed in deeply. They came to a room with a big table. She drew a chair for him to sit and she sat at the other end.

He said, "Some time back a young girl came to you about me."

"That was Elsie Francois."

"That's right. And I went to the country this weekend."

"To enjoy yourself? Or you just had to go."

"Why you asked me that?"

"I ask you questions as the spirit moves me."

"I had to go. It was a strange weekend. But in a lovely place. Far. With good people. And as soon as I reached back last night the ticket collector said you sent a message you want to see me." He wanted to tell her about the dream but he did not.

"Yes. I had the impression you were on the run. And when I prayed I realised there was no more danger. I saw you were safe. I wanted to tell you."

"Mamselle, I ain't sure I believe...I don't know how to put it."

"*I* know how to put it."

He looked at her.

She said, "What you want to say is this: you ain't sure I ain't a fraud. You ain't sure this is not a sham. You ain't sure you believe in what I'm doing. Don't worry. Just listen to me. How you going? What happening these days? What happened recently?"

His heart started to thump. "How you know?"

"How I know what?"

"How you know what happened recently?"

"If something didn't happen you wouldn't come. You don't believe in Mamselle Marie. You come today because you are frightened."

Butler was astonished. The pitch-oil light shone on both their faces. She was smiling quietly.

"You come today because you are scared."

He said nothing. He did not want his eyes to meet hers. He looked at the cluster of balisier in a corner of the room.

"Mr Butler. I don't know what moves me, nor what moves you. But I just believe in prayer. And I always liked wild flowers as a child. There are lots of good simple people around here, and they believe in me. And they come and we pray and they get their problems solved. The prayer brings in this good presence and maybe they get wiser. Maybe this is God, I don't know. But at times I feel prayer brings God into this house."

"You feel so? And what you feel about Butler, Mamselle Marie?"

"I know you are in danger, I know they are out to get you. *You* know it too. You fighting for the people but you feel you have no power. But real power is really on the side of right. You ever hear this saying: 'What stronger breastplate than a heart untainted? Thrice is he armed that hath his quarrel just.' Beautiful, eh? I remember it from 'Choice Quotations' in the West Indian Readers. Where the quotations came from I do not know. Who wrote that passage, I can't remember. The first thing is to be on the side of right and you could do anything. The first thing is to have your quarrel just. That's why I told Elsie you'll win. No magic in it. You bound to win. And I am with you. You come to me now, but when you speaking in Siparee or anywhere around I come to you. And I listen. You don't see me. But I'm there."

He was astounded. She continued speaking. "You admit that you frighten, but they more frighten than you. They'll try to kill you."

"Mamselle Marie they tried up to last week. A sharpshooter in a frigate. All the way from England. I'm not so sure if it was a frigate. I had to rush to a little village way on the east coast. Far but nice."

"Mayaro?"

Butler was flabbergasted. "You know this?"

She laughed. "It *must* be Mayaro. When you say a nice place on the east coast – well it has to be Mayaro. But they didn't kill you. You surprised I know this too?"

Butler laughed.

"I will pray. And I'll sing a few hymns in thanks."

"Yes, Mamselle Marie."

She began in a deep melodious voice, and in a chanting style. "Lord, I beseech you, bless this soul that is beside me. Bless and protect Uriah Butler. Help him Lord, and guide him, if Thou be pleased. Lord, he is struggling night and day, day and night, to save his people. Be with him, Lord, watch him as he walks this path of danger. Lord you know that truth is on his side, justice and right dwells in his heart. But to save the people of Fyzabad, Lord, and to save the people of Trinidad the journey is perilous, and he is singed by the flames of iniquity; protect him, Father, if Thou be pleased. Guide him, for he is a determined man, devoted to Thy works. He hath his quarrel just, O God. He is surrounded on all sides by his enemies and by the friends of his enemies. But he is brave, Lord, and thou hast given him courage. Some of the men with him who echo his words are jealous men, but bless the faithful couple that are with him, for they are with him in word and deed. Lord Jesus, Uriah Butler is strong in his love for Thee. Comfort him. Let not his heart be troubled if before him there's a lot to overcome. Give him strength to conquer all and to vanquish his enemies. Hear me, O Lord, stand with Uriah Butler. He came from Grenada and you brought him to Fyzabad, do not desert him now in the hour of need. Bless the Governor, Lord, who is working hand in hand with Butler. Guide the Governor to protect Butler, so that even if Friend Fletcher is persecuted and called away, Butler will lead your children from the clutches of iniquity to the Promised Land. Lord, it is the evil men who seek to gain everything from the oil without giving anything to the people. Butler is calling on them for justice. Butler is calling on them for fair play. Instead, they want his blood. Give him help, Saviour, to fight until victory. Lord, you have shown now is the time. Now is the hour. Let him tell his men to strengthen themselves and be ready at the call. And let him triumph in Thy holy name. Thanks be to God."

She bent and kissed the floor, then she kissed Butler's hand, and she rose and took the silver bell from the table. She rang it three times then, silently, she prayed again. Then she lifted her voice in song.

Butler remained on his knees. He heard her sing 'What a friend we have in Jesus', and then she sang 'God be with you till we meet again'. After that she wiped her eyes and sang 'The Greatest Love of All', and she ended with 'Fight the good fight'. Then she took Butler by the hand and raised him up. His eyes were full of tears, and his heart was racing.

He said, "What is the time, Mamselle?"

From there she could see the clock on the side wall over the table and she said, "Quarter to three."

"I think I'd better go now."

She looked at how his hands were trembling. She knew something was wrong.

He said, "You said the time to call the strike is now?"

"Yes. Get your men together and speak to them."

"I wish I could talk like you."

"Like me?" she said, surprised.

"You could speak nice, and…"

"And what?"

"And you is a nice lady."

"Thanks. But I want to be a happy lady. I feel as strongly as you about the situation, but I am not brave. So I always pray. I am a seer woman but I can't see further than my face without the grace of God. You are on the battlefield, a warrior for Fyzabad. You can't fail, Mr Uriah. There is a time for everything, and your time is now."

"Thank you, Mamselle Marie Vidale."

10

I N the still of the night, on the slope going up the hill past Vessigny village, the men huddled together to hear Butler. Men not only from Vessigny Village and Fyzabad, but from Forest Reserve too, from Penal, and from Point Fortin. Most of the men had come to Fyzabad by bus and had walked to Vessigny under cover of darkness. They did not want to strike, because if they did not get the wages which came their way fortnightly – however small those wages were – they did not know what they would do. They could hardly live from one week to the other without this money. They did not want to strike, but they came to hear what Butler had to say.

For he was so insistent. He had preached and pleaded with them, he had sent messages to them on the job, at home, even at church. At first they had thought of him as a man simply seeking attention, but of late they had come to believe there was really something they ought to hear. For the police did not give Butler an easy time. The way they hounded and persecuted him there must have been something to hear. Many of them remembered that night at Emporium Hall when Butler was speaking of the injustices the workers faced, and the huge amount of money Apex Trinidad Oilfields was earning. It was a public meeting and both of the Fyzabad policemen were there taking notes. And when Butler had condemned the injustices, the police had wanted to pounce on him and arrest him. But in a critical moment when the crowd moved up menacingly, they had released Butler but charged him with sedition. He had been summoned to appear in court but had never appeared.

They came to this secret meeting because they heard the strike was meant to run Apex into the ground. They heard Butler had said the secret was simple: unity, and that no strike was any good unless all the workers stayed away. Butler had said if this happened Apex was bound to collapse or pay higher wages.

This was why they had come. To know how to break Apex and force Hickling to pay more. They wanted to hear Butler explain. If he was convincing then they would sacrifice, once it made Apex fall.

It was well past half past eight in the night now and the silence of the hall was as deep as the darkness. The meeting was for nine o'clock and Butler watched anxiously as people stole into the hall.

There were three candles on Butler's table and two on the floor on either side of the room. Near the table, there were some sturdy young men on either side of Butler. A bunch of red wild flowers was in a jar not far from Butler's Bible.

A young man came up and as he approached the table the candlelight flickered on him. He bent down to Butler and he said, "Chief, it's time now. It's nine."

Butler asked, "Our fellers still out there?"

"Yes. But they have to stay there. Is only two ah them. Let them stay and watch out. Although somebody tell me is only John at the station. Gilroy Price went Siparia."

"He went to get straight?"

Hothead could not laugh.

"You want me to start now?"

"Yes, Chief."

"When you go home tell Elsie – "

"Elsie's right there in the front row. In front you."

Butler was taken aback.

Hothead said, "Start now, Chief. Is nine o'clock orready."

Butler started with a prayer. He kept his voice low. He said, "Just a prayer, my brothers and sisters. Just a prayer to keep us and guide us. And I want to ask you for a little hymn, 'I heard the voice of Jesus say'.

And he himself began singing, and in a moment the hall was full of song, not loud, but loud enough to make Butler think of the police, and loud enough to cause Hothead to leave the room and to join the two guards outside. He had something in his pocket which no one knew about, not even Elsie. Before he even got to the road the hymn died down. But as he looked out, he listened to the lilting melody, but it was the words that softened his heart:

> *I heard the voice of Jesus say*
> *Come on to me and rest,*
> *Lie down thou weary one, lie down,*
> *Thy head upon my breast.*

The hymn seemed to cast a serene atmosphere over the hall. Butler remained standing while the rest sat down and he moved from where he was and went to the front of the table, and he said in a soft, gentle voice, "My brothers and sisters, while we was singing that verse, I listened to the beautiful voices of the ladies from Vessigny and from Fyzabad and I felt as if we were already in the Promised Land. God be praised. We shall get there. With courage and patience, and sacrifice, and unity, my friends, we will get there."

Although the night was cool, Butler, who had his straw fan, fanned himself a little, then rested it down on the table. He said, "I asked you to meet me here tonight under circumstances in which anything could happen. We have to keep our voices low, and to keep the light dim, because the hand of injustice is raised against us. My friends, we have no right to hide to speak out for our rights, we have no right to hide to make plans for our future. In this country, in this land where you was born. But you know what the police is to us. But what I wanted to say first of all is that when we was singing I heard the ladies. In this darkness you can't see who is who. How beautiful the voices, my friends. Only that I didn't expect ladies at this meeting tonight, because as I said, anything could happen. I want to appeal to the men. If the worse come to the worst tonight, protect the ladies – even before you think of protecting Uriah Butler."

Voices in the hall cried, "Amen!"

"All right, my friends, not so loud. I can't see much as to whether the lodge is full or not, but when we was singing I had a good idea of the numbers and I know you answered the call. Amen. God be praised. I have something to tell you tonight. Every minute, as I speak to you, every minute I feel as if something could happen. I feel something will happen. So I'll have to talk fast. Yea, Lord. We are in a valley of tribulations, we are in a vale of tears, and I want you to stand fast and I want you to be strong, you know what's happening in this colony. You know what's happening in Fyzabad, in Forest Reserve, in Point Fortin, Butler don't have to tell you. No, I don't have to explain any more. I like how you bearing up, but Apex don't care a damn, and we have to fight the good fight."

There were muffled cries of "Amen".

"I am telling you tonight, my friends, that Uriah Butler is a man of peace, but if Apex want war I will lead you into battle, yes brothers and sisters. I would lead you into battle, for the Lord is with us. You have to get up and get and you have to fight for yourself. The stupid salary you getting from Apex, that could ever mind your wife and children? But Hickling want it like that. Yes, brethren, you better know it now. Hickling and Inspector Power want it like that. The Apex Company want it like that. Yes, my friends, you better know that all these foreign bas –, all these foreign gentlemen want it like that. Yes, brothers, I don't want to be dramatic, but this nonsense has to stop. You have to fight as if you in the trenches, Butler could only do so much and no more. You know why I called you here tonight? I called you here tonight because at the last meeting I told you let's wait and watch. Let's watch it a little I told you all. Because Hickling said he would talk to me and they said he told the police not to jail me because he want to talk to me. That is true, friends? I don't know. But I am damn dissatisfied. Hickling said he want to talk. I said if Apex didn't intend to increase the starvation pay there can't be any talk. There's only one thing for it. Because Apex declaring big dividends. You didn't see the papers? Apex declaring big profits. Millions of dollars for last year, 1936. So my friends, buckle your belts. There is only one thing for it. Hickling said he want to talk. I'm in Fyzabad but Hickling sent quite to San Fernando to tell me legal adviser he want to talk to me. Yes, he sent quite to San Fernando to tell Cola Rienzi that. Yes friends. And I am right here. You could believe that? Anyway, last week I spoke to Hickling – oh you didn't think I met Hickling? He called me in the office. You want to know what he told me? Friends, that is why I called you here tonight."

Butler drank some water from a glass on the table. He looked down the hall as if he was looking outside. He looked around for Jonas but Jonas was out at the gate, keeping sentry. With his eyes now accustomed to the flickering light he saw who had been in the front row next to Jonas. He saw Elsie. He put down the glass again.

He said, "You could imagine a man like Hickling sending for me to come to his office to talk and not talking about money? You could imagine that? Hickling called me into his office and tell me the Government getting fed up with me and me threats. He said this colony can't do without Apex, the amount of money Apex putting in the Treasury, and if the men go on strike it will cripple the country and if I don't want to find me backside behind bars I'd better behave meself. Not one word about any increase in pay."

There was a moan in the hall.

"But God is not asleep, my dear brothers and sisters. No, God ain't sleeping. Brothers and Sisters the great God of Israel is watching the suffering of his people, and the time for deliverance is here." There were several low cries of 'amen' in the audience, and a ripple of applause went right across the hall. Butler said, "The Lion of Judah was lying down but he's getting up now, because he is watching. The time is close. They think they chained the Lion of Judah, but the Lion of Judah will break every chain."

As Butler went on speaking, the plaintive, melodious hymn rose softly throughout the hall:

> *The Lion of Judah will break every chain*
> *And Heaven's redemption will bless us again,*
> *The Lion of Judah will come from the sea,*
> *And Heaven's deliverance will bring joy to me.*

As Butler neared the end of his speech he put up his hands and the singing died away.

He said, "I ain't saying no more to Hickling, but I want you, friends, to show him the power of unity." He dropped his voice. "I am calling on you to strike, and to strike as if it's one man. We calling a day and every man walking out on that day. And I talking about Apex now. Afterwards we will deal with Forest Reserve, and United British. If they can't hear, they'll feel. Look, Saturday next, the 18th, they having big Coronation Carnival in Port of Spain. Because George VI crowning. I like George VI, I love him bad. I ain't have nothing against George VI. But this is my country and yours. We was born here, right here, and if anybody have to enjoy the juice of this land it's you and me. And so this is a call to you, brethren, a call to arms. You ain't carrying any gun or stick, but you armed to yuh teeth with justice. Yes, justice on your side, and Butler with you and we going down fighting. When I say I am with you, you could believe I am with you, and is Butler till the final bell. So I'm expecting you to wait on the call, be on the alert, and when I give that call I calling on you to walk out of Apex as one man. And remember this, I am no hero. I am no big-time leader. When I'm with you I'm with friends and brothers and if nobody's carrying the banner then Butler will carry it. Right? With you I could be strong like a lion. And if Hickling saying this country needs Apex, I will tell him frankoment that Apex needs this country too. Apex needs us, yes friends, Apex need the workers. Because who will bring up the oil from the ground? So brothers and sisters, what I want to tell you tonight is that the call is coming soon. That is what I call you to tell you tonight. Band yuh belly, because the call is coming momently. As soon as the next two or three weeks, yes, as soon as that. Okay, the police didn't find us out tonight. I have the exact date of the strike but I still ain't giving it here because I ain't one hundred per cent sure who is here. A spy could have slipped in, we don't know. I want you to be on the alert and all of you will get a message. God be praised. God always guide the righteous. Okay, comrades, brethren and sisteren, we breaking up now. Just let's sing softly, 'God be with you till we meet again'. Softly, eh, brethren? Let us sing."

11

O N Monday morning Jonas went to Forest Reserve. He did not
pass through the main gate but through one of the oilfield
roads that went in the direction of the famous oil well 'Helena'.
This well, Helena, was the highest producing of all the wells of
Trinidad Leaseholds Limited and it always had a large gang of
oilfield policemen in the vicinity because the company did not
want hotheads to come too near.

Jonas felt he had to bring his message to the workers, even if he
had to be expelled from the premises.

As he drew near the well, many of the gang-workers stopped to
look at him. When he approached them he was taken aback because he saw an old friend. He said, "Hey, Emery, you here? I
thought you was down La Brea."

Emery spoke quietly. "Came down last week. We'll talk. That
meeting went off?"

"Yes. You knew about it and why you didn't come?"

"We had a blow-out on Number Three."

Jonas knew about that blow-out. They had been all crying sabo-
tage. As he looked around, with almost everyone's eyes on him, he
wanted to scream, "I didn't cause it. I only come with a message."

But he realised he should calm himself. He had seen most of the
faces at Butler's meetings.

He said, "Friends, what I come here for is this. I'll make it short
and sweet. Butler can't come here, you know that. And although I
ain't working on this side, ah thiefing a little chance. We had a
meeting in Vessigny last night and I come with a message."

"Message? Well give it," somebody cried.

As he was about to speak he spotted someone else he knew and
he just said, "Hey Mark," and watched him stride off. He continued, "Fellers, this is a message for all."

"Just give yuh message."

"Well shut – " He checked himself.

Emery Ford came to him and said, "Jonas this is a busy morning
for the boys. Don't lose yuh temper." He took him a little distance

away, then he said quietly, "The fellers here really like Butler but they can't show it too much. Just tell them what you have to tell them and that's that. The fellers have to work, you know. Tell them before the foreman come back."

Ford clapped and signalled the workers to come. Jonas said, "Friends, sorry. I'll just give you the message and go. I ain't going into anything like Hickling and so on. And what Uriah Butler have to put up with, etc. I ain't going into that. I just passing on the message and that's it. Then I gone."

Marcus came back and he said to himself, *Oh hell, the hothead still here*. He caught Jonas's eyes and he made a sign by opening his arms, and with his lips he formed the words, "We busy, man."

Without appearing to notice, Jonas said, "Well, I could see you fellers have a lot to do and I orready take up so much of yuh time orready. I know you busy. But ah come to bring a message from Butler and I have to tell you. It wouldn't take no time, it short and sweet. Those who here will tell those who ain't here. This is very important, and I'll tell you why. The message from Butler is that he decide to call a strike. Yes, friends."

There was so much applause and so many cries of "Hurrah", that Jonas was stunned. Many were asking "When?" and "How soon?" And a few started singing, 'When the Saints go Marching in'. Even Marcus had a smile – but it was calm and reserved.

Jonas said, "When? Friends, you asking when? Brothers and Sisters when the call go out, that's when. The call going out soon."

Somebody said, "Don't try to talk like Butler."

Jonas said, "There is only one Uriah Butler!"

He turned and he saw Marcus's eyes on him. Marcus repeated, more by the movement of lips than by words, "We busy."

"Ah finishing, friends, but let me say this before the foreman come."

There was laughter, and Jonas looked around puzzled. His friend Emery said, "Marcus is the foreman."

"Oh Christ. I didn't know. Okay boys, let me clear out so you could work. Sorry Mark. Okay, Butler say prepare to buckle yuh belt tight. And listen out. The call coming. Butler calling the strike on – number 19. I deliver me message and I gone."

There was applause.

12

WHAT with the delays, and the need to see Butler himself, it was late evening when Jonas got off the bus and walked through the track home. When Elsie came to the door dressed and with shoes in hand, he said, "You going out or coming in?"

"How come you stay so long? You forgetting I told you I have to go to the women's branch? I was waiting for you all the time. A little bit again and you wouldn't a meet me you know." Then after a little silence she said, "How the day went?"

"Good. Very good. We could count on – "

She interrupted, "Look, oh gosh. What ah shoulda tell you first of all I didn't. Mr Uriah was here."

"Butler was here? Jesus! I want to see him bad. I want to see him now. After Forest Reserve I went down to Vessigny you know, but he wasn't home. Then I went to Vance – look, you told him I went down Forest Reserve?"

"Yes. He couldn't remember if it was today you said you was going or if is tomorrow. He say he done give you a message." Her voice dropped and she looked around, and although there was nobody to see or hear, she whispered, "The message is the same thing you told me last night? About how the strike will call on June 19th? The Saturday?"

Jonas was nodding 'yes', and as he looked at how her face brightened up, he said, "But you didn't believe me."

"How you mean? Why I wouldn't believe you – who tell you that? You is me husband! Is only because I was excited. You see ah didn't expect good news. Look how long we didn't get any good news. But Mr Uriah did well know what he was doing. Anyway, I only hope the good news come out as good news."

"What you mean?"

"What I mean is I hope everybody stay home on that day."

"They'll stay home." The fact that she said this caused some doubts to stir up inside him.

She said, "You know how those boys can't sacrifice at all?"

He was disappointed in her. "Elsie, you saying that too? So you ain't leaving nothing for Hickling to say! After all, the fellers have to work like mules for 72 cents a day, when – "

"I ain't leaving nothing for Hickling to say? But it's the truth. We mustn't be afraid of the truth, Jonas. Hickling was saying we don't save, and that's the gospel. I remember telling you I agree with Hickling, although Hickling can't hide behind that. Because oil making money and Apex hauling in a big profit."

"Well, I could never agree with his stupid statement about workers not sacrificing because I want to know what the hell you could save from ten to twelve dollars a fortnight."

"But Jonas, *you* getting the same thing and we always have food on the table. Don't get me wrong, the money's still a damn scandal, but I ain't working nowhere because you don't want me to do domestic servant work or any menial work, but we still ain't suffering."

"Because it's you. It's due to you. You know how to save."

"You too. You is only a hothead."

"We come like Jews. I admire those Jews, O God. Thrift, girl. When I give you a dollar you save a dollar fifty from it."

"Well, it's the same blooming thing those other women could do."

He looked at her.

She said, "You hear me? You didn't hear me. It's the very same thing they could do. All they doing is complaining, but they rushing to excursions, they fulling up the dance halls. They going to cinema quite in Siparee. That is all the kinda sacrifice they making and that's why Hickling don't want to give us a damn cent more."

He said nothing. She said, gently, "Look, I have to go."

He was still silent. She looked round. She was placing some hairpins at the tips of her plaits, and she had one of the hairpins in her mouth. She took it out and said, "Let's just face the facts, Jonas, poor people spend money like water when they have it. You remember that little group when Cola Rienzi fought their case in court and win a little back pay for them? And they celebrated so wildly they couldn't even pay Rienzi?" And she said in her mind, *That's why the poor remain poor.* She tugged his sleeves. "Cheer up. That's how it is. They don't like to save. Butler's always talking to them."

"I, too. But we can't let Hickling get away with murder."

"I know. And if we ain't careful they'll trample us."

"Elsie, look, I'll tell you this. Don't say nothing when I tell you because I know how you is. Today, I think it was Emery Ford – yes, Emery Ford. Anyway somebody said something like 'Stop talking like Butler,' and I said, "It have only one Uriah Butler." Well I'll tell you now: it only have one Elsie Francois. If anybody could stretch a penny to reach a mile, it's you. Only one Elsie."

She laughed it off. "And it have only one Hothead." She kissed his cheek.

"On me cheeks? Good God. Come back here."

"Not now. I have to go."

Elsie took the news of Butler's decision to the women at the meeting and they were all thrilled, and in the room there was a buzz which came from their chatter. All these women were the women of the oil workers – a few were wives but the majority of them were in the category of 'house-keeper', and there were a few girl friends and 'concubines'. Once Lance-Corporal John was giving a list to Hickling of about thirty workmen and their female companions who were always talking about 'strike', and when they secretly investigated these people they found that out of the whole thirty, as many as twenty-seven of the men were just 'living with' their partners, and only three were married. Which led Hickling to say, "Mr Butler wants to fight for higher wages, why doesn't he fight for higher morals?" Which in turn stumped the lance-corporal for words. For it was not only that he himself wasn't married to the mother of his five children, but he did not see anything wrong with just 'living together'. And when Hickling said, "Just imagine the number of little bastards running around," the lance-corporal did not even know what 'bastard' meant. He asked what that was and when Hickling told him he said, "I was a happy bastard, Colonel, Sir."

All these things were passing through Elsie's mind as she stood in front of the women. Some had their heads tied to show they were defiant and militant. Elsie said, "Everybody all right? Okay. What I just told you is what Butler himself said. What I want to say to all of you is to band yuh belly because you don't know how long this struggle will last. Support yuh man. You mightn't have much in your home – in fact, yuh cupboard might be like Mother Hubbard's – you know who that is?" They stared with blank faces. And she herself thought she should have known better. She was sure a few of them had actually been to school but she could not guess which ones. She said, "You ain't plant sweet potatoes round your house, and a little bit of cassava and so on? Look, tell me this – anybody could starve in Trinidad?"

She was talking gently all the time but then she got firm and said, "Don't give in! Support the man in the house. Show him that you with him and that you believe in him. And you going up with him to – me husband like to say, 'to the final bell'. Listen, all the men in Fyzabad under a strain. All. Because as you know it's a tough battle going on, ah don't have to tell you. A battle for justice, let's face it. Our men in Fyzabad under plenty pressure. You have to pamper them – "

Someone said, "Pamper who? Don't make me laugh." And a ripple of laughter went round the room.

Elsie said, "These are *our* men, the fathers of our children. They belong to – "

Somebody said, amidst the chatter, "The fathers of our children but they does mind them? Ha, girl! You talking because you ain't have no children."

"None of me own, but it matters not. The children in Fyzabad is mine and yours. They belong to all of us. Not so? Ain't is we who bringing them up? We don't want these fathers to fall. Or fail. If it's a long strike and you don't pamper them they'll lose heart. We don't want this strike to break for no reason at all. Anybody here know me husband?"

Quite a few voices cried, "Hothead", and some said "Jonas". Only two said "Kid Fearless", and she snatched on this and said, "Me husband believe in Butler and he on his feet backward and forward so that this thing doesn't fail. Because he know the importance of it. Look, he have a boxing fight Saturday night in Emporium and he ain't train yet because of this thing. He ain't have no time. He want to –"

A lady in front interrupted, "If he ain't train yet, when he'll train? He ain't have time because of this Butler business? So Saturday Butler will go in the ring for him?"

There was laughter.

"Maybe," Elsie said. "I don't know. All I know is that *I* ain't going in the ring for him. Because I ain't train either. Of course the other feller, Kid Tiger, will knock him out, and I frighten and I ain't so like the thought of that, but I going to Emporium just to show him I support him. And if he stumble quick and fall and they count him out, that's the best thing."

The women laughed.

"But what ah came to tell you is about the strike. Take this date down: June 19th. Don't forget that date. Prepare for it. All the men have to come out. It ain't make no blasted sense if everybody don't come out. If half come out and half stay in, Apex will still run and all that will happen is after more weeks of penance and more pressure, when you have nothing at all in the house and nothing to send the children to school with, the men who come out on strike will have to creep back and ease back to work. And why? Because Apex still functioning. The strike ain't do a damn thing. And then Hickling will get more bold. Is then he'll be cocky! Because we losing again and again. We showing them they superior and we can't win."

She stopped to see if the words were sinking in. She said, "Sisters, there's where you come in. When Butler call the strike, keep them home. They don't know how much power we women have but we could be Tarzan when we ready. Not so? Keep them home, I say to keep them home. Don't give them a chance to say they going to work. Tell them they ain't going to no damn work this morning. And that's that. Be strong. These blinking men like to beat their wives but you stand up to them and tell them no work this morning. It's the only way. Hear me, sisters. June 19th is coming. You stand up in front of them. Stand up and tell these boys, 'It ain't have no going to work today.' If they want to fight with you, fight back. You don't know yuh strength and yuh power. The success of that strike depending on you."

She looked at them and it was a different atmosphere in the room now. She herself was a little overwrought.

She said, "My name is Elsie Francois and me husband is Hothead, and both of us swear to God if every one of you women do what I say now, June 19th will be the day of deliverance, so help me God! Because I could blooming well guarantee that if you keep your men home Apex bound to give in. Because jumbies don't know how to operate ah oilfield, and spirits can't drill. Take what I telling you today. True, me husband don't want to hear about the Coronation. But Coronation ain't nothing. So what? I ain't hate white people, you know, and neither me husband. But me husband sick with the blinking cross we have to bear. He sick with the struggle Butler have to put up without enough support. And the oilfield employers laughing. They saying we hungry – and that's true. But how could anybody be too hungry to fight? We have to sacrifice. When June 19th come, keep the men home, sisters. You could do it, because they can't do without us, you know. If you see how me husband rushing home, just to look at me."

She put up her hand, "Don't laugh now. Don't laugh now. This is serious business. It's a battle all of us have to fight. The men in the front line and we behind. When they think of the struggle they get bitter, but what's the point? Don't get bitter, get better. And fight back. That's exactly what ah tell me husband. Sisters, you fighting back? Yes? Amen."

13

WHEN Elsie got back home she was disappointed to see that Jonas had already gone to sleep. She tried to shake him and roll him over but he only groaned and snapped at her.

"Boy, what's wrong? You couldn't wait up for yuh wife?"

There was silence. She shook him again and he groaned and she cried, "Everything went well. The evening went good."

There was no answer. He was lying on his belly, and she pulled him over onto his back. She said, "You lying down like a dead man and only snoring." Although she asked herself if dead men could snore she did not even laugh. She watched his face, and then she said, rather loudly, "Jonas!" He turned and opened his eyes and rolled on the side, then he closed his eyes again. She said, "You up?"

He opened his eyes. He said, "Elsie, what in the name of heaven wrong with you tonight? Ah trying to get a little sleep and you there harassing me."

"And who you want me to harass? You is me husband. When you go out in the night I always up waiting for you but when I go out it's something different, you have no blinking time with me."

He rolled to his other side. His eyes were open now. He looked around him. When he saw her he said, "How it went?"

"Very good, boy." She sounded excited. She was about to kneel over him on the bed to harass him even more but now she quickly jumped down from the bed so she could change quickly to get into bed again before he fell back asleep. She said, "You was waiting up?"

She rolled his head and said, "Jonas, you was waiting?"

"Aha." His eyes were closed again.

"Look, before you go back to sleep, say if you still going to Point Ligoure tomorrow."

"Aha."

"Aha? You still going. You worrying about that silly Coronation parade? If you don't want to see it, just stay inside. Like me. You don't have to go to hell away in Point Ligoure."

He rolled right over onto his belly, then onto his back again, and he got up into a half-sitting position. He said, "Oh God, Elsie. Girl, you have the devil in you tonight or what! All day I up and down the place and I tired and want to sleep but oh Jesu lover of my soul, this woman wouldn't leave me alone."

Elsie laughed. She said, "It's because she love you."

His eyes were half open because of the glare from the light which Elsie had left on. She was wickedly amused. She took off the light hurriedly and got into bed and hugged him up.

She said, "Why you still going to Point Ligoure?"

He wrung himself away and rolled around. He said, "You asking why I still going Point Ligoure? Ain't it train I going to train, Elsie? Didn't I tell you ah going to spend the whole time there because I have to go in the ring Saturday night and up to now I ain't do nothing yet?"

"Nothing yet? And Saturday is the Coronation Carnival? You said you spending three days in that old house down Point Ligoure. In any case, good, listen to this: the village is Point Fortin. Why they have to come and call the beach 'Point Ligoure'? That make sense?"

He did not answer. Because he knew that she knew very well the beach was named for his grandfather who lived in that old house.

She shook him and said, "Okay, another thing. Tell me this: tonight is Tuesday night. You staying until Saturday. So what time you coming for the fight?"

She knew all these answers already but she just wanted to keep him awake. When he told her he was coming at seven p.m. and that he was going straight to Emporium Hall, she said, "Where is Emporium Hall, deary?"

The question could not have been more ridiculous because even from the back window of the house they could see Emporium Hall. There was silence.

She shook him hard this time and she said, "I told the girls how you always like to rush home just to see me."

He opened his eyes. When he took in what she said he gave a little smile. Then he said, "Yes, but tomorrow morning I'll be in Point Ligoure."

"You want me to come?"

"But Elsie, we talked about that orready last night. I going to train. It's only three days I have – well, let's say four. How I'll concentrate? And I love you so much orready."

She hugged him up tightly. A strange feeling just rushed up in her and she felt it in her nose. She wanted to cry but she didn't. She had told the women to be strong, and now she wanted to be tough, but she couldn't. She said, "Yes. That's true. But you'll train just three days before the fight? That make sense? Eh? Mr Uriah Butler going in the ring for you?"

"But Elsie, you know how things was. I still have to try me best." And he yawned.

"But don't let that blasted tiger-man knock you out, you know. Else I coming in the ring."

There was nothing but silence. She kissed his closed eyes and now it was she who yawned. She said, "Okay, Sweetie. You orready in dreamland. And I ain't far meself. We'll talk tomorrow morning, eh? We'll talk before you go."

14

In the still of the morning Jonas got up and dressed by the light of the pitch-oil lamp. He looked at Elsie sleeping and he gave her the slightest touch of a kiss on her eyebrows, scared to wake her up. Then he took his packed grip and stole out of the bedroom.

Two nights ago he had told her of his predicament. Having given his word, and having signed up to fight Kid Tiger, he could not back out. In fact, backing out might even land him in jail. He just *had* to appear. Posters about the fight were stuck up in Emporium Hall and all over Fyzabad. Today was Wednesday 15th May, and he had not done anything much except his skipping, and some shadow-boxing. He knew his bobbing and weaving was good, and he felt that for him this was the most important thing now. More important than a good punch. Because although Tiger was slow, Tiger, for a middleweight, packed the heaviest punch in Trinidad boxing. His punches were even heavier than those of the heavyweight, Gentle Daniel. So some boxers said. He had never fought Tiger, so he didn't know. But he had talked to some of the men Tiger had beaten – he had seen some of the fights, and he particularly remembered that revolting night when Tiger despatched Speedy Collins. He remembered the left to the head which stunned Collins and had blood streaming from under the left ear, and he remembered how Tiger crossed a right uppercut and Collins's knee buckled, and when Collins wouldn't go down Tiger swung a bolo punch to the top of the head and this made Collins stagger – and still Collins's corner would not throw in the towel. Madmen! Because people were shouting in Emporium Hall and it was almost a riot. Collins's handlers were only hoping for the bell to ring and for the round to end, so that their boxer would get a moment of respite – a breather, to regain the strength of his legs, which were rubbery, and for them to wipe away the blood. And for him to recover. Madmen! Because anybody could see the only place Collins would recover was on the canvas.

But he remembered the bell *did* ring just as Speedy Collins looked as if he could take no more and would go down. And he remembered how he was so annoyed when Collins's handlers, while wiping away the blood from Collins's face, were telling Collins what to do in the next round. The *next* round, mind you! It was cruel and scandalous to send Collins back to fight! Yet they were telling him how from the time the bell sounded he must skip away and dance and let Tiger throw punches and miss. He remembered how awful he felt to have to be a part of that barbarity. Could Collins 'skip away' at that stage? In fact, what were they really wanting? Did they want Tiger to kill Speedy Collins, for heaven's sake? Couldn't they throw in the blasted towel and stop the show? For even if Collins could have danced on those rubbery legs he wouldn't have been able to dance on that bloody canvas. And 'bloody' was the word, yes, because the canvas had been slippery with blood. The blood running from Collins's ear and nose.

Hothead looked at the sea in the direction of the white streaks of foam in the distance with gulls flying low over the water, but he was not seeing anything at all. He was only seeing how, when Speedy Collins resumed the next round, Tiger, fierce now as a real tiger, simply pranced, and did some unnecessary footworks then pounced on his prey and unleashed a left uppercut, which lifted Collins's chin, and then came down with his usual bolo, and sent Collins crashing to the canvas, and he remembered how amidst all the shouts and screams, amidst all the uproar, Collins rolled over and got to his knees, not knowing where he was, whether he was at Paramount in Siparia or Emporium in Fyzabad, but as he tried to rise at the count of nine, there was another tigerish bolo, and he dropped to the floor as a log.

Just to think of this made Jonas feel more angry and revolted and a little bewildered. Because he was re-living the shrill noise all around him, and the rush to ringside, blocking his view. Maybe some rushed to see whether that bolo had killed Speedy Collins! But what upset him most of all was that when he stood up so he could see above the heads of those who had stampeded in front of him, what could he see but Speedy Collins, who had just fallen like a palmiste tree, on his knees again, ready to get up! He wanted to cry, "No, Speedy!" But in any case who could hear in that din? But it would have been a waste of time, anyway. The referee didn't stop counting, and Tiger was jumping around menacing the battered Speedy Collins. Then the next moment Jonas could not help but turn his head away. For at the count of nine Speedy Collins rose, and with a flurry of lefts and rights Tiger rushed in for the kill, and as Collins staggered and stumbled, mercifully the towel was thrown into the ring, and the referee stopped the fight.

Jonas felt sick as he remembered that night. Just to recall it made him feel to vomit. And yet Sharkey had been saying it was a great bout. And even Rafael, the promoter of Speedy Collins, was bragging and saying his middleweight taught Tiger a thing or two. Yes, Collins taught Tiger how to eat them raw, and without a tooth pick! Jonas wondered what was it that had made he himself, Kid Fearless, sign up to fight Tiger in the first place. Because in a way it was like a sheep going to the slaughter. Well, a sheep did not have to practise to go to the slaughterhouse. He laughed at himself, but even saying that did not make him afraid. In fact, had he trained he would have been confident he could put Tiger down. For the only weakness Tiger had was what he, Fearless, could capitalise on. It was simply that Tiger did not bob and weave, he moved in a straight line. He just kept coming in to you. It was only when he had you in trouble and he knew it, that he began showing off, pretending he could shift and feint and skip. Pretending he could dance.

If he, Jonas, had trained, by the time Tiger thought it was time for the dance it would have been too late. He knew that his own strength was in bobbing and weaving and making boxers miss, he wasn't fooling himself. But Tiger was strong and only kept coming, and the problem was that while you could run, and even backpedal, there was just no place to hide.

He felt a little embarrassed and annoyed for his lack of training. But what could he do? It was just the wrong time. What could he say? The Butler events had come up and he could not turn his back on them. Because the Butler affair was for one's country and for human dignity. Boxing was for personal glory. For the roar of the crowd. But he just had to be in the ring on May 18th – what could he do? He had no choice; he had given his word. He had entered a contract. He just had to fight, even if he was eaten raw!

He tried to throw this off his mind by thinking of how the breeze was blowing cool and nice, and how there was the green clump of mangrove running so beautifully to the Guapo River – things he had seen dozens of times before – and he considered how white the sand was. But the colour he was thinking of was not white but red. Red for blood and for the colour of what was a good part of the so-called canvas when Kid Tiger had butchered his friend, Speedy Collins.

Horrified, he got up and turned to walk towards the mangrove clump. God forbid! The canvas was not going to be red. That was why he came out to Point Ligoure to live like a hermit in his grandfather's old boathouse until Saturday. And only train, train, train. Train to move out of the way, and of course, train to stay.

He came back and went inside the old boathouse and changed his clothes and his shoes. He put on a pair of blue shorts and a red jersey and a pair of newish washekongs. He said to himself, *Ah wonder where the name 'washekong' come from*. They were really canvas shoes and because the soles were of crêpe people also called them 'crêpe soles'.

The red of his jersey was very stark. Having thought of blood a short while ago he was not keen on seeing any more red, but these were always the colours he chose, ever since he went to Vance one day, where Uriah was living at the time, and saw Uriah's wall papered in those colours. When he had asked why so much red, Uriah had said, "You don't know those parasites sucking the blood of these workers? That's why I have red. Red for blood."

He remembered himself saying, "Blood again, Uriah?" and Butler answering, "Hickling wouldn't ask that, though. If when we strike he could get Fletcher to call out the army and shed some blood, you think he'll hold back?"

And Butler had added, "The white strips, though – the white strips is for hope. Yes, I always have hope. In spite of Hickling. Yes, Sir. If you ain't have hope you can't cope."

He had liked the sound of that then, and he liked it now – although his own hope was like that white cloud hanging there on the horizon. It didn't seem to be resting on anything solid.

He remembered asking Uriah, "Why the black rafters?"

"Black is strength. You need strength to win. You know why we'll win? Because we have right on our side."

Jonas came back to the present. He said to himself, *Look, you didn't leave Elsie to come here and day-dream*. He promptly got up and went out of the cabin and looked around him. The sea was blue and rippling and there was a strong breeze blowing from the south. But there was more than a hint of low darkening clouds just before him to the west. He did not want rain today. He looked straight across the water and although he could not see the hazy outline in the mist, he tried to imagine rain was falling across there in Venezuela and that it would not come here.

He went into the boathouse to get his skipping rope, and when he came out again, in that short time the western sky definitely looked like rain. His heart thumped, but then he suddenly remembered what day it was. He was astonished how that had entirely slipped his mind. He said aloud, "Let the rain fall and wash out this blasted Coronation parade. I wish it could do just that when Saturday come, and let it wash out the Carnival too. Because that's all people thinking about – fête and bacchanal." Then he looked around and said, "But look how I forgot them completely and yet they is the cause I come out here this morning!"

He took the skipping rope then went out on the hard sand and began to skip. Then he dropped the rope and went back and brought out a piece of rectangular board, not very large, and he put it down on the sand and he began to skip on it. He was there skipping for at least one and a half hours, and as he was skipping he was thinking. In his wandering mind he even heard the siren blow at nine a.m. to start the parade, and he was very upset but he kept on skipping. He had quite forgotten there would be the parade over at Point Fortin too. When he had skipped for about an hour and three quarters he glanced at his watch and felt he would do the final hundred. But when he reached the next hundred he continued skipping because he was feeling good.

He skipped and kept watching the landscape here at Point Ligoure. He watched the curve of the beach. Suddenly, the weather changed and got very bright, although it had been threatening to rain. There was nobody on the beach for miles, and he enjoyed this very much. He was glad for the solitude. Still skipping, he looked up at the sky and saw that the threat of rain had completely gone. He continued skipping until the sweat was beginning to ooze and run off him. The truth was that, physically, he was in shape. His body was responding. He was just jumping, calmly, and turning his wrist, and the rope was just passing under his feet and over his head. He felt glad because he hadn't trained much and he was in form.

* * *

Back in Fyzabad it was still early when Lance-Corporal John walked through the track. He stood up in front of Jonas's house and called and in fact it was his voice which woke up Elsie. She came to the kitchen door, opened the top half and peeped, then seeing the police uniform she rushed back and put on a dress quickly. Sleep, which was in her eyes, now fled for good. When she came back she opened the front door and said, "Morning Constable, what happen?"

"Where Hot–? Where's yuh gentleman?"

She could hear her heart thumping inside her. That was what she wanted to know. For she realised now Hothead was not on the bed. The voice had brought her straight from dreaming about pigeons and ducklings to a state of stupefaction, and right now her mind was in confusion and disarray.

She stuttered out, "Constable, I don't know. Where he is? Tell me, please."

She bit her lips so that she would not cry and break down. She was a strong woman, and lots of people told her so, including Jonas himself. But now she felt as weak as a strip of straw, and desperate.

Lance-Corporal John, who knew nothing whatsoever as to Jonas's whereabouts and was simply checking up, said, "You asking me? You want me to tell you where yuh husband is? He in jail!"

"What for? What he do? Oh my God!" She started to cry. She held on to the kitchen door and nearly slid to the floor. But she had the presence of mind to know crying would not help and there had to be action. Right away she thought of bail. Someone to stand the bail. She thought of Chee Fong. She looked at the constable standing at the bottom of the steps, and she wanted to go and get dressed properly if she had to go out to try to get bail. She had asked what Jonas did but she was sure that it had something to do with the Butler struggle and the Carnival merriment she was already hearing. She said, "Constable, please, me brain addled. I so confused I can't tell you nothing. I know me husband is a hothead but he is not a bad man. What he did? They'll take bail for him?"

The policeman stared at her. At first he thought it was a performance but now he was beginning to suspect Elsie was going mad. He said, "Look, Madam, I talking to you. It ain't seven o'clock yet, I come here and ask for yuh husband and you crying and jittery and you can't tell me where he gone this Coronation Day, and I – "

"Constable," she interrupted. "All right, all right, sorry. I didn't know what was what. As you come here and call and wake me and I ain't see him on the bed – you know I got all mixed up. You know how it is when police in front yuh door, and you ain't see your husband. But everything orright now. As you mention 'Coronation Day' ah come back to me senses. Oh God, I so happy. He gone out."

Her face was bright, almost smiling as a contrast to Lance-Corporal John's. He did not like to see people smiling so early in the morning and he felt he missed an opportunity. He said now, "How you mean you come back to yuh senses. If you did come back to yuh senses you'd answer me question. I asked, where's Hothead?"

She was in sufficient possession of herself now not to let this constable come here and insult her. She knew exactly where Jonas was. She knew he was skipping and shadow-boxing at Point Ligoure. But of course she would not let John go there to harass him.

She said, "Well he got up early this morning, nah, and he went down Erin to get some fish, but – "

The lance-corporal's hand went up. "Stop right there. What story you cooking up? Erin? Why you didn't say that all the time?"

"But Constable, is you who confused me. I was dreaming about ducklings and you come and wake me up and tell me my husband in jail. Is only when you mention 'Coronation Day' I remember – I remember – " She had been on the point of saying she remembered the bout for Emporium, but realising that this again would lead to further questions, she said, "I remember we'd like some fish."

The lance-corporal all but laughed. He said, as if to himself: "She said 'when you mentioned Coronation Day'. Who you think you giving that to! Hothead ain't in love with no Coronation. That is why his head hot today and I want to know where he is and what mischief he up to."

"Well, I told you where he is. On Erin beach."

Lance-Corporal John considered for a little while whether he should go there. Erin was not far. But just at that time, with the parades starting up, he heard a little commotion. He walked away without even telling Elsie he was going.

15

IN Port of Spain, Coronation Day broke on a Queen's Park
Savannah still covered in mist from the hills. It was eight o'clock
and the blast of music announced the arrival of Governor Sir
Murchison Fletcher. Sir Murchison, with his party, was escorted to
the Governor's Box. The Local Forces were lined up in front of the
grandstand ready to begin the parade, and as one looked around,
the stands were full for such an early hour, and crowds from the
lower orders stretched away on either side of the green.

There was a lot of pomp and ceremony in front as the parade
started, and although Sir Murchison Fletcher was appearing to
look on attentively, his thoughts were far from anything like a
coronation parade. On one side of him was his wife, Dorothy, and
on the other was Olga Mavrogordato, the wife of the Inspector-
General of the Constabulary. Despite the pomp of this
Coronation Day the Governor was feeling quite uneasy, but he
was being careful not to look it. He was ill at ease because today he
could hardly be in touch with what was going on in the oilfields.
It was not that he was unpatriotic and not filled with happiness for
the crowning of George VI, but he was Governor of the Colony of
Trinidad and Tobago, of which oil was the most precious possession of George VI, and by God, if things were to get out of
hand in Fyzabad, why, it could be –

His wife jerked him from his thoughts: "Murch, isn't that a
lovely formation? Unbelievable!"

"You took the word from my mouth, dear."

She seemed aghast at the formation on the green before her, while
Sir Murchison tried to look amazed. He had noticed when the various contingents of the local military forces and the police, together
with fire-brigade men, were beginning to form the letters, but his
mind had drifted from the Queen's Park to the oilfields.

He whispered, "Dorothy, this is really charming. This is
the greatest expression of loyalty we can imagine, Dot." And
he read out the letters the soldiers had just formed: **G-O-D
S-A-V-E T-H-E K-I-N-G.**

Lady Fletcher said, "So you see, 'out of evil cometh good'. And last year you were so upset when the Prince of Wales abdicated."

He turned swiftly to her. "And weren't you?"

"Yes, but as I always say, what could one do about love? He met Mrs Simpson and fell for her. That's all."

Governor Fletcher was not going to argue with his wife in the Governor's Box. This was not the place for it. In any case he had sworn he was not going to argue with her on that matter any more. Neither in his box nor in his sitting room nor in his bedroom, nor in the garden. The end of last year was a wonderful season for the argument. Apart from Dorothy, whenever and wherever he met people, and he met most of them in his own ballroom – the ballroom of Government House – whenever he met them, the abdication was the main topic. It was always, "Your Excellency, how do you see the matter...? Your Excellency, how do you feel about the succession...?" They all forgot he was the Governor and he wasn't supposed to see and feel anything. And if Edward VIII was fool enough to give up his throne for the woman, what could he do about it? But this was the morning to end all argument, the coronation of Edward's brother, George. God save the King. The only sad thing for him was that the brightness and joy of this ceremony was overshadowed by the storm clouds hanging over the oilfields.

As the Local Forces paraded he could see the mist as if slowly lifting from the St. Ann's valley before him – before his very eyes – and also lifting from the mountains beyond. Although the atmosphere over the Queen's Park was somewhat cool, there was not a speck of cloud in the sky. So it was going to be another hot day.

And perhaps a hotter day in Fyzabad!

As they watched the Local Forces parade on the patch of green encircled by the racing track, Governor Fletcher turned to speak to his wife, but she was taken up with looking at the sergeant-major of the armed forces. Sergeant-Major Cox was marching in style in front of his detachment, throwing up his staff and catching it. She always liked to see that sort of thing.

Fletcher turned from her to the other side of him. He said, "The Savannah's like a picture postcard. What a beautiful morning."

Olga Mavrogordato smiled. It could not have been a more beautiful morning. In fact she was just thinking about what looked like a dusty pink and yellow against the green background when between the two pink pouis in the distance she caught a glimpse of the Governor's mansion. She had just said to herself, *Gosh!* She had been thinking of pointing this out to the Governor sooner or later, but now as he broke into her thoughts she would not say anything.

He said, "But the mist is thinning fast. It'll be a hot day."

Olga smiled again but the Governor's wife laughed. She said, "Murchy, so what sort of days have we been having? Ever since we came here last year it's been hot, hasn't it? Even when it rains."

"It won't rain today. It wouldn't rain now. There's not even a patch of white in the sky."

Olga was listening to them. They were talking as if they were experts on Trinidad and as if Trinidad was like this all the time. *She* could tell them about Trinidad, if they would only ask. They were not even a year here yet, because Claud Hollis returned in June. Yet they knew it all. She looked towards them with her sweet smile.

Dorothy saw her and said, "Is everything all right, dear?"

"Yes, Lady Fletcher."

"Sir Murchison says it will grow hotter as the day wears on."

Olga said nothing, but she felt riled. It was still early, so wasn't it obvious it would grow hotter as the day wore on? In any case, could they tell *her* about Trinidad? She was born here!

She leaned back, caught the eye of the Governor's wife and said sweetly, "But Lady Fletcher, you know, in Trinidad this is the hot season."

"That's it, my dear." Lady Fletcher gave a broad smile.

Governor Fletcher said, "That's right."

Olga looked at them puzzled. They probably thought her a damn fool.

She looked in front of her again and chided herself. Then she said to herself, *Why am I so piqued this morning?* She was really piqued and sensitive and it really wasn't their fault that her husband had to be in the oil belt night and day for the past three weeks. Night and day, day and night. She hardly saw him. That was not the Fletchers's fault, she told herself. It was because of those stupid oil workers who were threatening strikes and making trouble. Especially that man, Buzz Butler.

As her thoughts wandered a blast of music distracted her, and looking to the west she could see only brightness and glitter in the morning sun. The drums were rolling like the pattering of rain and the soldiers changed their march and were goose-stepping from the western side back towards the grandstand. The band-leader was throwing up his staff and catching it with such precision that it took over her mind completely. Also, the glistening trumpets and trombones were playing such stirring music that she could hardly help feeling moved. She gave a sidelong glance at Sir Murchison and saw that he had his eyes on the long line of uniformed men and women marching towards the paddock. There was the khaki of the volunteer brigade, the black and glistening white of the constabulary, there were the browns of the ex-servicemen, and the ceremonial dress with brilliant red sashes of the officers of the Light Horse. The musicians were now in the foreground, and they were playing the stirring march, 'Land of Hope and Glory'. She felt as if her pores opened. This was her favourite patriotic song.

The band was in front of the grandstand now and as the music swelled to full blast, Sir Murchison leaned his head towards her and said, "That's 'Pomp and Circumstance', dear."

Olga said, "Oh, I'm sorry Your Excellency, but that's 'Land of Hope and Glory'."

Sir Murchison smiled. His wife looked towards him as if to ask what was it, but he just whispered, "The honest truth, Dot, is that my mind is both here and in Fyzabad."

She did not answer.

He mumbled to himself, as a joke, "Couldn't George VI choose a more convenient time to ascend the throne?" Then he turned to Olga, "Well, it's a nice Coronation holiday. By the way, how's Colonel Mavrogordato coping?"

Olga's thoughts were so lost on the parade that she was taken unawares. But she knew the Governor had spoken to her, for she had glimpsed his head lean. She said hastily, "Your Excellency spoke?"

"I was asking, how's the colonel getting on?"

She put on a truly sweet smile and said, "Oh, you know, he has to cope. For the past three or four nights he had to be up and down, but what can one say? It's all for the British flag."

"Of course. I should think so too."

She did not quite understand that.

Dorothy was paying attention, and leaning in front of Governor Fletcher she said, "At least that trouble-maker will be behind bars."

The Governor said, "That's right."

Without looking at them Olga mumbled, "Hope so."

Then suddenly she was all seized. For a while she had been looking around the green and now she spotted the police contingent and she was tense as she watched her husband marching at its head. And at least this time she felt proud to be with the British. For her heritage was not British and she knew little about Britain. So she was not usually worked up and she had not got worked up even for the Coronation. Because she did not always like the British. She was a little girl during the 1914 war, but at least she had been old enough to know how stupid the British administration had been towards foreigners. Especially towards the Germans. They gave her father hell, just because he had come from Germany. They insulted him, kept a watch on him and restricted his movements. She had never forgotten that, and last year, when Edward VIII had abdicated, she had said in her heart that it damn well served them right. What the calypsonian had sung, 'It's love, love, love alone that cause King Edward to leave the throne,' of course it might have been true, but what she had said was that it had made love an extremely expensive commodity indeed. But it served the British right. Those limeys hated the Germans and because her father's name was Boos he had been like a cat on hot ashes. But now it was love which scandalised the British. Love alone. Although they kicked her father around she lived to see the day when his daughter's husband would be in charge of their safety. Perhaps he was the most important officer around – yes, even more important than the Governor. And infinitely more important than the man who was in charge of bringing up their oil from the ground. She glanced towards Hickling, and there was a sudden sweet and serene smile on her face. Because as he was looking at the parade he could not help seeing her. She said in her mind, *You all see where I'm sitting? This is Karl Boos's little girl. And you see who's marching down there, leading the constabulary? That's Boos's son-in-law. But we'll reap a harvest with this 'love alone' because with this parade and your big coronation who you think*

*gaining in Trinidad? That feller Butler! Keep Stephen in Port of Spain
in this ceremony and you'll see what'll happen.*

As she thought this she felt a genuine concern. The concern was
there all the time but it now came to the surface of her mind.
Because although she felt the way she did about the British, she
was sure it would not be good for her nor for any of the white
people if Butler got his way. And of course the main thing was that
it was Butler against Stephen Mavrogordato. The rebel against the
Police Chief – against the head of security in Trinidad. Although
Stephen had hundreds of men and a military force to call upon at
any moment, she was usually nervous about his safety. And wasn't
it justified?

She could not understand how the Governor could have him on
the parade this morning while the forces of mischief were sure to
be running loose in Fyzabad. She always knew that Fletcher and
his Colonial Secretary were hopeless blunderers, but where were
the others – the advisers, or even the senior and respected members of the Legislative Council? Stephen was surprised this morning when instead of being despatched on an intelligence mission,
he was gazetted to parade. She was pleased about the little rest he
was getting yet very concerned about what might be happening
down in Fyzabad. She had made several attempts to touch on the
subject with Fletcher but did not. She did not want to be seen as in-
terfering. But in her mind it was clear that it was sheer madness to
have both Stephen and Hickling away from the oil scene.

She looked round. There were a lot of military exercises going on
in front of them but she was only interested in looking at her husband. She was sure that she would be seeing him only for a brief
space more. She felt convinced that after the parade Fletcher
would despatch him to the hot spot but she was not sure Fletcher
was that sensible. But after all, could he do anything else? People
said the Governor was dim but surely he was not *that* daft.

She looked at the Local Forces doing their drills but she was
thinking that Stephen would obviously not be spending time with
her today. He himself did not know what was going to happen. For
although he was in charge of things he was cautious about not
suggesting to the Governor what the Governor should do.

But Olga thought now that if it was she who was playing such a
crucial role as Stephen was playing she would blinking well tell

Fletcher and Nankivell what to do. Because it was their blundering that made it so much more difficult for him. She got worked up. Stephen would not have to be all over the oil belt at all times if Fletcher and Nankivell were doing their jobs. As Stephen always said, they were too bleeding soft on that bandit, Butler. In fact, although Butler was charged with sedition for that speech Sunday, Nankivell had said plainly he did not think Butler had broken the law. Just imagine! Nankivell had told him that Butler's words: 'Even if the King...' were not strong enough to be considered sedition. But Stephen had made it quite clear emergency powers had given him the right to arrest and charge, and the court would have to decide whether it was fair or not. Nankivell had backed down.

But Butler was still on the loose in Fyzabad because the blighter had been given bail! But the point was he was summoned to appear in court and did not, so why did they not arrest him?

The sudden chiming of the joy bells startled her and shook her out of her thoughts. This was about the third time for the morning she had heard them, and she saw now that every time it came there was a shift in the programme. It was only now that she realised the music had stopped.

She looked around, her face wearing a sweet, placid smile. She looked towards Hickling and his wife and made a dainty little wave of the hand. Hickling was the man who wanted to see Stephen all the time, either to find out what was going on or to tell him what a certain Lance-Corporal John had said. She and Stephen always laughed at Hickling. He was so forceful and authoritative in the Legislative Council but without Stephen's vigilance he would be a sitting duck for the oil workers. Stephen also felt Butler would talk about striking but would never call a strike. He would use all those fiery words and scare poor Lance-Corporal John, but he wasn't going to call any strike because the workers could not endure it.

As she looked around she spotted Charlie King by the side of the paddock. He was not in the parade because he had on his simple police uniform and she became a little alarmed and wondered what the hell all these senior police officers were doing in Port of Spain when Fyzabad was like a powder keg waiting to blow up. What were they doing here? Inspector William Edmund Power had been right there behind her in the Governor's Box, and this had perplexed her because this was the officer next to Stephen in rank, and now she wanted to know what the france was going on, why didn't Stephen insist that Edmund Power be sent to Fyzabad?

As she thought of all this, alarmed, the Governor leaned over. "It was jolly good, wasn't it? They're coming to an end now."

She was taken aback. She had not noticed. She said, "It was beautiful, Sir Murchison. A nice setting, too."

She was not sure what she meant by that.

"This is going to be 'The Last Post'," Sir Murchison said.

The Governor bent on the other side to talk to his wife, then he turned again and simply glanced to see what Hickling was doing. All morning he had been wondering if Hickling had any late news. They would talk later. There might not be the time to chat before entering Trinity Cathedral at eleven o'clock for the Divine Service, but certainly when they met in the Legislative Council afterwards in the session for loyal addresses there would be a minute or two.

Joy bells, ringing every fifteen minutes, had kept interrupting his thoughts. But it was really a joyous coronation morning and he wished he could have felt more joyful, but the problems at Apex were big in his mind. It was a real puzzle to know how to deal with them. Hickling was in favour of strong-arm methods, and even Colonel Mavrogordato was not averse to it. And what made it so much worse in his view was that even the local keepers of the peace were anxious for war. Charlie King, who he had glimpsed a while ago, seemed bristling for blood, and from what Hickling had told him, both Lance-Corporal John and his acting corporal were anxious to teach the strikers a lesson by the use of the baton. As he looked towards his wife he realised her eyes had been on him. He raised his brows. She said gently, "What's the matter, Murchy – are you tired?"

"Me?"

"Well, you do look tired. Or worried. Because you keep dreaming away." She was all but whispering now as she turned and held his arm. "You are paying not the least bit of attention to the parade. Is it that fellow over…?" She stopped.

"Which fellow?" He looked over to the right of him where the Colonial Secretary was sitting with his wife.

Dorothy had to laugh. "I don't mean Howard Nankivell. Howard is no trouble. In fact Howard is more like you. I am referring to that man down in Fyzabad. The butler."

Sir Murchison laughed, "The butler? Not *my* butler!"

"Sometimes I think he is. Anyway, enjoy the parade a little more. Those boys are good. Very smart and efficient. And," she whispered softly, "and they're doing all this for you, Murchy."

He said in her ears, "Not for me, for King George VI."

She leaned over to his ears. "You represent him in Trinidad."

"That's right," Sir Murchison said, and chuckled.

They both looked now at the various contingents of the Local Forces marching back from the New Town end of the Queen's Park Savannah towards the paddock. The joy bells had already rung several times and now it was nearly nine o'clock. The mist had completely lifted from the Queen's Park Savannah and had also cleared the Northern Range. In the hot sun the poui which Olga had admired looked stark and brilliant with its mass of pink flowers.

As the Local Forces neared the paddock the Governor was getting ready to go down to take the salute. Even now he could not help thinking of the unrest in the oilfields and of the man Dorothy called 'the butler'. He hoped things would remain under control and that everything would be peaceful. With all his friendship and cordiality to Hickling, who felt the oil workers were overpaid, and who also felt 'the butler' should be put in jail, he himself was not so dense and unfeeling as not to know that these workers had a just cause. As the head of the parade neared the paddock the Governor prepared to go down to the dais to take the salute.

Olga was paying attention as Bandmaster Rupert Dennison made a right wheel and brought the band just before the Governor's dais, where it formed up. All the rest of the Local Forces formed up behind it, which was just in front of the Governor's Box. Then, while the volunteers and soldiers presented arms a huge Union Jack went up on the flagpole, and as the band broke into 'God Save the King', even she, Olga, was moved. She even felt a little too weak to stand up. When everybody sat down again and Sir Murchison Fletcher walked down the decorated stairway to address the Local Forces, she turned to Dorothy Fletcher. "God bless George VI."

The Governor's wife did not answer. Tears were in her eyes.

Olga said, "At least everybody is looking forward to this king."

"Yes."

Olga was looking straight ahead of her, not at the Local Forces, but at the beautiful setting in which the Queen's Park Savannah was framed. There was silence now as Sir Murchison began to speak, but the atmosphere was so calm and nice and peaceful that she could not help saying to herself, *A pity about that madman.*

"What's that?" the Governor's wife said.

"Sorry. Didn't realise I was talking aloud. Just said, 'Sorry about that madman in Fyzabad.' Let me shut up 'cause I want to listen to Sir Murchison."

In her mind she said, *Just fancy I have to listen to this hogwash. There's always something to spoil things. This patriotic talk's a waste of time, not because I ain't British. Though I have to support them because here in Trinidad we are one sort of people. They call us privileged, so what's wrong with privilege? I like it!* Then her thoughts shifted and she said silently, *Anyway, after this I expect Stephen will be going down to Fyzabad so I'll be going home. I ain't entering Trinity Cathedral for any blessed Divine Service and I ain't going in the Red House to hear any stupid set of loyal addresses. I had my Coronation Day already and this is good enough for me. But I'll tell you something, that man in Fyzabad will have a good Coronation Day inciting the workers. I want to see Stephen and then I'll go home. The Queen's Park Savannah's pretty but it's blooming hot already. Oh God, Fletcher, you don't have to talk so much. You don't know when to stop?*

16

WHILE the loyal addresses were still going on, Corporal Charlie King, Lieutenant-Colonel Hickling and Colonel Stephen Mavrogordato were having a little chat. They had retired just outside the Legislative Council Chamber in the little passageway overlooking St. Vincent Street. Hickling had told them he had had no news at all from Fyzabad, nothing this morning, but that last night he had heard from Acting Corporal Gilroy Price that all was quiet. At least there was no move to call any strike, and the police were keeping sharp vigil on any meeting Butler might call.

When Charlie King heard he looked away and smiled wryly.

Colonel Mavrogordato turned to Charlie King and said, "I feel just as strongly as you, Corporal King, but you've got to realise I don't have absolute powers. If I had my way I would have you on the San Fernando post throughout this crisis, and I would be down there too, most of the time. But with this coronation affair Governor Fletcher insisted that both the military and security forces had to be on parade, because, he said, this is in the Official Standing Orders and Procedures, and the situation at Fyzabad does not merit any change. I could not argue, and to tell the truth I could not say he was not right. It's just that I am uneasy. You smiled when the lieutenant-colonel talked about Gilroy Price, but – yes, Corporal?"

Charlie King said, "Gilroy Price don't know nothing. And he can't say nothing about what will happen, because he don't know. Constable John is a much better police but he ain't in charge. In any case I always tell you this, Lieutenant-Colonel Hickling, and I mention this to you, Colonel, just the other day. In this situation you want at least four good police in Fyzabad, not two."

He looked at Colonel Mavrogordato. Colonel Mavrogordato shifted his eyes from King and looked across St. Vincent Street to Police Headquarters. The lieutenant-colonel said to himself, *Who does Charlie King think he is? He wants to tell me how to run my police force?*

The corporal continued, "Okay Lieutenant-Colonel, and Colonel Mavrogordato, Sir, I know this is Coronation Day and the British Empire rejoicing. But my feeling is while we rejoicing we should have somebody keeping watch on what going on in Fyzabad."

Lieutenant-Colonel Hickling was going to speak but Colonel Mavrogordato cut in excitedly. "I'm in total agreement with you, Corporal Charles. Do you hear me? We are in agreement. But I want you to know that Governor Fletcher does not take orders from me, I take from him. In other words I am not the Governor. I can only make recommendations to the Governor. But I have to share your concern a little because if Fyzabad goes up in flames we are all going to hell."

Hickling said to the colonel, "You saw him this morning?"

"No. From the green, yes. When I was marching. But not to speak to. In other words I did not see him to speak to."

Hickling said, "Corporal Charles King, I'm afraid I must take issue with you when you say, 'We *must* have somebody in Fyzabad.' I guess you mean police. I am saying we do have somebody in Fyzabad. Two good policemen. Okay, you might not think much of Acting Corporal Gilroy Price, maybe because he does not seem as alert as you would like. Or flamboyant. But you told me you weren't impressed. But I can tell you Lance-Corporal John is excellent. An excellent officer with his nose to the ground. He reports everything that looks suspicious, and in fact sometimes I think he is too damn excellent because he interrupts me all the time to let me know what is going on. I'm not saying there should-n't be another officer or two at Fyzabad, but I think the colonel would agree with me and talk about the accommodation – " as Hickling looked towards Colonel Mavrogordato Charlie King thought, *Well, build a bigger station!*

Hickling was looking at Colonel Mavrogordato but the colonel deliberately did not say anything. Whether Fyzabad had two policemen or four was not in Charlie King's province. And if it came to it, why did not Hickling himself improve the accommodation? With all the money they were scooping up why did not Apex give the police more facilities? It was irritating to listen to this tripe.

The loyal addresses were still going on, and Colonel Mavrogordato, with his brows knitted, looked now to see what was happening, and to see when the session would start coming to a close. As he looked he felt a little embittered inside because Governor Murchison Fletcher seemed to be sitting as if on a throne – as if he was King George the Sixth himself – and it looked as though speeches would go on forever. He said to himself, *Do these blasted people know what we are facing in Fyzabad?*

Charlie King said, "How it looking, Colonel?"

Mavrogordato said, "Well, as you can hear, they are still at it."

Corporal King stood there fidgeting with impatience. Then, pretending he was looking at how the corridor was made, he glanced at the ceremonial dress of the police chief, the buttons on his lapel looking not like brass but like real El Dorado gold.

He could not help shaking his head just that little bit. He said in his mind, *Look how the government pampering these two British blockheads, eh?* He knew that the only reason Mavrogordato and Hickling were being chummy with him and inviting him to the corridor to talk was because he was Charlie King. The one and only. The terror of criminals all over Trinidad. In whatever part the criminal was causing trouble, just call on Charlie King. His mind went to the time in 1935 when he arrested Dalgo – Dalgo, the great thief and highway robber that no one could even see, let alone find. Dangerously armed, Dalgo cared nothing and feared nothing – even jumping out of a speeding train. Not only did he, Charlie King, arrest Dalgo but he didn't even have to raise his hand. People were stunned. Now the authorities had him on the Butler case, but with Butler it was different. It was not a case of not being able to find Butler, it was just that they were all afraid to put hand on him in Fyzabad because of the people. But he, Charlie King, wasn't afraid of the people. He was just waiting to –

"Thank God," Hickling cried, startling Charlie King.

Colonel Mavrogordato smiled. He said, "Well, the session was pretty long but all good things come to an end."

Charlie King said, "That's right, Colonel," and he said in his mind, *You see those hypocrites?*

It was about half past twelve when Colonel Stephen Mavrogordato hopped out of the buggy at his house on Cipriani Boulevard, and when he went into the house and Olga saw him she shrieked and ran and threw herself on him.

She said, "How you do, boy? This morning I hardly saw you at all, except marching. So what? How things? You hungry? You know how long I had Bernice lay the table, because, somehow, I don't know, somehow I felt we'd see you, and see you around now. It's just God, ain't it? Kiss me, please. Stephen you don't have to go out again? I don't want you to, but if you have to go you have to go."

He chuckled. He was holding her tight and now he released her and said, "Gaga, you know what I'm supposed to be? Chief of Constabulary. You yourself were saying Fletcher would have to be mad to have both me and Power at the parade. And you know what? He even had Charlie King up here."

"Yes, I saw King. I saw King at the Savannah."

"Sometimes I wonder if Fletcher is all right in the head. He and his Colonial Secretary, Howard Nankivell. I mean Nankivitch."

She laughed at the name 'Nankivitch'.

"That's what they call him at Headquarters. He's a dyed-in-the-wool Russian communist. The more I hear him in the Legislature it's the more I have to say, 'My God, this is a shameless communist.'"

Olga looked concerned. The colonel turned towards the window. "Anyway, Ga, after lunch I have to head for you-know-where."

"San Fernando? I hope this Butler to-and-fro business finish quick you know. I hope it doesn't take up the whole year."

The colonel was looking out of the window. He said, "I don't think Fletcher wants to finish it. They could easily detain that terrorist. Simple as that. In fact they even have a warrant out for him and scared to arrest him. I was with Hickling in the Red House. King was there. Hickling's scared that a strike will kill Apex because it could last for months. But without saying it he's scared to have them take Butler, too. He told me confidentially that the people could attack the camp if the police take Butler. Personally, I don't think these hungry people will do any such thing. I think what Hickling would like to see is soldiers with guns down there but Fletcher will never do that. Hickling already left for Fyzabad. And you know what Fletcher said to Charlie King? After the silly loyal addresses I went to Fletcher, and Hickling came up. Fletcher agreed that I should hurry down to the south. When he saw

Charlie King, he said, 'Corporal King, are you in Port of Spain?' It was so amusing even Charlie King had to laugh."

Olga said, "If ever I saw a madman!"

The colonel said, "He thinks it's we who are mad. You know what he said to Hickling at the last emergency meeting? He said, 'With all respect to you, Lieutenant-Colonel, Apex has the key – "

"Oh yes, I heard that one. You told me. That's when he told Hickling to open his hand to the workers!"

"And Hickling said, 'I won't only open my hand I'll empty my bleeding pockets if you want.' He spoke to the Governor like that."

Olga laughed. The maid who had come and was now laying out the colonel's lunch on the table smiled too. The colonel said, "The thing is, Gaga, Fletcher feels deep in his heart that it's us white people who are causing the crisis."

Olga did not say anything. When he was sitting down to eat she went to him and said in a low voice, "Stephen, you mustn't speak freely in front of these maids. I noticed something. How her face changed about something you said. I hope things will blow over in Apex, though. You'll be busy again for that Saturday business?"

"The Carnival? Yes. But up here only. Power will be down there though. And Charlie King. I think I really have to hurry up."

"Poor Stephen," she said.

Down in Fyzabad Coronation Day was bright, beginning with loyal processions in the morning. The Coronation affair itself did not bother Elsie. She stayed inside and heard the music and the drums. What she was anxious about was that appointment for Jonas – the boxing. And of course, weighing heavily on her mind was that big and over-riding issue of Uriah Butler.

So far as she could see, the confrontation was coming. It could not be avoided. That date, June 19th, would tell. It was Mr Uriah against Hickling and against all the forces who wanted to trample on the rights of the people. That phrase sounded big and she did not like it but she had no regrets that she was living with a hothead who would help change things in Fyzabad and the whole island.

As she went about her work sweeping the house and cleaning up, she could not help thinking of Hothead and wondering how he was getting on. He had enough to eat. He did not want her there at Point Ligoure. She knew that. And all she said to herself now was, *Let him train. He just have three days.*

When she was finished all she was doing and when she had eaten, she went and took up something she had been knitting. It was after midday and she just felt she wanted Coronation Day to pass quickly and then the day after and the day after that and let Saturday come and let Jonas come back home. And of course she wanted him to win on that night but she would be mad to expect he'd win. Not unless Kid Tiger took in ill. She did not mind Jonas losing, she expected him to lose, and she accepted it. But let it be honourable. Let him fight the good fight and fail, or let the referee disqualify him for some thoughtless infringement. That would be nice. The money did not matter. They could keep the money.

She was knitting, but she was missing Jonas in a way that was becoming unbearable. All of a sudden she put her knitting aside and went and threw herself on the bed.

17

No sooner had Thursday morning dawned than Lieutenant-Colonel Hickling was back in his office. Apart from the fact that he had been eager to be back in this region, Fyzabad, to know what was happening with security, this was his home ground. He had been here as manager of Apex a little time now, and the place had grown on him, and if he had to be honest he really only felt comfortable when he was here. The truth was that he liked Fyzabad. He liked everything about it; he liked the very entry into the village after the long drive from Port of Spain, the Opel motor car racing down the hill from Avocat, then the big junction, the wooden, rickety workers' houses around you – houses with tin sheets on top and sometimes on the sides, with box-boards, just as those one passed at Vessigny. Although he wondered how people could live in them, these houses comforted him because he knew the rich flourished because of the poor. How could you have the rich without the poor? And where would the domestics have come from? He liked to see these box-like shanties and he liked the clumps of big trees on the sides of the hill, then the broad stretches of green and brushwood and tarred roads with the oil wells pumping – the great iron arms which pumped and pushed up the oil were always a thrill to his heart – and oddly enough he liked the very smell of the petroleum in the atmosphere.

He liked everything about Fyzabad except the people.

As he sat at his desk his face tightened and he got serious and concerned. All the way down from Port of Spain he had been wondering if they had taken the courage to clamp that impostor, that guerrilla, behind bars. In fact, when he had got past Mosquito Creek, and was crossing the Godineau Bridge, he had seen a big log floating down in the water and he could not help wishing it was the corpse of that bold-faced bandit. What had made him think of this was a matter touched upon by Lance-Corporal John several weeks before. It was when Butler had begun the campaign in earnest, stirring up discontent amongst the oil workers. John had come into his office one morning and had given him some roundabout story, or description, or explanation, but which seemed to amount to the same thing: to let someone have Butler floating like a log in the Godineau River. Of course he had rebuffed John and had chased him from his office and threatened to get him slung out of the police force. Could he have done anything less? But oh how he wished John would do it! He wished John would just do that.

As he thought of this he could not help feeling bitterly disappointed about the sharpshooter. What a remarkable case of British bungling! He had heard the sharpshooter came to Fyzabad and yet drew a blank. He thought, *Good God!*

He raised his head and looked through the glass window in front of him, and the person he was looking for was the very Lance-Corporal John he had been thinking of some while before. He just wanted to know how was it in Fyzabad and if there was anything to report. And he wanted to know if the man charged with sedition was still on the loose. Because if anything had developed after he had taken to the road, he would not know. Although he was feeling more concerned he was feeling stronger and better equipped. For both Charlie King and Inspector Power were at the San Fernando headquarters. What was of even more significance was that the Legislative Council had given Colonel Mavrogordato authority to call on the Local Forces for help in any emergency.

He heard voices outside and he realised it was getting close to seven, when the workday started. He had wanted to call down to the police station to see if Lance-Corporal John was about, and to summon him, but had realised that if he had done that the lance-corporal would get a sense of importance. The lance-corporal was always around him, always trying to say something to him, always trying to get a nod from him, always trying to get a smile. He himself was a firm believer that things should be like this, for what would happen if the natives were not kept in their places?

As he was thinking this, his secretary came in and the two men talked a little. In the middle of the conversation he saw the personnel officer through the glass and he sent his secretary to summon him.

When the personnel officer came Hickling showed him to a seat and he said, "Albert, the Oil Employers would like to see the attendance figures for the whole of May so far."

"Yes, I gave you for April – "

"Yes, but they want for May up to this point. We might meet in Port of Spain on Saturday."

"Saturday?"

"Why not?" Hickling said. "The Coronation Carnival wouldn't affect us. We'll have our normal meeting in the Red House."

"I'll prepare the figures. So you'll want them up to Friday?"

"That's correct. And as detailed as you can supply them. I want the names of the workers concerned, and the hour they reported for duty, and I want the names of the absent ones."

"You wouldn't be able to get all that for Saturday, Sir. Not with all those details. Today is Thursday already. We'll have to work all day on this alone – "

Hickling was going to make a quick retort that it did not matter to him whether they worked all day and all night, when as he got up from his chair he spotted Lance-Corporal John walking along the main road. He immediately looked around for the office boy. Then he said to the personnel officer, "Find the office boy and send him to call that policeman. I'll be here in my office."

"Yes, Sir."

When Lance-Corporal John came it was already half past seven. The lance-corporal was so pleased that Colonel Hickling had needed him that he walked in with his chest high.

Lieutenant-Colonel Hickling said, "Lance-Corporal, by this time you are usually under the almond tree."

"That's not me beat, Sir. I always there because since those workers so hogstylish nobody know what they'll do and I standing up there to see nobody break open yuh office to get at you – because you is the chief."

Hickling did not know how to take that. He did not know if by saying 'you is the chief' the lance-corporal meant chief of Apex or chief troublemaker. He could not imagine the lance-corporal would address him like that, although he noticed a trace of pomposity.

The lieutenant-colonel said, "I know the almond tree is not your beat. Nor is the breadfruit tree. And it is clear that you are not working for Apex. But I'll tell you something not generally known. Apex is drawing up more oil than any other company. I am not ill-speaking the others because they are all run by English gentlemen. And what Apex and Trinidad Leaseholds Limited are doing, and what United British is doing, is simply this: they are keeping this island running. Do you understand this, Constable John? Because that guerrilla, who is stark staring mad, does not understand that. The whole of your civil service has to get paid, your Governor has to get paid, your whole police force – do you know where the money comes from? The oil companies, which Apex leads."

Lance-Corporal John looked amazed and as if brutally enlightened. Hickling said, "So it is quite understood that you are not working for Apex and the almond tree is not your beat. By the way, do you know what Apex means?"

"No, Colonel, Sir."

Hickling was going to speak, then he paused. He was going to ask, "Why do you always give me a higher rank?" But he checked himself, and he decided he would accept the higher rank. In fact he was sure the fool did not even know whether 'colonel' was higher or lower. He looked at the lance-corporal and was going to ask him if he went to school at all but he checked himself again for the lance-corporal was bound to lie. He said, "Officer, I asked you if you knew what Apex meant and you said no. Well, Apex means the top. And we are there but we are still going for the top. That's where we are going. Get it?" Then he looked out of the window, then pulled it in a little, and he turned to the lance-corporal again. "Look, there was a lot of things heating up and boiling up when I was about to leave so I just wanted to check on you to see if everything's normal. But everything looks nor- "

"Everything ain't normal, Colonel, Sir."

Hickling looked at him. He asked him to sit down.

After sitting down the lance-corporal leaned forward and said, "That's why I wasn't under the almond tree this morning. Because ah was busy. Because things ain't normal. I didn't even know you was back here but me mind was hot this morning. I see a few faces, but as the hall was dark I wasn't sure."

"What are you talking about, Constable John?"

"They want to call a strike any day now. He say he'll paralyse Apex. The meeting was in Vessigny the other night."

"Constable, are you sure of what you are saying? Who informed you of that?"

"I informed meself. Ah did hear about the meeting in the rumshop, because I always pass in the rumshop to hear what ah could hear, and sometimes you does hear the real thing when a feller getting booze. So I went there playing I looking at the calendar and this man – he wasn't booze yet he was what you call 'sweet' – this man was talking about a Butler meeting. Ah know him good. He's a king ah draughts. So when he talk about the meeting ah pull back behind the door, and I hear him say the meeting is in Heart and Hand tonight – that was the other night – and Butler want every man there. But he didn't say what time so ah went in and ah tell him we have a little draughts tournament in the station tonight – that's the other night. He said he can't come, he can't study about draughts, he have to go down Vessigny for seven o'clock. So I say all right, I so sorry. So ah went to the station and ah put on me old civilian clothes, l with ah old felt hat deep down on me head – " Hickling turned away. "Deep down on me head, don't laugh, Colonel, Sir. Ah take the bus and I went down to Heart and Hand in Vessigny. And I went in the hall. The hall dark like pitch. Only one candle burning. And I hear everything."

Lieutenant-Colonel Hickling said, "Constable John, you are amazing. What shall we do without you?"

"He begin the meeting singing a hymn, soft, soft. They just sing two verses of 'Oh God our help in ages past'. No, it was 'I heard the voice of Jesus say'. Then he tell them something about he couldn't see who come but he could hear from the voices that the house full. He tell them he call them there for one thing, to tell them he almost ready to give the call for them to strike and when he give that call they have to strike as one man. Not some out and some in."

"And when did he say he would give that call?"

"He said he have the date but he won't give it there, because he couldn't see faces and he didn't know who was who. He watching Hickling. He said he tired with those white people."

Hickling's face grew red. "He said that?"

"Yes, Colonel, Sir." There was a bitterness welling up in the lance-corporal against Uriah Butler and he felt the urge to lie even more. But he could not readily find anything else to lie about. Hickling said, "Well, I'll have to put Charlie King on this right away. And Inspector Power too. They'll have to arrest this man now."

Lance-Corporal John was happy and excited. He said, "They come down yet or they still up there in town? In Port of Spain? I could tell them meself. Police to police. They come down, Colonel, Sir?" He was looking into Hickling's face. Hickling ignored him.

The lance-corporal turned back and looked through the glass and saw many people outside and was amazed how the place could have awakened to life so suddenly. As he turned again to Hickling he heard the cling-cling of a bicycle bell, and he said, "Oh yes, Major, he said something about bell. When he talk about the English people, he said he'll cripple Apex and is Butler till the final bell."

18

WHEN Charlie King walked into the Fyzabad police station, Acting Corporal Gilroy Price was there, but Lance-Corporal John was on the beat. It was a little after six p.m. on the day after Coronation Day. When Charlie King, in plain clothes, went up to the counter the acting corporal did not recognise him and said, "You want to make a report? Let me get some paper."

Charlie King was so taken aback he said nothing. Acting Corporal Price brought the paper and said, "Write here. On one side alone, eh? Okay, okay, you look as though you can't make it, ah better do it." Then he looked up at the ceiling. "What date this is again? We in May. Yesterday was Coronation Day so this is the 16th. Now what yuh name is?"

Charlie King was so astonished he stood staring at the corporal. He said, "What is me name? Charlie. What's yours?"

The acting corporal was on the point of insulting the intruder and driving him out of the police station when he paused, and looked hard at the man. "Charlie? You say you is Charlie? But yuh face look like – Yes, I see you before. Wait, you is Charlie King?"

Charlie King just stood there looking at him, his eyes not even blinking. He was astounded. Even though he was in plain clothes, he did not expect there could be anybody in Trinidad that could be so ignorant as to ask him his name. Especially here in the far south where he had taken Dalgo, Bango, and Castillo all the same day.

Gilroy Price said, "The more ah see you the more ah think you is Charlie King. You ain't Charlie King?"

Charlie King could find no grounds to arrest him, so he nodded his head and let it pass.

The acting corporal said, "We so glad to see you down here. We having a bit of a hustle. You mightn't know, but one of the fellers giving Apex trouble."

"Um hm?" Charlie King tried to look interested.

"A feller name Butler."

"And you saying I mightn't be aware of the situation?"

"Ah don't know but ah see you here with the lieutenant-colonel. The boss, nah. Hickling. So – "

"When was Dalgo arrested?"

Gilroy Price looked up at the ceiling. "Aha, we in May. They take Dalgo was last year. It wasn't you who arrest Dalgo and Bango?"

"*And* Castillo," Charlie King said with emphasis. "That was in 1935. You wasn't at this station?"

"Yes."

"And you ain't know Charlie King?"

"But how you mean? Ain't you is Charlie King? Ain't we chatting?"

Charlie King said to himself, *I only wasting time with this asinine acting corporal.* He looked around him, then he said, "I want to chat about Butler. Uriah Butler. What's the situation?"

"Well, you know how it is. Butler – "

"No, I don't know how it is, that's why I asking you. Inspector Power in San Fernando and I want to brighten him up on what happening. I didn't have to come down here but since the Governor and Colonel Mavrogor – what? Mavrogordato keep on saying they want a man like me here, ah come down. What is the present problem with Butler?"

Charlie King knew well that from the time he mentioned the Governor and the Chief of Police he would get results.

Gilroy Price was suddenly agitated. He had known that the name 'Charlie King' was a big name in the police force, especially since the arrest of Dalgo. And after he had fully recognised him, he had wanted to bring him down a peg or two. Just for wickedness. Because after Charlie had taken Dalgo, people were saying the police down south were no damn good, that's why they had to send down Charlie King. So he had despised Charlie King. Especially after he had seen him afterwards strutting in Fyzabad with the lieutenant-colonel. And especially after – who was that calypsonian? Was it the Mighty Growler? – Yes, especially after Growler had sung what became the most popular calypso of 1936. A calypso beginning:

> *What a big uproar*
> *When Charlie King arrested*
> *The great Dalgo…*

He knew Charlie King had become a famous policeman but he still did not visualise King rubbing shoulders with Governor Fletcher and Colonel Stephen Mavrogordato. He quickly realised that this officer had a lot of influence and could make or break him. Just fancy if he had chased this man out, not even knowing he was police, let alone the fact that he was Charlie King, and then Charlie King had gone and reported him to Colonel Mavrogordato! That could well have been the 'big uproar' of his life; the end of him as a policeman. And for the other side: if he was to please Charlie King now, who knew what could happen in the future?

He said, "Corporal King, I could tell you about Butler. All the underhand moves. It's yuh plain clothes what fooled me while ago."

"You want me to come here wearing police clothes? Eh? To advertise a 'Charlie King in town' sorta thing? You want me to pay the price, Constable Gilroy?" He had lingered on the word 'price'. Now he said impatiently, "Come on, give me the latest on Butler."

"He ready to call the strike. He call a meeting last week in Heart and Hand in Vessigny. He said he'll cripple Apex."

Charlie King took out his notebook. "Where and when was the meeting?"

"In Vessigny last Saturday."

"And you say he calling a strike?" Charlie King looked around, "When he planning this for?"

"He say it could be any time. Next week, next month, any time. He said he have the date."

"He say this out in the open?"

"No, Corporal. It was in the close. A sneaky meeting in the dark in Heart and Hand, with candles and all sorta incense, and hush-hush, and no policeman could go but – ah – but John get inside."

He was going to say *he* got inside.

He said, "As I in charge here as Acting Corporal I have to stay here and send the lance-corporal out on this sorta mission – "

"Well, it's a damn good thing you did that." Charlie King's heart was beating faster. His mind was flitting to all manner of schemes for he intended not only to stop Butler right away but to capture him and to give him a good beating with the baton.

The intrigue of inviting Butler to a conference at which Governor Fletcher, Nankivell, Mavrogordato, Hickling, and he himself would be present, and then seizing Butler, was not going to work. He had already suggested it and Fletcher had turned it down right away. He knew Fletcher and Nankivell would never lure Butler into a trap. Indeed, his opinion was that those two were encouraging Butler in his scampishness.

He said, "You know if Butler in Fyzabad now?"

"He in Fyzabad now but I could tell you those Butler people wouldn't let you take him. It might have riot and even blood."

Charlie King smiled. That was exactly what Butler was thriving on – the police being afraid of the Butler people. And that was what was causing the Butler people to act like hooligans.

He said, "Acting Corporal Price, I want you to understand one thing. You living here in Fyzabad, and you know what you know, and you know what you 'fraid. Just one thing I want you to understand. I name Charlie King, and I ain't 'fraid no man."

Acting Corporal Gilroy Price did not reply. He was anxious to see Butler held by the back of his pants or the scruff of his neck and thrown into prison, but all he was thinking about were the consequences. And not the consequences for Charlie King, nor for the police in general, but consequences for himself, most of all. He watched Corporal Charlie King looking uneasy and agitated. He was sorry he had told him about that meeting in Vessigny.

Then all of a sudden Charlie King turned round and said to him, "Where's Emporium?"

"Emporium? You mean the hall?"

"Yes, where the Butler meetings – "

"Emporium is just by that corner in front there. You have to walk as if you going to the corner, then a little before you come to that house there, by the junction on yuh right, when you swing, you'll see the sign on it saying 'Emporium Hall'."

"Okay. Leave it to me," Charlie King said, and walked out in the dark.

19

In Port of Spain, the Saturday of the Coronation Carnival dawned hot and bright, and when Colonel Mavrogordato awoke he opened his windows, which were high up and overlooking Cipriani Boulevard. As he opened the windows and looked down, the peacefulness of the place astonished him. The scene was calm and beautiful beyond description. He had been in San Fernando but had come back to town today, firstly because he had to be in the Red House by noon, and secondly because he had his duty to carry out. Carnival called for alertness. He shouldn't have had to come to town just for that, because he had planned to have Inspector Power in charge of the Port of Spain scene. Just to leave himself free for any emergency, so he could dash from south to north or north to south. But he had had a discussion with Governor Fletcher over the telephone and he realised that the best thing for him was to be available. So he had left Power in San Fernando and was handling the Port of Spain scene himself.

He looked around and wanted to call Olga to show her how peaceful was the scene below, but she was still under the sheets and he did not want to wake her up. He looked to his left, over Tragarete Road, and at the sea not too far away. And as he saw the water he at once remembered the gunboats, and he made a mental note that when he got into the Legislative Council this morning he would raise the matter of contacting the naval station at Barbados and of putting them on the alert.

It was really good that the constable had told Hickling about that clandestine meeting but he couldn't just go and pounce on Butler just like that – as Hickling was suggesting. By golly, wasn't Hickling an Englishman? How could he expect that? Suppose, for instance, the illiterate lance-corporal had made up that story! Hickling himself had said the policeman so hated Butler's guts, no Englishman could hate Butler like that.

The colonel shook Hickling out of his mind. He wouldn't get too agitated until he heard a little more. In fact the managers of the oil concerns were living in permanent fear and stress, and that was exactly what the guerrilla wanted. All he, Mavrogordato, was going to do in the Legislative Council this morning was to ask them to alert the frigates at Barbados in case there was trouble in the oilfields, and he would tell them what Hickling had told him. They all knew Hickling!

He was a little restless and he decided he would go downstairs and have some coffee and relax as best he could. It had just turned eight o'clock and if by nine Olga was still in bed he would have to wake her up. He threw his dressing gown over his pyjamas and began to descend the stairs.

Olga was not asleep. She was thrilled with the thought that Stephen had come home last night and at the same time she was feeling wretched that he had to return to San Fernando after the Coronation Carnival. What the hell was William Edmund Power in the constabulary for? Were they going to let a stupid, raving madman like Butler get them all stupid too? She had raised that question with Stephen last night and they had almost quarrelled. Which was a pity, for it had been such a beautiful night. They had saddled the horse and had ridden up to the Savannah, she sitting in front of him, side-saddle. On the Savannah they had tied the horse around one of the poui trees and had gone arm in arm around the pitch-walk. The atmosphere was so enchanted. The smell of the blossoms on the cannonball trees was so overpoweringly sweet. It was when they were passing round by Government House that they had begun talking about Fletcher, and this had spoiled the walk. For they had gone on to the subject of an interview between Nankivell and Butler – something she had never even heard of before – and they had gone on to security and what the police were doing in the oilfield – or rather what the police were not doing – and the talk came on to him, and she had said, "Why you? Why not William Edmund Power?" And they had got into harsh words.

As she lay down there, keeping motionless under the sheets, she heard him walk downstairs. Then she heard him call two or three times but she did not answer. In a way she felt sorry for him; he was doing his best. The present situation was none of his making. It was just the usual British bungling. They had sent a bad Governor, a bad colonial secretary, and they had introduced them to such a bad situation that it was bound to give rise to bad men.

She thought of the number of things Stephen had taken upon himself this morning. Needlessly. This question of detailing men for duty in the town and their precise assignments; that was for Power to see about, not Stephen! But where was Power? Way down in San Fernando, or maybe Pointe-a-Pierre, pretending he was protecting the oil refinery. Now Stephen had to take an early breakfast, then go to Headquarters to give final instructions, particularly to those men who had to do patrol duty on Marine Square and Frederick Street. Then he would have to busy himself in solving all the disputes there were to solve. Then right up to about six p.m. he would be having to check on the various points of the downtown area to see that the Carnival did not get out of hand. And then there would be no coming back home. The Carnival would finish at twelve midnight, and soon afterwards he would have to be in San Fernando.

She listened for his movements downstairs and she did not hear anything. Then she suddenly sat up and threw off the sheets. She had not talked to him since they had returned last night. She had decided that she wasn't talking to him. But just as she had thrown off the sheets, she had thrown off the feeling. She got down from the bed, put on her dressing gown and went down the stairs.

When she got to the kitchen she said, "What you doing here, Mr Mavrogordato?"

"Oh, it's you? I thought you were still sleeping."

"Let me tell you something. I was just lying down there. I wasn't sleeping."

"Oh, you weren't sleeping? And you wouldn't answer me?"

"Because what you think I am, Stephen? You have authority but you only playing the fool, you don't have to work today. And in general you making that man Butler make a general fool out of you. This is nonsense, you never in the house. The first thing is, if you all really want to capture Butler you'll capture him. He's only one man. Then what about Charlie King? Charlie King could more than deal with Butler. You yourself tell me Charlie King took Dalgo, Bango, and Castillo the same day. All of you making heavy weather out of this blasted Butler. What's it? What's going on? If you all scared to touch him in Fyzabad, invite him to talks in town and hold him!"

"Watch your auxiliary verbs, Olga."

She looked at him. She said, "You always talk about me English. I want you to know that this is Trinidad and I was born here. My father is German and yours is Greek. Okay? Remember that. The other day you told me I'm talking like the maid. You ever stop to listen to Bernice? You watch that, you know, because I'll really talk like Bernice and put some good spice in me language. Okay? Because I'm on the subject of Butler now, you want to put me off, but this is nonsense, Stephen, and that silly point you were labouring on last night, about Fletcher being Governor. Look, you in charge of security and neither Fletcher nor Nankivell could tell you what to do. And then, about this Coronation Carnival – you have no right to give yourself so much work. So much unnecessary work."

The colonel did not say anything. While the wife was talking she had been attending to the kettle. He had lit the stove and put on the kettle and now she started preparing the coffee. And her mind was working like a clock.

She had mentioned Charlie King. According to what the colonel had been saying last night Charlie King should by now be in Fyzabad in plain clothes, looking to see what plot was hatching and what Butler was doing. This was because of certain threats to the oil wells. These threats were merely based on rumours, but although rumours were flying until they were even coming through the window, some of them just had to be true. Her husband had said he had given strict instructions to Charlie King not to take Butler in Fyzabad. Not unless there was some insurrection or violence. She was vexed about that. Must the police give in to the mob? Must the police give in to criminals? As she put the coffee on the table in front of him he looked at her twisted face and smiled.

"Olga, take it easy. Relax a little."

"You and this government relaxing too damn much."

"You get too worked up about Butler and it isn't worth it. We have him under strict surveillance."

"Surveillance my eye! Butler have you all just where he want you."

"Well, go on. Get a heart attack. Get a heart attack and die. My dear girl, when you fuss and froth and then kick the bucket the problem will still be there. Take it easy. We'll hold Butler all right. But just that we can't get too excited. You think we could lay hands on him in Fyzabad? If you think so you're living in a fool's paradise. Edmund Power is one of those people like you who feel we could take him anywhere. Nonsense. That's why I didn't detail Edmund for Fyzabad. Those oil workers are just waiting for us to touch Butler. Any policeman would rouse them, but especially one of us. Let's face it, we are the target. But in for a penny in for a pound. If we get Butler anywhere out of Fyzabad, that's it. But I understand he doesn't go anywhere outside of Fyzabad."

He was sitting quietly on the chair and looking at her now – waiting for her response. He hadn't told her yet about what Hickling had said about the meeting and about the strike, and he didn't intend to.

He said, "But I take your suggestion, you know. What you said about inviting him to talks and capturing him. A damn good idea!"

As the police chief got upon his grey horse to ride into the city he thought again of what Olga had said and he said again, "Damn good idea!" But although it was a fine idea to invite Butler to Port of Spain for talks and then hold him, it was an idea that Governor George Murchison Fletcher would never smile on. Nor would Howard Nankivell. Neither was it an original idea – not by a long way. Fletcher had already tongue-lashed many of the members of the Legislative Council who had suggested that move, describing it as dishonest and traitorous and an insult to British justice. On those occasions Fletcher had also spoken of the extreme poverty among the lower orders and the particularly bad conditions in the oilfields, and had said that the oilfield employers should meet Butler at least half of the way. That was what had horrified the Council, and especially the president of the Oilfield Employers Association, Lieutenant-Colonel Hickling. In fact, oddly enough, it was only Nankivell who supported Fletcher in the Council. On Butler. The Council felt that Nankivell, who had met with Butler, had been completely brainwashed by him. As Colonel Stephen Mavrogordato reached St. Vincent Street and had a glimpse of the huge crowd in the distance, he hardly reacted to it because he was still thinking of Butler, and Fletcher, and Nankivell, and the present unrest in the oilfields. And he was remembering a personal discussion with Fletcher, when the Governor had said, "Colonel, the oilfield area is rich in black gold, but also in poor black people. Do you find this a coincidence? Colonel, it is easy to put Butler behind bars, but do you see the problem?"

Colonel Mavrogordato shook the thought from his head and as he drew nearer the crowd he began to hear the faint rattling of tin and the thud of bamboo as well as the high-pitched rhythm of what was called 'bottle-and-spoon'. He said in his mind, *I only hope you people give me an easy day*.

Whether they would or not, the colonel did not have the least intention of shirking his duty – even if it was Coronation Carnival. That was why he was alerting the gunboats.

In Fyzabad, the Coronation Carnival had waxed hectic and heated. When Lance-Corporal John had left the station early and walked out onto the main road he had realised that the commotion he had been hearing was from a band coming along the Avocat Road towards the junction down the hill. In the first sunlight of morning he saw people jumping up and making merry, and he saw people waving branches and green twigs and the men in front were beating spoon on bottle and there were some with lengths of bamboo keeping up a thick, steady rhythm. He noticed about six men in front banging on big oil drums and pitch-oil tins and jumping high, dancing, and there were others thumping on even the buckets with which they went to the wells for water. For these revellers it seemed a truly glorious morning, and as he climbed the bank to watch them he heard the chorus of voices from behind blending with the drums.

For the first time since he joined the police force he looked at reckless, celebrating crowds without wanting to make an arrest.

He stood high up on a mound, above the drain, to allow the free flow of the band, and he strained a little to hear which patriotic song the band was singing. He was wondering if it was 'Land of Hope and Glory', an anthem which usually brought tears to his eyes. The sound of spoon on bottle, of bamboo on macadam road and of the rattling of tin, blurred the voices a little, and he knew he had to wait until the front of the band got past him.

He watched the women wearing housecoats and carrying banners – which he could not see clearly – and there came the powerful, strident voices of a group led by none other than Swithin Paul.

He felt good to see Swithin, whose face was whitened with talcum powder as if it was a normal Carnival day. Swithin's usual portrayal for Carnival was 'drunken sailor' – which suited this drunkard very well. In fact, Swithin would be drunk even if he wasn't playing sailor. He felt very kindly now towards Swithin who he looked upon as a good man, even though he had had to put him in jail at the normal Carnival, last February.

Lance-Corporal John smiled to himself, the first time his face had relaxed while looking at a crowd in such revelry. He looked at the band, which was now passing him, and then suddenly, without anybody being close to him, he groaned, as though stricken down. For what could the revellers be singing? The words came to his ear:

To hell with Hickling, to hell with Charlie King,
To hell with Power, we want Uriah Butler.

And bringing up the rear, a group of about a dozen people were shouting out:

Long live Nankivell, and Fletcher
Rienzi, and Butler the saviour!

His heart beat fast and he could not stop himself from getting into a sudden rage. For in the full light of the sun he saw that the banners displayed were all in praise of Butler. Getting down from the mound on which he stood he glimpsed an orange banner with large letters saying: BUTLER WILL BLAST APEX OUT AH FYZABAD, and not too far from him was a huge cardboard placard with the words: TOUCH BUTLER AND FYZABAD IN FLAMES.

He breathed hard. He moved in the direction of the placard but the crowd was too thick and he could not get near enough to snatch it. His heartbeats raced like the thuds of the bamboo drums which had just passed him. He was enraged to the point where he felt hot and bewildered. Being now on the side of the road he ran down the hill to get in front of the band, but seeing so many big sticks in the band, he looked around to see if he could spot a police uniform. He had previously agreed that Gilroy Price should stay at the station, so he knew he wouldn't see Gilroy, but he was hoping and praying that Charlie King would be somewhere nearby.

He was in fact walking backwards, glaring at the band and in between, turning back to see how far the junction was. He was trembling with fury. The banner of those people he thought of as criminals had talked about Fyzabad being in flames but he was feeling now as though his whole head was in flames and, gripping his baton, he did not care who had to pay for it.

He knew the band was going to pass up the little incline by Chee Fong, then take the La Brea Road, then go through the centre of Fyzabad, then up the Vessigny Road, before wheeling round again and coming to the junction. Although he could see no Charlie King and no prospect of help whatsoever, he decided to teach these revellers a lesson. He intended to stop the band. He screamed to a little boy, and pulled him aside so no one would hear what he said. He said, "Sonnyboy, go up to the gate by the Camp. You know the Camp – where the English people living? Tell the gateman to telephone Hickling and ask him to phone Inspector Power in San Fernando and tell him to send soldiers here because it have riot. Run quick." He had to end up speaking loudly but because of the din no one could hear what he said.

The band was still coming merrily down towards the junction when Lance-Corporal John, running towards the junction, blew his whistle, then put up both his hands ordering the band to stop. The band came to a stop, but directly afterwards four big, angry men squeezed to the front and one said roughly, "Constable, is you who stop the band?" The speaker had a red cloth tied round his head and an iron pole from which a banner had been flying. He had a bottle of White Star rum in his back pocket and a little hammer sticking out as if he had been tuning a steel drum. Another of the men said, "You don't know 'im? He is Lance-Corporal John. What *I* want to know is what he stop the band for?" The other two stood by and simply glared. They had massive pieces of wood in their hands and looked as though they were ready to use them. They were not drunk yet, just sweet, but looked furious. Then a woman eased up behind the thick crowd, threatening with an empty rum bottle in her hand.

Lance-Corporal John's face was soft now, and the frown was giving way to a smile. He said, "Well, I never see more. This is Coronation Day, you about to enter Fyzabad proper, you don't want to enter nice? In a sort of formation, like? That's why I stop the band. Because I don't know if they having a competition, but I say this band looking so nice, I'll stop them and let them enter Fyzabad properly, in style. Dancing, like. And you fellers vex for that?" The four men glared a little longer then slid back into the band. The woman showed him the bottle then pushed it up to him, saying, "Smell it. Any trouble this morning and you'll find out!" He could hardly contain his embarrassment. He felt to beat her up like soft-candle, but not in that volatile crowd.

The men took to their banners again and the others resumed beating their oil drums. They didn't quite believe in the 'formation' the lance-corporal had spoken of, for the simple reason that the lance-corporal had never bothered about formation before. Nor bothered about Carnival bands looking nice before entering Fyzabad. Either Fyzabad proper or improper! When the band started up again it just swept into the village, dancing, lit up by the morning sun, and by the revelry, and by the fluttering of banners, and by the rhythm of drum beaters, bottle-and-spoon men, and men with buckets and pitch-oil tins.

Lance-Corporal John wasn't seen again for that day, and Inspector Power, who had suddenly sent for Charlie King during the early morning to take over the controlling of crowds in San Fernando, almost sent him back when Hickling had telephoned him to inform about riots. But when Power had asked where exactly were the riots and how big – just so he would know how many soldiers to send and what kind of ammunition – and also, when he had sent to know who exactly were rioting and why, Hickling decided to drive down to the village centre to see for himself. And when all he had seen were happy crowds making for the Vessigny Road, and singing and dancing merrily, he was so vexed with Lance-Corporal John, yet so relieved, and yet so ashamed to ring back Power and say, "It was all a mistake," that he went home and just shut himself up in his study. And would not talk to Mrs Hickling. But he simply *had* to telephone San Fernando, or what would he do with the soldiers?

He rang, and when Power asked why had he taken so long in this emergency, he replied, "Well it *was* an emergency, but it is under control now. Handled it myself. That's why I took some time."

Inspector Power was very concerned. He replied, "I told Colonel Mavrogordato and he was worried stiff. He wanted to know if the oil wells were attacked. Were they? And did this trouble have to do with the Butler business?"

And Hickling had said, "No, Inspector. The crowd wanted to riot because Lance-Corporal John did not want them to use the Vessigny Road."

"But Lieutenant-Colonel, you did not say the crowd wanted to riot, you told me rioting was going on and troops were needed urgently. Before I sent soldiers to Fyzabad I took the precaution of notifying Colonel Mavrogordato. And now this is the tommyrot you'll tell me?"

"Look, Inspector, I was told by – " The noise of a wall telephone being replaced violently, hurt Hickling's ears.

He was so angry and humiliated that it was the first time since he was a child he felt like bursting into tears. He did not know who he hated more, Lance-Corporal John or Inspector Power. He said to himself, *That stupid Lance-Corporal John. Could you credit him with causing war between two respectable Englishmen?*

20

A LL afternoon and early evening the crowds celebrated free and unmolested. And just around six p.m. the Carnival began to fizz out. And maybe it was because of the boxing that the Carnival ended so early. Busloads of people came from the villages around Fyzabad, and in Fyzabad itself the people took their Carnival straight from the streets into Emporium Hall. Just that those who really knew about boxing strongly suspected that it would not end in Carnival mood – except for Young Tiger and his followers.

At this point, Emporium Hall was packed to capacity and the crowd was buzzing. It was already about eight p.m. and, in any case, the boxing contest was about to start. Uriah Butler was sitting near the door a little restless and on tenterhooks, and he was only in the hall because of Jonas. But he was already vexed because so far as he was concerned, eight was eight. If they were not going to get a move on he was soon going to get on the move. From the start everything was contrary. When would they learn to do things?

For instance, the referee was Orosco, and Orosco was from Siparia just like Kid Tiger. Could he be a fair referee? Was that justice? Was that fair play? Was that democratic? The referee was in the ring with Tiger and Tiger was jumping about and waving and playing the fool, and the silly crowd was waving and clapping and croaking, but so far as he, Buzz Butler, was concerned, both boxers were working class, and two working class men had no right to fight each other. Of course he could not tell Hothead that, nor could he tell Hothead how he really felt because Hothead meant so much to him. But it was nonsense to have two working class boxers squaring up to fight each other when now more than ever the workers needed solidarity. He could not stand being in that hall when that sort of thing was going on. And the worst was that they were calling that square space in which the boxing was going to be, and which had ropes joining the four corners – could anybody believe they were calling that a ring? How could a ring be square? It was just like Apex saying that eight cents an hour was a reasonable pay. And some of the very workmen did not contest that! Eight cents an hour for a labourer and twelve cents an hour for a skilled workman. Did anybody ever listen to such rubbish? Did the skilled workman need more food than the labourer? And many of these workmen did not even want to strike. No wonder, because a lot of them did not know a damn thing about unity.

As Butler moved uneasily in his seat a big roar went up. It was Kid Tiger reappearing. He had been sent out of the ring because of the unbearably noisy applause, but now he came up again and began to dance around the square ring to even noisier applause. He was dressed in tiger-skin shorts and a pair of spotted boxing shoes. Then, after a few moments, Kid Fearless came up, bowed, then lifted the ropes and slid under them, wearing cheeky-looking red shorts. But he certainly was not feeling cheeky. For although he was the hometown boy there was so little commotion, so little applause and shrieks when he appeared that it was embarrassing. Butler felt badly. But there was no doubt the crowd wanted Kid Fearless to win.

The boxers stopped jumping about only when the referee called them together in the centre of the ring. The referee spoke loudly, for all to hear, warning the boxers that they had to obey the rules, and how they must neither punch nor pinch in any clinch, and how they must listen for the bell and not hit after the bell else they'd be disqualified forthwith; and he warned about so many other things, that Butler said in his mind, *Who Rosco think he is? He playing Hickling! He could disqualify somebody?*

As the referee explained the rules, Butler noticed that the eyes of Kid Fearless were on him and so he slowly turned away his head. This was another reason why he did not want to come. He realised that it was because of him Hothead did not have time to train and he knew he was going to feel particularly badly when Kid Tiger knocked him down. Down and out. That was why he, Butler, was sitting where he did, on the side of the ring, towards the door, where he could make a quick exit. And that was why when he had seen Elsie standing before the crowd at Emporium Hall, obviously looking out for him, he had swung back and moved out of the way until she went in. Because he did not want to meet her. He did not even know where Elsie was sitting, and as the bell went for the first round he was not sure he wanted to know. He watched the two boxers in the middle of the so-called ring and he was suddenly glad that Kid Fearless was wearing red to hide the blood. And he was so happy to see that Fearless kept bouncing and dancing at a respectful distance instead of jumping in and 'mixing' punches. He had warned him about this some time ago because, although he did not know very much about Kid Tiger, he knew enough to know about the law of the jungle, where the tiger would use sheer power to tear up its prey. He had heard enough about this particular 'tiger', and he had already seen enough of the grimaces to convince him there was very little difference between this one and the real thing.

At the moment, with just about a minute gone in the first round, Jonas was just jumping around, bouncing on his toes and simply throwing out jabs to keep the tiger at bay. He looked nice, for his style was pretty. The crowd was roaring and you could hardly hear anything, but on occasions clear voices came across the roar: "Go for him, Tiger!" and some 'jungle' men were telling Tiger, "He could run but he can't hide."

But more of the Fyzabad crowd were now turning to their own boy, and more frequently one was hearing shrieks of "Fearless!"

Half the round had gone and not a single effective blow was landed yet. Kid Fearless was now bobbing and weaving and he was moving his head away from the punches so smoothly and so fast that he had the crowd spellbound. Although he was moving back all the time, skipping and back-pedalling as though he were on a bicycle, he did not give the impression that he was running away. Now, towards the end of the round, Tiger was impatiently pouncing upon him time and time again but the punches were always out of range. And as Tiger grew tired, every time he was made to miss he stumbled, and there were clear signs that he was getting weak. One sign was that his punches were slower, and as a result of this Fearless was becoming so bold that at one stage he stood up toe to toe to Tiger and simply ducked the punches, making Tiger miss about six before skipping away again. The crowd went wild. When the bell rang to end the round Tiger was so furious that he pranced and groaned and punched the ropes, and when the referee warned him he threw such a punch it was a good thing Orosco knew how to duck.

Orosco cried, "You think you is a real tiger? Bet ah disqualify you!" Lifting Tiger's hand, he signalled to the judges he was deducting one point.

The second round went so much like the first round that Sharkey was getting nervous. He had come all the way from San Fernando to see this fight not only because it was his own promotion and his own Kid Fearless, but also because he had dreams of luring Tiger into his camp. Then, too, Tiger had told him about a 'Boxing Iqbal', who he might wish to match with Kid Felix for the Discovery Day card. But Tiger had also told him that if Kid Fearless did not get knocked out too badly, Sharkey could match Iqbal with Fearless, and the fact that Iqbal was unknown now was nothing, for with the right promotion, such as saying Iqbal was from Venezuela and calling him 'Kid Diablo', he could draw a crowd.

So he had come to see Tiger, too, and was counting on seeing Iqbal afterwards, but at the same time he tried to give the impression to Fearless that he was at Emporium solely to support him. Yet this morning when his wife had said, "Shark, you think Fearless could pull it off?" he had answered, "Pull what off! Felix come quite here to tell me the man ain't training he only studying Butler, and I know for a fact Tiger ranting and raving and only flooring sparring partners. If Fearless last one round tonight he last plenty."

Now that the bell had rung to end round number two it was amazing to Sharkey that Fearless had not gone down yet.

Sharkey left where he was sitting and went around to the handlers of Kid Fearless. He got there just before the bell sounded for the third round. He said to Fearless, "Is me, Sharkey. I want you to dance and skip as ah tell you. Keep it up. Bob and weave." Fearless glanced at him but his own breath was coming fast. And he was beginning to feel tense, for in spite of everything he did not give himself much of a chance. But now things looked as though they were beginning to change. Amidst Tiger's frustration and impatience and anger, Fearless had heard what surely was heavy breathing. And he was now urging himself to keep it up and stay there. Keep up the bobbing and weaving. Keep up the evasion. Make Tiger chase him and get tired. Put into practice all those little things he had tried out at Point Ligoure. Try to keep on. To the final bell.

When the bell rang for the third round he found every time he feinted Tiger, and ducked to make him miss, he heard Tiger's grunt. He told himself, *It beginning to look…Beginning to look… as if… Tiger…Tiger…As if Tiger wouldn't last…*

The third and fourth rounds again went as the first two, with Kid Fearless just managing to 'back-pedal' and keep out of the way, because sometimes he could not help getting the feeling that Tiger was faking tiredness to catch him off guard. For he could not believe Tiger was *that* tired. It might be a trick. In any case he was taking no chances. Because he did not want to come so far and get knocked out. He never expected to be there at the fifth round but since he was, he wanted to go, yes, he wanted to go to the final bell. He wanted to go to the end, whether that end was bitter or sweet. Just that he did not want to be knocked out.

He was exceedingly tired now, and his dancing no longer had the bounce of the earlier rounds. But he was still making Tiger miss badly because he was seeing the punches coming. Tiger had got so slow. He himself was panting, and was running away now so blatantly, that the referee stopped the proceedings for a moment, took him to his corner and said to his handlers, "If he ain't standing up to fight he ain't going to win no round you know, and on top of that I might have to disqualify him." He did this because these men, knowing that Tiger just had to land one good punch to floor Fearless, were brazenly urging Fearless to back-pedal.

And the more Fearless back-pedalled, and danced, it was the wilder Kid Tiger got. And now Tiger, getting desperate, started throwing the crazy punches which worried his corner. And the roar of the Fyzabad crowd was beginning to grow.

But it was in the opening of the sixth round that the uproar broke out. As the bell sounded Tiger rushed out and wildly launched a flurry of blows to put Kid Fearless down, and Kid Fearless, in a desperate effort to evade the onslaught, crouched and, more through frustration and instinct than knowing what he was doing, came up with the most devastating uppercut of his whole career. The effect of that lucky punch was to drop Tiger heavily on the canvas.

Pandemonium broke loose, and the whistles and shouts and screams and yells were so sharp that one could not hear anything else. Scores of Fyzabad people jumped into the ring to embrace Kid Fearless. In the din, the referee, Orosco, decided he wasn't counting until the ring was cleared and this itself nearly caused a riot. Lance-Corporal John jumped over the ropes to force the crowd to clear the ring, when he came upon Butler in the turmoil. He quickly lifted his baton to take advantage of the situation but the crowd, seeing the baton, made a sudden lunge to escape and this all but pushed him down. In the panic the lance-corporal did not see Butler again.

It was only when the ring was cleared that the referee started to count out Young Tiger, who was still flat on his back. The din was so great that nobody could hear Orosco and there was a storm of insults. Butler took off his jacket to go up and warn Orosco, but someone held him back. But there was concern too that Kid Tiger could be hurt – although the fact that he was writhing a little meant he had not lost consciousness. When Orosco finally stopped counting, Young Tiger was still flat out on the canvas, and in fact Orosco could have counted to a hundred. It would have made no difference. Tiger did not even know where he was. He looked so completely dazed that Orosco got in a temper and cried to his handlers, "Why you ain't lift him up instead of talking yuh stupidness!" And when they eventually took up their boxer from the canvas, they had to hold him when they put him to stand up or he would have fallen again. Orosco roughly grabbed his arm and on the other side he had the arm of Kid Fearless. He looked at Tiger's face and it was blood-clotted and disfigured, but the eyes were wide open. The roar soared as Orosco raised the hand of Kid Fearless.

"Ladies and Gentlemen, by knockout in the sixth round, the winner and new champion... ."

No one could hear him in the deafening roar, and no one was listening. It was just about twenty minutes to nine, and now, with the Fyzabad boxer crowned – like George VI – there seemed plenty of time for the real Coronation Carnival.

21

IT was about two the next morning when, on coming out from Jonas's track, Kid Felix met up with Lance-Corporal John. In fact, at first he did not know who it was. The night was black and when he reached out of the track onto the main road a light flashed on him and a voice said, "Who's that?"

"Me, Felix. Kid Felix. And who's that?"

"You is Kid Felix? You coming from – from Fearless?"

"Yes. The feller they calling Fearless." He had realized it was one of the Fyzabad policemen that was speaking.

"What they having in that house, fête? I standing up here since midnight and ah see a lot of people going in there."

"So you don't know about the big boxing bacchanal? The sensation. Fearless knocked out Young Tiger, the middleweight champion. You don't know that? Strange. To me is as if I saw you in Emporium."

"I didn't say I didn't know Fearless knocked out Young Tiger. Of course I was there and I saw the lucky punch. And afterwards all these bands on the street they saying Fearless crowned and is a fresh Coronation Carnival. And ah was waiting here ah was ready for them because whatever Carnival it is it ain't going on after midnight with me – ay ay, what the hell they think it is! And so when ah run them off the street ah see lots of them going in here."

Kid Felix said, "It had lots of people in that house. It was like a Carnival again."

"I was coming to hear what going on but I have to watch the streets." Then he lowered his voice, "I hear *that* feller in there."

"Who you mean, the strike-man? The mischief-maker?"

Lance-Corporal John's heart thumped. He had heard about Kid Felix but of course he had had no idea whether Kid Felix was for or against Butler. He was thrilled now to hear, 'Who you mean, the strike-man? The mischief-maker?'

He said, "He there? That skunk. I stand up here waiting to interrogate him. You think he coming now?"

Kid Felix laughed in the dark. "Coming now? Not that man. Not where he anchor in that morris chair. He and that Jonas so thick, you can't get a razor blade between them, and I ain't think he leaving there till in the morning. You know although Fearless won he really get a bad bad beating up?"

"When he was going home and I was backing the crowd for them to bring him out, I only spot his face, and I could tell you, the cheek round one eye was swell-up as big as a breadfruit."

"Well, it swell-up worse now. It looking like a football. And the face cut up, and the chin raw, and when he reached home, you know he couldn't even stand up?"

"Why he couldn't stand up, ain't he was near the Lion of Judah? That is what ah hear his friend saying now. He's the Lion of Judah and he'll break every chain."

Kid Felix sneered in the dark.

The lance-corporal said, "Where you heading for now, Partner?"

"I was thinking if I could get something for Siparee. I didn't want to stay in that house no longer. Only that as a boxer, you see, I have to make him feel – you know what I mean. I had to make him feel I supporting him – "

"You mean you'll support a big stiff good-for-nothing?"

"Oh no, no, Constable," he laughed. "I can't support him that way. You mean to mind him? I think the so-called Lion of Judah could do that. I wondering about the bus. If I did bring me bike – "

"We could lend you a police bike in the police station. That is, if you'd bring it back."

"But of course, Constable."

Lance-Corporal John contemplated this new friend, Kid Felix. It was crucial to have a man like him who was in the confidence of the other side. He could be the finest informer the Fyzabad police could have. The lance-corporal said, "Come on then, why we don't walk up to the station? Perhaps we could get some coffee and talk a little bit, and then you could ride down to Siparee." And as he moved off he glanced back and said, "God! If I coulda ketch up with that blighter!"

When they got down to the police station Lance-Corporal John put on the kettle and they both sat talking in the still of the night. Acting Corporal Gilroy Price had not come back from San

Fernando, and Charlie King was nowhere to be seen. It was now nearly three, and as the lance-corporal looked west towards the Gulf of Paria he could see the faint lightness of dawn. He was feeling thrilled by the information Kid Felix had just given and he could hardly wait for the morning.

The lance-corporal said, "You was there in Forest Reserve when he went down?"

"No. It's a Butlerite who told me. You know they calling them 'Butlerite' now? A feller name Emery Ford. He told me he was on the site where they preparing for a new well near the 'Helena'. He was so excited. He said at last Butler calling the strike. So I asked when? I pretend I was excited and you see I used to work in Forest Reserve so they thought I was Butlerite too. Because that's a stronghold, you know. So when I asked him the date he tell me the 19th of June."

"Oh," said Lance-Corporal John. He felt so nervous he could not sit down in one place. The kettle had boiled until it was almost dry and now he saw it but when he went to get the coffee there was no coffee at the station. He came back to the front, and then he chuckled and said apologetically, "I forget Charlie King like his coffee."

Felix said, "He like what?"

Felix had forgotten all about the coffee and the lance-corporal realised that, and he said, "You know they send Charlie King here for a little time?"

"Yes, everybody know Charlie King in town."

"I was just saying he must be gone San Fernando."

"Could well be."

Lance-Corporal John looked at a few files and then drifted back and sat down. The cocks were crowing all over Fyzabad but neither the lance-corporal nor Kid Felix took notice of them. Nor did the two appear to notice the fast-breaking dawn. The lance-corporal was thinking of what could be done to forestall the strike of June 19th, but Kid Felix already knew the solution. He said the matter was so easy, simply invite Butler to Siparia to a conference of four or five people to discuss the future of boxing in Fyzabad, and kidnap him right there, in Siparia. The lance-corporal felt it was a great proposal to suggest to Charlie King, but where was Charlie King? As the lance-corporal looked out at the front door he was taken aback. The dawn was already light grey. He walked to the pitch-oil light on the ledge and snuffed it out. The room was still in half-light.

Kid Felix said, "What? You know I didn't notice how it's morning? I'd better take the bike and ride down. Ah feeling tired."

Lance-Corporal John said, "No, you'll get a bus now. It's nearly six. Ride down by bus and you could even lie down on the seat and rest."

It wasn't long afterwards that Charlie King came in. He came in limping on a crutch. He had on a rather loose black jacket, a brown felt hat, old baggy white drill pants, old boots that may have been brown at one time, and he was also wearing heavy eyeglasses.

At first the lance-corporal did not recognise him. When he had approached the station Lance-Corporal John took the report-book from the shelf and was about to ask the person to write his name first before making any report, but when Charlie King pulled off the hat and took off the eyeglasses the lance-corporal, shocked, cried, "Corporal Charlie, where you was? Where you come from now?"

"By me friend. By Fearless. In the house."

"In the house? And what happen? I thought you went San Fernando. You get hurt? Because this morning you wasn't walking with crutch! – I mean yesterday morning."

"Nothing ain't happen. We was drinking coffee and talking and we was saying what a sensational fight. But Fearless was flat out on the bed. I hardly even see him. When I asked about the strike, the guerilla said, 'Old man, I haven't seen you before. You from Fyzabad?'

"When I said I was from Forest Reserve, he said, 'Oh, you working at all?' I said, 'I can't get a job.' He looked at the crutch beside me and he said, 'Don't worry. All we want now is unity. When we call the strike on June 19th we want every man out. When you go back to Forest Reserve and you see the fellers tell them Butler say so.' He tell me, 'Don't forget, tell them the strike is June 19th.'"

Lance-Corporal John laughed, and yet he felt sad and a little jealous. Because Charlie King's resourcefulness always put them all in the shade. He knew that was why the police authorities always sent Charlie King when there was a problem. Still, he himself, Charles John, did not have to wear such a dramatic disguise to get the date.

22

Two weeks had passed and it was already the opening of June when Jonas, after the sensation of Coronation Carnival night, felt himself on the mend again.

For he had taken more blows than he could ever remember.

When Elsie, Marie Vidale and Butler had managed to get him home that night, lifting him bodily and somewhat in triumph, with the roar in Emporium Hall making the roof vibrate, he was just weak and lifeless, but it was the next morning that he felt the full force of the pain, and it was then that his cheeks and the area round the right eye were swollen to what Elsie saw, not as a grapefruit but as a calabash. The week after the fight he had lain almost completely in bed, stiff and hardly able to move.

The swelling had gone right down now. It was the poultices of Chee Fong that had done the magic.

Elsie said to Jonas, "You almost ready for the road, boy. You almost good again."

"It's the poultice."

"Yes, it's the poultice. We have to thank Chee Fong."

She was lying down beside him, and she had lifted her head to watch his right eye. She rested her head down again and she squeezed Jonas's head to hers, temple against temple, and she thought whatever lay in the future, she was happy now. She just lay against Jonas and squeezed him to her.

There was silence, and Jonas's mind drifted to days ahead, because there was a lot of work to be done, and not much time. And there were things he could not leave to anybody else. He felt more and more concerned. Nineteenth June was not all that far away.

He said, "Elsie, how me face looking? Something on me mind."

"How you mean how yuh face looking? You want me to bring the glass for you to see for yuhself?"

"No. *You* tell me. I find things taking long. I have work to do."

"How you mean work? You worried about Forest Reserve? In any case they excited about what you did in that fight and they don't mind you taking a rest. You didn't hear Kid Felix? You is a hero. Felix said even the manager, Korkhaus, was laughing all over his face. And even drinking whisky, for you."

"Tell me how me face looking. Apart from the swelling on this side." He touched the poultice. "Tell me, but don't fool me. Tell me if I could go out in the street."

"But Jonas, how you could say 'don't fool me'? I would ever fool you? You is me husband. Ay, ay. Anyhow, if you thinking of going out like that, forget it. Look, you want me to let you go out with a poultice on yuh face? You want – "

"No, I'll wait for that swelling to go down and then we'll take the poultice off. But the rest all right? I still feeling me nose funny."

"Well, I could tell you, yuh nose come a long way. The remedy what Mr Uriah give you really worked, boy. And the swelling over yuh left eye almost completely gone."

"When I reached home that Saturday night I couldn't see outa it. It was bad."

"Bad! Is bad you say? The swelling was like a lime at first, but next morning it was a calabash – "

"I hope that swelling where you trying the poultice, I hope it go down quick. Good God the strike calling in three weeks, I have a lot of work to do, I can't keep lying down in bed."

"So what would happen to the strike if you – " And then she said to herself, *I'd better not talk about that.* He sensed what she was going to say, and he thought, *Girl, you so right. But the thing is, I ain't dead yet.*

She turned her head towards him and she said, "I know you anxious. But a little patience, Jonas. God wouldn't forsake his children." She sat up thinking. She put her hand under his head and she felt it very warm and she squeezed his head to her. She said, "Ah hurting you? Talk you know." Then she said, "You ain't have fever? How yuh head so hot?"

"No, I ain't have fever; sure about that."

He squeezed her and she knew he was happy. She said, "Now listen to this. Talking about Mr Uriah. Why he like to walk all over the place like that? Sometimes I get so scared."

"I can't explain anything, but I feel Butler have some kinda magic. Nothing to do with superstition. I can't explain it, but look at that sharpshooter. The man came quite Fyzabad, oh Christ."

"But Mr Uriah escape because of Fletcher."

"That's true." Then he said, "All I want to see now is the 19ᵗʰ."

"Me, too. Oh, and you know something, Jonas? I forget to tell you because you was sleeping when I came back with the poultice. I met Gustav in the shop and Gustav called me outside and tell me all the workmen say they'll come out on June 19ᵗʰ because you make them feel so proud."

"Gustav said that? Gustav, the informer?"

"Yes. Why? He's the only Gustav round here."

"Well, tell Gustav he could go and inform Lance-Corporal John."

23

COLONEL Mavrogordato sat with Lieutenant-Colonel Hickling on one side and Inspector William Edmund Power on the other, and Charlie King sat between Inspector Power and the Governor. Colonel Mavrogordato said, "Your Excellency, we want to bring up a matter that has been presented to you before. We bring it up again because of the delicate nature of the situation. It is the country's future that is at stake and we seem to think it is justified to take an extraordinary action in an extraordinary situation. What we are proposing is this: today is Wednesday the second of June, and one could, with justice, call this the eleventh hour. The reactionary element is still at large, and as far as we can see, everything is pointing towards a strike. Lieutenant-Colonel Hickling assured me, as he has kept assuring the Legislative Council, that any strike lasting more than a week will cripple Apex and therefore will cripple the economy. It seems to us that to avoid hardship and untold suffering the best thing to do is to let us take Butler."

Governor Fletcher was taken aback. He said, "You want to avoid a strike. Now the act of striking itself is perfectly legitimate. And being perfectly legitimate I can't do much about it, can I? I am saying the same thing that I said some months ago when you made a suggestion of this nature. I want to be fair to everybody and to myself. Do you want to indulge in forced labour? Do you? Because that is what your proposal amounts to – in so many words. I am taking no side at all in this. If the alternative to taking Butler is so bad, why not give him what he asks for? I am saying this because, quite frankly, Butler's request is reasonable. But in any case, you gentlemen cannot think much of me. You want me to sanction the kidnapping of Butler. In any case that is not British, is it?"

Hickling said, "This is our last chance, and I am desperate. All these fine points about being British, I don't know what they would mean. If the fellows strike, thousands will suffer, black and white. If we prevent the strike only one man will suffer – a terrorist."

Governor Fletcher said, "When I talked about being British, I simply meant being fair. We British pride ourselves on being fair, don't we? This is my argument but I want to stop short of industrial affairs. Petroleum is a fine thing for this country but it is also making it into a tinderbox. I cannot help you if the oil-workers withdraw their labour but I must also warn you that there is nothing illegal about it."

Colonel Mavrogordato said, "But Your Excellency will of course advise that law and order will have to be preserved at all costs."

"Sure, Colonel."

Lieutenant-Colonel Hickling said, "It seems to me a simple matter. All the colonel has to do is to call a conference; it could be just amounting to the four persons here now. We call a conference and we put the case to him and, Your Excellency, I know you will stress the protection of British lives and property. And I would say if he is of a different opinion, in a few days time I am sure it would be all right to detain him."

Sir Murchison appeared to weigh it in his mind, and he said aloud, "Yes, sure, on the basis of the prospect of unrest, yes, civil unrest. That should allow us to detain him."

When Governor Fletcher had seen the determined look on the faces of the three men, knowing very well that the Colonial Office had already condemned him for being soft on Butler, and especially knowing what a sterling part the oilfields had been playing, he had suddenly changed his mind. He was no more for the taking of Butler than he had been before, but he decided to try a different strategy.

He said to Colonel Mavrogordato, "It seems to me that this is the only thing we can do. If there is the threat of civil unrest – if there is evidence of this – we can detain him. But first we'll have to have that conference you spoke of, and put the matter to him, and unless he gives a clear-cut undertaking, the only thing one can do is to detain him. That is as I see it."

Colonel Mavrogordato, Hickling, and Inspector Power glanced at each other. They could not believe that they had achieved this victory without a fight. They really could not believe their ears. There would be no need for the secret petition of complaint to the Secretary of State for the Colonies.

Hickling said, "Your Excellency, you said 'if there is evidence of civil unrest'. Of course there is evidence, Your Excellency. Abundant evidence. Lance-Corporal John has always brought information as to what the oil-workers are saying and of course what the people in the street are saying, and – well – you know, Your Excellency, that Colonel Mavrogordato is dead against taking Butler in Fyzabad."

Charlie King said, "That is why Butler's feeling so powerful. I meself could take him easy, easy. People wouldn't know, let alone to make trouble. When we having this conference?"

Only Governor Sir Murchison Fletcher answered. He said, "I don't know when Colonel Mavrogordato proposes to have this conference but I would advise it should be early, for the sooner we have peace of mind it is the best for everybody. This is just the beginning of June, and of course as you say, the 19th is the crucial date. I would suggest for the latest we do this by next Tuesday."

Lieutenant-Colonel Hickling said, "I was thinking in terms of this week." He looked at Colonel Mavrogordato.

The colonel said, "It depends on where we are going to invite him. If it is to San Fernando, for example – "

"Why not here?" Hickling interrupted. "Government House. We could have him arrested right here and taken to the royal jail just across there."

The Governor warmly agreed.

Colonel Mavrogordato said, "It makes sense."

Charlie King got up anxiously. He bent to Hickling, "If we could agree now on when we could hold the meeting, and perhaps if we could hold it on Thursday, we might be able to have Butler behind bars by weekend. Because when…"

His voice trailed off, as Hickling, paying no mind to him, began whispering to Colonel Mavrogordato. Governor Fletcher looked at this and shook his head ever so slightly. Fletcher thought, *Is it any wonder there's no compromise whatsoever in the oilfields? Is it any wonder there's a rigid line between the oil bosses and the native workers? Or I should say natives on the whole. Corporal King is one of the most efficient police officers, and at the same time one of the most loyal – if it's anything he's too damn loyal; and that's what they do to him. He's speaking to Hickling and Hickling turns away and whispers to the colonel. That's how they insult him.*

After the discussion between Hickling and Mavrogordato, Hickling said, "Excuse me Your Excellency, what do you think of this decision, between myself and the colonel?"

"Which decision? I wasn't listening. I was just thinking of how we could get a better relationship in the oil belt."

"We decide we'll have the meeting here on Thursday."

"Well, that is exactly what Corporal Charlie King had been suggesting to you."

"How does Thursday sound to you? Good?"

"Yes. I'll make it do."

The three men appeared very contented. The Governor watched them. Charlie King was as usual the enthusiastic, cheerful person, and he did not seem to feel in the least bit slighted. Colonel Mavrogordato got up and then Lieutenant-Colonel Hickling got up. They were smiling. They could not quite believe that the Governor could make such a right-about-turn.

Colonel Mavrogordato said, "All right, Your Excellency, we shall see what we can do. We'll get through to his legal adviser and put the proposal. Of course we shall say that *you* have invited Butler to talks – just to make sure that he comes. We expect to have good news and if that is the case we shall all be here on Thursday."

Governor Fletcher got up. He said, "That will be the greatest pleasure."

The guard, having seen the Governor on his feet, approached the conference room to escort his guests out.

As soon as the guests went out of the gate the Governor went upstairs to his private telephone. When he got through on the line he said, "Mr Adrian Rienzi? This is Government House. The Governor."

"Yes, Your Excellency."

"Are you alone?"

"Yes, Your Excellency."

"Are you alone and can I speak?"

"Absolutely, Your Excellency."

"There is a proposal to invite your Mr Butler to Government House. The Chief of Police and Hickling will be there. And Charlie King. And it is proposed that I should be there. Butler must on no account accept the invitation because the plan is to detain him. And he must stick to Fyzabad. He must remain in Fyzabad."

"Yes, Your Excellency."

"Very well. Thank you."

"Thank you, Your Excellency."

24

ELSIE felt so good about Chee Fong that she had already resumed shopping at his place. She felt good about him because he was the first one from that shop and first among those people who were always in it, to send congratulations to Jonas. When she had dashed there to get some poultices the morning after the fight, although it was a Sunday, Chee Fong had flung the door open to her and his smile stretched wide across his face. He had said, "Velly good, velly good, Elsie. Give boy many congre – congregations," and even *he* had laughed at himself because he knew he had not said it right.

Elsie had told him, "Well, he got velly good punches too!" She didn't know who had discussed the fight with Chee Fong. At the time it was barely daybreak.

Chee Fong had replied, "Punches *too*? Even good boxer he getting more than two punches."

She had laughed. Afterwards she had thought of Pa Jakes, who she regarded as a snake-in-the-grass. He had never shown any genuine friendship for Hothead. Yet he was always pretending and at the same time backbiting. She had spotted him in the yard of Emporium Hall that evening. When he had seen her his eyes had quickly turned towards the southwest, as if he was inspecting one of those new derricks. He did not see her at all! No, he did not see her! Yet if she had called him, his answer would have been so sweet, you could have skimmed the sugar off it. Chee Fong could teach them all how to live with each other. In fact he had not even taken money for the poultices and wanted to hear nothing about payment.

She went to the bedroom to Jonas, "Just skipping across to Chee Fong."

"You mean you have to skip, Elsie? Okay, take the rope. It in the gym."

"Could see you getting better!" she chuckled.

He had been in a good mood because he had been thinking of the strike and victory. He drew himself up into a sitting position and said, "Elsie, what you think will happen Saturday?"

"Well, to tell you the truth, I can't guess, but I know what *should* happen. Today's Wednesday. It have three days more."

"You think we'll shut down Apex so Apex will have to settle with us? Eh? What I mean is, you think we could make them close down, or give us the pittance we asking for? You think we could break them?"

"Well, I don't know. Mr Uriah told the workers plain: 'The issue is in *your* hands.' They know what they have to do."

He looked bewildered. "Elsie, but why all the time it's *we* who have this kinda thing to go through? Why it's *we* who have to beg and cry out for justice? Why it's *we* who have to fight out our soul-case to get what's ours. This isn't fair, Elsie. This world isn't round, you know!"

She stood up watching him and listening to him. She said, "There he goes again. Talking about what's fair. You think those oil people care about what's fair? Butler told the workers: 'The issue is in your hands.' When strike day come all they have to do is to stay home. We ain't quarrelling and we ain't begging for nothing. The oil in the ground belongs to us!"

"But it will be in the ground. Look Elsie, sometimes I get confused. You think if the strike last some little time these poor people could stand up to it?"

"Sometimes I meself get worried about this. Because when you poor in this world you don't have any blooming chance and I don't know why in the name of heaven our people want to be poor. Yes, you vex? They want to be poor. Me? I like money. That's why I went quite San Fernando and put every cent of that money in the bank. That money you win in the boxing. Why you vex now – we always quarrelling about this. The Bible say: 'Blessed are the poor for theirs is the kingdom of heaven.' Well, keep the kingdom. I don't want to go."

"The Bible said what? You sure?"

"Ah, I don't know. I think the line is: 'Blessed are the poor in spirit for they shall see God.' Something like that, ain't it? I ain't so sure now but it's something like that. And there's this other one about it's easier for some camel or other to pass through some needle's eye than for a rich man to enter the kingdom. Anyway, if I had my way this is one woman who wouldn't get through that needle's eye. I feel the people who have money don't want you to have money too, so they – "

"Wait a minute. I ain't see that point. Why they wouldn't want you to have money too? They already have money!"

"Yes, but if everybody have money, nobody wouldn't work for anybody."

He had to laugh.

"You could laugh if you want but I know it's those rich lazy sultans who like to write about this blinking camel."

"Elsie, take it easy. Sometimes you have good ideas but I for one ain't agree with this one. And please, Elsie, don't talk against the Bible. As fiery as Uriah is he always love the scriptures. You know what he said once? He said, 'That is me refuge and me strength'."

She was silent.

"And Elsie, he's always calling for unity."

"He'd better call for thrift too. So that it just wouldn't be unity in poverty. Because poverty could break the strike – they'll crawl back. We ain't rich but if everybody in Fyzabad was like us those people would damn well have to respect us. Because then we'd be fighting fire with fire. Right now we can't fight fire with nothing because we ain't have a damn thing."

He said, "That's true. But unity's still a weapon?"

"For now it's the only hope. That is the only thing I counting on and hanging on to. That is if we prove we have unity when strike day come. But I don't want you to mope and moan and feel sorry for yourself. When you out in the street again and you meet yuh friends, what you have to get in their tough head is not only the extra three cents or four cents an hour that we calling for but that we have to fight back."

She looked at him with his hands covering his face again. She said, "Look I want to go. I have to go. You not in pain or anything?"

"I only feeling a bit – you know."

"Depressed. And Jonas, I don't think you back to strength yet. And I think I talk too damn much, anyway. And I know you upset about what going on. You'll let Hickling and those fellers upset you so bad? That's why, on the whole, I like Uriah Butler. He told the workers straight, 'The issue is in your hands.' Butler is a fighter but he can't do no more. And the referee tell you plain, in Emporium Hall – when he was calling out the rules, he tell you and

Tiger: 'Go back to your corner and come out fighting.' I like that. I hope that's how the fellers coming out on the 19th."

When Elsie entered Chee Fong's shop, as soon as she noticed who was leaning up against the glass case, her mood changed. She simply bought a few things without saying anything. She bought bread, rice, black-eye peas, butter, but there were other things she had come for, which she forgot. Even Chee Fong was surprised. He was surprised but of course he knew why she was in this state. She said, a little confused, "I'll have to come back. Add these up, Chee."

She paid and left without saying anything, not even to Pa Jakes. When she left the lance-corporal kept his eyes on Chee Fong and smiled. He remained leaning up on the glass case in the same position he was in when Elsie had walked in, and not even his head had shifted. But his head shifted now as he looked at Pa Jakes. The old man smiled.

Then Meelin appeared from behind the curtain, and Lance-Corporal John said, "Ma Chee Fong, you ever see more?"

She laughed "Kee kee", and she said, "She no likee Coral John."

Lance-Corporal John mimicked, "And Coral John no likee neither."

Which made Pa Jakes laugh. Then Pa Jakes said to the lance-corporal, "That's funny. Since that night you ain't ketch up with him?"

"Well, I ain't see him. Me? I ain't taking him here. Here in Fyzabad. Not with these hooligans. In any case, Charlie King in town. But what ah was saying was, ah know he have a place in Vessigny – that's the madman – and he have a place here too. But he ain't in Vessigny and he ain't here. But Saturday night he say clear the strike will be in a few days. Well, I know the date. He talk plain. He tell them frankoment: 'Babylon have to fall.'" The lance-corporal smiled a sour smile and looked away. Then he said, "But I have to see his backside fall first."

Meelin laughed "Kee kee" again.

Chee Fong said, "Elsie no buy 'cause police here."

Pa Jakes said, "Good people don't 'fraid the police. If yuh heart clean you buy any time, and especially when police there. Eh, sah! But from the time she come in and see you, Constable, hm, I nearly laugh. Her face changed, boy. And this bitterness, it's all through you-know-who! He want a strike, but he ain't working. And you think he want a job? He just want to see Apex come to destruction."

Lance-Corporal John said, "But he said so. I was there. So you didn't believe me? I sitting down right there in the dark room and Butler right there on the other side. Candles burning, lavender, people singing. I have me hat pull down over me face. They singing 'Hail to the Lord's annointed'. The man calling Hickling name, Judge Gilchrist name, he said these foreigners so bad. I nearly arrest the brute right away. I had to bite me teeth because if I did only arrest Butler those ignorant people woulda kill me. They woulda – Oh God, look who going down the road!"

As he was looking out into the road he saw the limping figure cross the far junction and he said, "All over Fyzabad I can't find this man. I hear somebody say he could make himself invisible, and perhaps is true. Look, I have to shadow him. Look, ah going. Till later."

He was so much in a hurry he nearly tripped on the steps.

By the time Lance-Corporal John reached the nearby corner Butler was out of sight. The lance-corporal did not know what happened. He looked around but he had no idea where Butler went. Ashamed to go back to the shop, he went to the police station.

Butler wasn't even aware that Lance-Corporal John had been looking around for him. He was standing on the far side of Ma Ramsingh's green grocery shed, because it was in the shade, and so it was cool there, and the day was really beginning to grow warm.

He was waiting for the Siparia train which was due in at ten o'-clock, but he did not want to go across to the railway station yet. He had not wanted to be here at all, but since Mamselle Marie had whipped up a big following for him in Siparia and, also, since she was coming to Fyzabad because of him, he felt he had to try and meet her at the railway station. Because she had sent that message by the guard.

Since he had gone down there that first time she had been very kind to him and was in warm support of the political party he had organised. True, she had found the name odd: 'The British Empire

Workers and Citizens Home Rule Party'. 'British Empire'? She thought that did not sound like Butler. But he was able to convince her very easily. For he had told her, "If yuh have you hand in the lion's mouth, you'll jerk it out? Eh? You wouldn't ease it out? Well they have me down as a revolutionary, but I want to tell them that I'm really for the British Empire, I love the British Empire. Because I want what I want. And when the Secretary of State for the Colonies read my petition, and the petition come on letter-paper which have on the top, 'The British Empire so-and-so', he must say, 'This man might indeed be revolutionary, but revolutionary for the British Empire!'" She saw the point and was amused.

Apart from that she held prayer meetings and spread his name throughout the length and breadth of Siparia. So what could he do when she sent the message saying she wanted to hold a prayer meeting to bless his house? He had talked to Jonas about it and asked if the prayers could be in *his* house instead. Both Jonas and Elsie were thrilled. As he was waiting he thought of this, and he felt happy to be able to bring a little joy to Elsie and Jonas.

He looked at where the sun was, to guess the time, and it seemed so late that he listened to see if the train was coming. He heard nothing, and as he walked round to Ma Ramsingh, she turned to him and said, "That was a good get-away, Mr Uriah."

"A good what? How you mean?"

"He was right here. He come right up to here."

"Who is 'he', Ma Ramsingh?"

"I ain't know how you calling them. By name, ah mean. He come right up to here when you was hiding."

"I wasn't hiding. I went there for the cool. Who it was?"

"The police with the big eyes and the mark under the chin."

"Lance-Corporal John was right here?"

"I ain't know how you calling them. I was trembling. I didn't want him to see you."

Butler was taken aback. "You didn't want him to see me?"

"I hear they have a warrant for you."

"Well let them bring it!" His eyes flared. "Let them touch me. They say is sedition. Well let them come and take me! Let – "

Somebody approached Ma Ramsingh's stall and Butler was silent. When the person walked away Butler said, "It was the same meeting I had just the other day in Emporium Hall. The police charged me with sedition. Because ah say, 'Even if the King...' I was telling the workers look how Hickling expect people to work for starvation pay. Then ah said, 'Justice is yuh right, and even if the King come you have to fight for justice. Yes, even if the King!' They say that is sedition. They say – Look, Ma Ramsingh, ah think ah hearing a rumbling. The train coming." He walked away. Then he turned and said, "We can't just get frighten. We –"

He stopped abruptly because of her antics and he said, "What happen?"

She did not speak but something *did* happen, because she was shaking. Then she began trembling violently. Butler did not know what to make of it, but he just looked behind him. And walking to Ma Ramsingh's stall was Lance-Corporal John. Between Lance-Corporal John and the open space beside Emporium Hall he could see the train coming.

He said, "Ma Ramsingh, I have to go. Remember we have to unite. It is the only thing. Butler party only fighting for a better and a brighter day."

Then, limping, he hurried to the railway station.

25

I T was not long afterwards that Lance-Corporal John saw Butler walking across the road with Mamselle Marie Vidale. He was shocked. When he had heard the train chug off he had been hurrying to the Apex office to tell Hickling that Butler was going to San Fernando. And it was only because he looked back to cross the road that he saw them.

He stood up and watched them going through the track and he did not have to wonder what house they were going to. It was just about half past ten now. He continued toward Hickling's office.

As he made long strides along the gravel road to the Apex buildings the picture of Butler and Marie Vidale crossing the road was vivid and burning in his mind. The wanted man with the blue dock shirt opened at the neck and the brown pants. And beside him the woman in mauve. Was it mauve? He was not sure what you would call that colour but he would say mauve. And not just a mauve dress, but a flowing mauve gown. And a mauve head-tie. At a certain point as he was walking he was not sure if he should go to the police station first or continue on to Hickling. He even stopped and turned it over in his mind, and then he decided to go on.

The reason why he had thought of the police station was because it had occurred to him he might need some sort of reinforcement, but it was no sense going back to the police station because in any case if reinforcement had to come it would have to come from San Fernando. And although Hickling was not of the police he had a lot more weight than the Assistant Corporal, Gilroy Price, because all he had to do was to telephone Inspector Power and in a few hours' time policemen would be in Fyzabad.

When the lance-corporal reached Hickling's office and knocked on the door he heard Hickling say, "Come in," but when he pushed the door open and Hickling saw who it was Hickling got up and said he had to go out.

"This is a little important, Colonel, Sir."

"So my job isn't a little important too?"

"Is about Butler. Butler and Marie Vidale."

"And who?"

"Mamselle Marie Vidale."

Hickling's heart started to race. "But Vidale is in Siparia so far as I know."

"She in Fyzabad today. I just see she and Butler crossing the road. They gone by Jonas house."

Hickling sat back down on his chair. What was the meaning of it? Butler and the sorcerer. He wanted to collect his thoughts.

His mind went to the workers who were still rebellious and on edge but since the Coronation Carnival that Saturday everything was quiet. He had frequently asked himself if that was the calm before the storm, but there had been no reason to think there was a storm brewing. In fact he had already informed both Colonel Mavrogordato and Governor Fletcher that there had been an improvement. However, now things looked ominous.

Butler and Marie Vidale together in Fyzabad! He felt uneasy, because through the stories of Charlie King, he regarded Marie Vidale as evil. He was particularly uneasy about the fact that she was so near to the Apex oilfields.

He looked up towards Lance-Corporal John. "Well, I had the impression that things were improving, however..."

"Yes, Major. Things improving, but for a big bacchanal here in Apex. Marie Vidale doesn't make fun!"

Hickling sat up in the chair. "Look, Officer, are you trying to frighten me?"

"No, but we might need reinforcement."

"To do what?"

"Surround the house."

Hickling said, more calmly, "Officer, do you wish to make me laugh? Would you surround someone's house just because he is entertaining a friend?"

"Marie Vidale is ah obeah-woman."

Hickling said nothing. He was hoping there was some justification for surrounding the house. He was hoping that there was some law against obeah. At least, against what he was told was obeah.

The policeman continued, "And Butler is ah wanted man."

"But do you think the people would let you take him? You your-self know it wouldn't be easy. We all want him behind bars but I feel now nothing like this should be done in Fyzabad. I told Inspector Power about this already, but he's game to arrest Butler anywhere. I don't want to be a party to it. About this present situation, I have a feeling Butler could associate with whomsoever he wants. By the way, is Marie Vidale a criminal?"

"You asking that Colonel Hickling? And ah done tell you about Mahal? And about – "

"Okay, okay. So far as you are concerned she's a criminal. I want to ask you this, and answer me straight out, yes or no. Has she been convicted of any crime?"

"No, Sir. But – "

"I told you I don't want too many words. The answer is 'No'. That's good enough."

Lance-Corporal John kept standing there. Hickling looked about him. Then he said, "This place has too many hotheads. You told me about one hothead – "

"There's where Butler gone, he and Marie Vidale."

Lieutenant-Colonel Hickling went on as though he had not been interrupted. "This place has far too many hotheads. Butler is a hothead, you are a hothead, Charlie King is a hothead," and he said in his mind, *Sometimes I think Inspector Power is a hothead too.*

Lance-Corporal John was talking. The lieutenant-colonel was not listening at first and then he said hotly, "Yes, I think you are a hothead too. And please, Lance-Corporal, please let's not have too many words. Sometimes you are so long-winded and what's more I can't stand your English."

He got up, walked towards the window, then turned back and said brusquely, "What about the meeting tonight, are you going to the special meeting?"

"Which special meeting, Colonel, Sir?"

Hickling said loudly, "See what I mean?" Then he turned to the lance-corporal. "Do you mean I have to mind my business and mind yours too? Yesterday I came across a handbill written in red and stuck upon the front of the Labour Office. It said red was for blood!"

The lance-corporal hardly waited to hear everything the lieu-tenant-colonel said. He saluted and said, "Colonel, Sir, let me go and see."

The handbill stuck on the Labour Office was hand-written and in red ink. It was not signed by Butler, like the rest. It simply said: *To all perspective strikers, a special, emergency meeting tonight to discus the charge against Buzz Butler. We hearing that the authorities planning to hold him any time now, for Sedition But any such atempt mean blood. We meeting at seven tirty tonight at the house of Charles Smith – you know where it is. Turn out and support your Chief. Hail to the Lord's Annointed.*

Lieutenant-Colonel Hickling had not taken the notice seriously and he was not even going to mention it to Lance-Corporal John had not the lance-corporal disturbed his mind with the mention of Marie Vidale. He had almost disregarded the notice because the way it was written, the way some of the words were spelt, it was not like the usual handbills, but seemed to come from someone trying a prank.

But this was not taken the same way by Lance-Corporal John. When he saw it he tore it violently off the door of the Labour Office, and became nervous and furious. Then the very next thing he thought of was the house of Charles Smith. The notice had said 'you know where it is', but he, Lance-Corporal John, did not know where it was. He did not even know Charles Smith. Right away he thought of doing what he was no stranger to: disguising himself in plain clothes and going to the meeting. But he could not think of who was this Charles Smith and he had to find out.

As soon as Lance-Corporal John left, Lieutenant-Colonel Hickling perused his diary to see what his day would be like. Usually his secretary told him, but he had no secretary today.

He said to himself that he would have liked to know what Marie Vidale told Butler, or what they had told each other, and in any case why was she here? He wondered if it had anything to do with the meeting at Charles Smith's house. And he felt it probably also had to do with that warrant. He wondered since when Marie Vidale became this great ally of Buzz Butler, because he had never heard anything about that. But even so he had only just got to hear the name Marie Vidale when Charlie King was here recently. He himself had been here for a few years, and before Charlie King came, he had never known she existed. So had she really done that to Mahal and his family?

Hickling was confused, and he was annoyed that he was confused because he had never had any intention of letting these natives occupy his thoughts. And being in this state now he was particularly harsh on Butler because this was the man who was causing all the trouble, here and in Port of Spain, and all over Trinidad. And he was the man who had caused the government to go stark staring mad, else why should Nankivell behave like a clown, forever talking of the plight of the workers; and why should Murchison Fletcher himself, the very Governor, appeal to him over wages, saying, "Lieutenant-Colonel Hickling, see what you can do for the oil workers." See what he could do, indeed. Charlie King had shown him something called a bull-pistle, an extremely injurious whip, and if he had one in his possession he would certainly try and see what he could do for the oil workers!

Hickling was blowing hard, so angry he was. He looked outside through the glass windows at the activity going on, and afterwards he looked again at the diary.

As he looked through the diary, the thoughts of Marie Vidale came to his head again. Not that he believed in black magic, but he had seen Mahal himself, nobody had had to describe the man to him. In these little colonial backwaters there was so much talk of so much nonsense that could not possibly exist. For instance, Charlie King had even told him about soucouyants, old ladies who flew by night to suck blood. How in the name of reason could an old lady fly? Or a young one, for that matter. He respected Corporal King but he could not help calling him the king of all these superstitious, illiterate baboons. He could not explain how such a man could be so successful. God forbid! But he had seen Mahal himself, and he had looked out particularly to see if this man was faking.

What special powers did Marie Vidale have, he did not know. The only thing he was sure about was where the powers had come from. For it had to come from one source only – the Devil. It had to be either witchcraft or obeah that did that to Mahal. Somebody had to cast that spell. He did not know anything about witches and spells, but he knew something had happened to Mahal and he hoped, vaguely, but nervously, that nothing would happen to he himself, Hickling. He hoped he would never cross the path of this woman in mauve.

As he sat there thinking, a most unlikely idea came to his mind. It was more like a suggestion than an idea. It was as if that ape, Lance-Corporal John, had been standing beside him and had made this outlandish suggestion. And what was the suggestion? It was as if Lance-Corporal John, that half-wit, had said to him, "But Colonel Hickling, Sir, instead of thinking about Marie Vidale and wondering bout she powers, why not invite her to yuh office, Colonel, Sir, and talk to she?"

And doing just that was in Lieutenant-Colonel Hickling's mind now.

He began looking at the diary again. It was the second Tuesday in the month and at two in the afternoon he had the oil employers' meeting. There was no question as to whether he was going to this meeting. At this meeting a lot of things had to be decided. He wrote something against that entry and put down the book.

He could not concentrate. He thought about a few telephone calls he had to make. The way things were going he wanted to ask Inspector Edmund Power if Corporal King could not remain at Apex for the rest of the crisis. Since King was feared by all, the situation demanded he remained in Fyzabad at this time. He also wanted to talk to Colonel Mavrogordato. It was this whole question of reinforcements he wanted to discuss. He did not like how things were shaping up and he had to take precautions.

It was getting late and he decided to do some work on the statistics the secretary had provided for the oil employers' meeting, and of course he had to adjust a lot of the figures to show that Apex was still the outstanding producer of petroleum in Trinidad. He had a lot of respect for Trinidad Leaseholds Limited and for United British Oilfields of Trinidad, but it could not be denied, after he fixed up his figures, that Apex was at the apex of them all. Of course, Trinidad Leaseholds Limited and United British Oilfields would say that they were also refining, and that was all well and good, but let them be content with that. They could not be good in everything. Let them not claim that they were leading in production. Even if that were true, his figures would show a different picture.

He knew that one thing they would all be united in is in not giving in to Butler and his band of hooligans. Butler was talking about the profits the oil companies were making, and had caused even Colonial Secretary Howard Nankivell to refer to it and to say the oil workers were living in misery. Living in misery, mind you, with low pay and bad conditions. What damn nonsense was this? So how would they have been living if Apex and Trinidad Leaseholds and United British were not there? In luxury? These people should stop talking of profits and be grateful the oil companies were there, so that they could have jobs and have incomes. Butler was inciting on every front. He was even attacking Judge Gilchrist, saying Gilchrist was giving the Apex land to foreigners and not to the workers. So who owned Apex?

His blood boiled. It was high time to put a stop to Butler and that was why he was looking forward to Thursday. The man was charged with sedition and he was walking about with impunity with the police afraid to arrest him, and he was continuing to incite. There was that meeting at Vessigny that Constable Gilroy Price had told him about, and there was going to be one again tonight. With God's help, though, Thursday should see the end of this. King had promised him, secretly, he would take Butler in Fyzabad, but he, Hickling, did not want any such thing, and he hoped King would not try any nonsense. Because that could lead to riots and bloodshed, and damage to installations at Apex. True, King did have a reputation for arresting even violent people without any show of resistance – he did not know how King accomplished it, but it seemed to be a fact, for a lot of the natives had told him of it. But he wanted nothing of that, and had warned King. Yet King was the main man needed in Fyzabad. To detect plots and frustrate evil moves. Apex could not welcome a strike. Even the planned detention of Butler could lead to chaos. Hickling took up the telephone and dialled. When he heard Inspector Power's voice he said, "Look, it's urgent. I want to see if you could arrange something for me."

The inspector asked him what it was and Hickling went into great detail, telling him what the latest situation was at Fyzabad, how things were becoming more and more dangerous – thanks to Butler – and, irrespective of Thursday, how they had to act now if they wanted to save the Apex Oil Company. Of course, he made things sound more dangerous than they really were, talking about the agitation of Butler, the threats Butler had made, how the men were becoming more and more agitated and talking about striking. He even spoke of the fact that Butler was holding another meeting that very night. He said Thursday just had to be the day.

The inspector listened and he became so concerned and furious with Butler that in the conversation, although Hickling had asked for Corporal Charlie King, he thought quickly as to whether he, in fact, was not able to go instead. But he could not go, since Colonel Mavrogordato had specifically posted him to San Fernando to be in charge of the whole south-western region, ready for any alert in the industrial town, in the sugar areas to the north and east of it, and the oilfield areas to the south of it. When Lieutenant-Colonel Hickling was finished talking, Power said, "Okay, so Butler's playing the jackass. That's what Nankivell and Fletcher want. Unless some oilfield don't go up in smoke – "

"No, no, no. Please don't say that!"

"Well, that's what Fletcher wants. And Nankivell. *I* don't want that. That's why I want to come down meself and apprehend the brute."

"Let Charlie King come. You said he's down but I haven't seen him yet. You don't bother, send Charlie King. Not that you aren't a finer detective than Charlie King. You are. But Charlie King knows his people, you don't. He can mix with them, eat with them, drink with them. And he can take Butler like nothing. Just that I meself prefer to wait for Thursday. King will take Butler so easily he wouldn't know when he's in the van."

Inspector Power chuckled at the other end of the line. He said, "I understand the rank and file talk about Charlie King as though he is divine. I suppose it came from that Dalgo incident. I hope for your sake it's justified. Because I sent King down. You'll see him. Don't worry. So Butler – "

"By the way, I nearly forgot to tell you. You heard about Mahal, of course."

"No."

Hickling was surprised. "You don't know about Mahal, who walks barefooted throughout the length and breadth of Trinidad, believing that he's driving a car? Turning the steering wheel, stepping on brakes, all day – "

"Yes, yes. That's right. I have heard of a character like that."

"Well the woman who did it is with Butler as I talk to you."

"How do you mean, 'the woman who did it'?"

"It's obeah. Haven't you heard of obeah either?"

"No."

There was the silence of disbelief. Inspector Power said, "In your job at Apex you move about talking to the natives, and you get to know them. In my job I don't get to know them but I get to lock them up." He laughed, "Haw haw." He continued, "In any case you have a policeman there always on the beat, always investigating, poking his nose – that's good, mind you. I'm talking about the lance-corporal now. I suppose it is he who told you about obeah!"

"It's Charlie King who told me about obeah."

The inspector could not say anything. He could not think of anything to say. For Charlie King was a policeman who was working with him all the time. The inspector changed the conversation. "So how are things on the oilfield itself? Isn't everything normal now?"

"You're right to say 'now'. Yes, everything's normal now. But as I told you, if Butler gets his way things won't be normal for long. And we are not sure about Thursday because – "

"I sent Charlie King. Also, Butler'll be held in town Thursday."

"Well, all right, Inspector. I'm not very confident this morning. Will Charlie King be here while this crisis lasts?"

"Yes, but there'll be no crisis. And there'll be no strike."

26

MARIE Vidale spent all day in the house of Jonas and Elsie. They had converted the house into a chapel and the whole place was reeking with wild-senna leaves, balisier, the sweet-scented lavender, laburnum, cyp, pois doux and man-better-man. There was also the sweet smell of rosemarie and khus khus grass and metivier grass, and the faint sickly smell of fever grass and chandelier. Two candles were lit, one on either side of the room.

The house was not closed but Elsie had got out old bed-sheets and converted these sheets into a heavy draped curtain at the front door. And they had spent the entire morning in prayers.

Butler had made himself easy and flexible up to now, not because he was afraid of the sedition charge, but for the want of not driving away those who loved and supported him. For unity was the key so far as he was concerned. That was why at intervals during the prayer meeting he answered questions from Marie Vidale that he would have hardly answered from himself.

It was when she had said, "What is sedition, Mr Uriah?" that he was taken aback. He could hardly believe it. This was a person who was going to intercede for him with the spirits to save him from sedition and she did not know what sedition was? It was only then he realised that despite the impressive mauve head-tie and gown, and the imposing presence, Marie Vidale was, underneath it all, a woman as ignorant as the scores of other women around him in Fyzabad. Not that she was a sham. He could see the power of her faith. Just that her question to him was unbelievable.

He had said, "Sedition? That is like if you say something against the people who rule you. You remember Christ was tried for sedition?"

"It wasn't treason?"

"No. I think it was sedition. He said something against Caesar."

"And what is treason?"

"Treason will be like if Hickling say something against – well, it have to have a war, let's say you have a war, if you help the enemy, well that is treason."

"So you *did* say something against Caesar, I mean, against the Governor, like."

"Against the King."

Marie Vidale opened her eyes wide. Looking away, she said, "I did not believe when they said that."

Butler smiled quietly. He said, "Marie Vidale, Butler is not afraid of the King."

She stared at him. He said, "It's only God I fear. Not Man." His voice was soft but firm. His eyes were on her. Her big eyes were fixed on him. He said, "This is why I am giving myself to this house today. It is not only because you people love me. How nice it is for brethren to dwell together in love…" He forgot the quotation. He said, turning round, "Jonas and Elsie, bless you both." He had hardly realised they were not in the room. He continued, "And Marie Vidale came in from Siparia to pray for Butler not to make a jail. But let not your heart be troubled, my sister. If there is a just God above, if God is just he will know I am fighting a just war. Yes, friends, the Lord is my shepherd, and I am fighting for the poor and suffering. Not the rich, but the poor and suffering, and even if … ." He stopped short as Marie Vidale made a sound of surprise. Butler smiled. He understood. The people in Fyzabad would fall on their knees to Hickling, let alone the King. So what he was fighting for was not just better wages and better working conditions. He was fighting for self-worth, self-respect. Dignity. Whether he succeeded or not depended on the people. The issue was in their hands.

Mamselle Marie Vidale and Butler went into another prayer session, and Butler felt transported and relaxed and as if he was in the presence of someone truly divine. For he felt an inner peace. Jonas and Elsie were still out of the room. For Butler, the scent of the flowers, and the candles burning seemed to have brought a tranquillity he had not felt since he had left Grenada. He looked at Marie Vidale sitting there with her mauve dress and her head bent in thought, the great head-tie almost touching the table. He looked at her and said nothing. At length she raised her head, and with a soft smile she said, "God is good. Justice will come in the end."

"You feel so, Mamselle Marie. You make me strong."

"And you make *us* strong. When I say *us* I mean the working class. Everybody knows what's happening, but few are willing to do what you doing."

"Somebody have to do it."

"That's why I come to pray with you. This is Tuesday 15th. You know what I fear, Mr Uriah? I fear they'll panic and try to kidnap you. You are brave and bold but we need God's help. Watch how you're walking."

She continued, "And if I were you, in future meetings I wouldn't say 'even if the King'. Because even if it's not sedition, Caesar want to get rid of you and he'll just jail you. He'll cry sedition and clamp you in jail. We don't want to take any chances with a man like you going to jail. Because what will happen to the oilfield workers and to everybody? That's why you shouldn't say 'even if the King.'"

Butler did not want to argue but he felt his blood getting warm. He continued to smile, although the smile was a little forced now. He said, "The King is flesh and blood just like you and me. He born just like us and he'll die just like us. But my God will never die." He felt genuinely overwhelmed at the wonder of it all. He said, "Some place in the Bible say 'kings and queens and princes go forth in golden raiments', but I ain't fighting for riches and I ain't fighting for splendour. I'm just fighting for better times for those workers. Marie Vidale, you'll be surprised what Apex could afford to give to the workers, but Hickling will never do it. He'll never bend, so we'll have to break him. We'll have to fight the good fight."

This was a moment for Marie Vidale to slide into prayers. And then after a short while she broke into the hymn, 'Fight the good fight', and then she sang, 'Oh God our help in ages past'.

It was getting on for four o'clock when Marie Vidale brought the prayer meeting to an end. To Butler, she appeared powerful now and impressive and to him it was certainly not the same person who had asked: "What is sedition, Mr Uriah?"

She stood up and said, "Well, it was a long day and a nice day, but now I'm looking to go. Don't forget, be careful. We gain nothing if we lose you."

"You can't mean that. Please don't say that."

"You getting humble now. Thanks be to God. And for yuh meeting tonight, take things as I tell you. Wish I could stay but I can't.

A long day and I have to go home. But take things easy. No big strike talk. Because Charlie King will be there and he'll be only too glad to clamp you in jail. Play it easy and Saturday we hope every man come out. Don't blow no trumpet. Hothead tell me Charlie King in town."

"That's what they saying. I ain't so sure."

"He'll be there at the meeting. They call me an obeah woman but you ain't have to work obeah to know that. They want you bad. Charlie King will be there listening to you. You wouldn't see him."

"I'll watch out."

"You wouldn't see him. But mind what you say. Sometimes you could be a hothead."

"It have only one Hothead," he said and laughed. Then he got serious and looked up at her. "Ah really fiery sometimes because ah feel it in me guts – the pressure, the frustration. You could beg and you could go down on your knees – you could cry blood, these b– " he stopped. He said, "These wicked people wouldn't give you nothing. But I know sometimes I should calm down. I'll take yuh advice."

She said, "They have guns and bullets, and that's how they'll answer you. Be meek. Meekness could be power too, you know! Oh yes. Who you say that police officer is? The one who they sent to San Fernando?"

"William Power?"

"That's right. Well that's just what they want. Power over us. Our policemen so glad to do their dirty work."

Butler said, "Well the hour is coming. After me meeting tonight we just have to wait to see what will happen Friday. If the Friday night shift walk off we could be sure the Saturday shift walking off too. I'll be so glad. I going in Emporium yard Saturday early to address all the strikers. I feel so happy you came to pray with me."

"No, it's my happiness. Good luck. I'll come back, you know. This is only Tuesday. I'll be here by Friday."

27

Butler's meeting that night was very brief. He had been so influenced by what Marie Vidale had said that the meeting turned out to be extremely low-keyed. It did not look like a Butler meeting at all. It was kept at Emporium Hall where all Butler's meetings were kept, and after opening with the hymn, 'O God of Love, O King of Peace!' he told the men he had reached the limit of his patience with Apex. He was very calm in saying it, he did not get worked up, and he certainly had no intention of making a fiery speech.

Before he began he looked around the room, and it seemed strange to him that although there was a good attendance, with scores of workmen attending – rig men, pipeline men, and machine shop men – he thought it strange that although there was a full hall there was not a policeman in sight. He confidently expected Lance-Corporal John to turn up while he was speaking.

As it happened Lance-Corporal John did not turn up at all, and this was not because he did not think it useful to be there, but because Charlie King had advised him not to.

And Charlie King himself was there, disguised as one of the rig men. As brilliant as the move was he knew he had already been overshadowed, for Lieutenant-Colonel Hickling had told him what the Acting Corporal at the station had done. But he did not want to admit that Gilroy Price had shown the way. He did not want to admit this even to himself.

When he had arrived here and had called to see Hickling after a few days he had not even had time to mention anything of his intentions to disguise and infiltrate when Hickling told him what had happened at Vessigny. He had become very irritated to hear of it even though he figured that a great deal of information had been got by Gilroy Price which could have been got in no other way. He nevertheless resented the method used because in using it now he could not be original. He could not raise a gasp of astonishment as he always did.

Not that he was going to arrest Butler tonight, though. As he sat there before the meeting began, while candles were being lit and flowers were being arranged on the table, he at one moment actually thought of it and the method in which it could be done. But he quickly dismissed it, for it made no sense at all. Because he did not even have Lance-Corporal John as a back up, let alone the squad of men he really needed, a squad of at least twenty men, heavily armed. For this group of workmen, who he saw as illiterate thugs, would not let him take Butler away under those conditions. He was sure of it. They would kill him even before he got out of the yard of Emporium Hall.

He had looked around the room. It may not have been as dark as Hickling told him the one at Vessigny was that night but it was far from bright, and this lighting was certainly a Butler strategy.

But it was also a strategy which helped him now because nobody could see his face clearly. By the light of the candles his eyes scrutinised the faces of Butler's henchmen, and indeed the face of Butler himself, a face he had seen just once before. He was looking, too, at the women close to Butler, and he saw at once that the woman they were calling Elsie was one of the most attentive. There were a few things he would have liked to write down, but of course he could not be so rash in that room. Would a rig man take notes at a meeting? He just had to remember faces.

He sat there now, pretending to be one of the most disgruntled of the rig men, but not wanting to draw attention to himself. He wanted to appear as any other rig man, and he tried to get into snatches of conversation, but he could not chat, because he knew nothing about rigs if he was asked about them. He was sitting at the very back of the room, and when Elsie Francois was sprinkling the incense just before the opening prayers, the sharp scent had made him cough. People turned round to look at him then and he took the opportunity to bury his face in his hands.

His heart had raced. He had said to himself then, *Oh God, they'll find out I ain't no rig man but is a police spy! Oh God, oh God!*

But the emergency soon passed because everybody gave full attention when Butler began to speak.

As Butler began speaking Charlie King set his brain in action to try to remember exactly what words were being said and what

threats made. But it was a big let down, for there was nothing seditious and no threats made. In Charlie King's opinion it was a waste
of time. Considering the lengths to which he had gone in order to
get a rig man's outfit, he felt he had never been so cheated.

The corporal sat with a smirk on his face. He sat there at the back
of the hall looking around him while Butler was winding up. He
stood up, pretending to look at some of the notices stuck up on the
notice boards behind him. He got out of the row and went in the
direction of one of the notice boards in particular, anxious not to
attract too much attention. He was thinking neither of notice
board nor notices but one of the notices surprised him and made
his blood rise. It read: *Brothers and sisters, the time is ripe. Be pre-*
pared. Stock up. Get your pitch oil, put rice and flour in your safe. When
the strike come, and that will be soon, be not like the seven foolish vir-
gins. Put a little more oil in your lamp, brethren. Also watch your
tongue. Do not let them know of our plans. The enemy spies are all
around us. Love your neighbour but don't trust him. Is people like you
and me who go back and carry news to the police. Let us unite with the
Chief Servant. God is our judge and our salvation. Let's unite and rise
up.
He had hardly finished reading it when there was a burst of applause and people got up from their seats to go and embrace
Butler. He turned around. He did not know what Butler had said,
but in any case the meeting was over. Corporal King took advantage of the rush of the crowd towards Butler, to slip outside unno-
ticed. As he left Emporium Hall going past the police station back
to his Apex quarters, he was accosted by a policeman who shone a
torch on him.

"Who is you?" Lance-Corporal John said. "You come from the
Butler meeting? You blasted rig men don't know what to do with
yuh bleddy time. You just want to cause ruction to give Apex
trouble?"

Charlie King was so taken aback he did not know what to say. It
was such a long time since he was last spoken to like this that
although he welcomed the lance-corporal's attitude to rig men,
he nevertheless felt hurt and shocked.

The policeman said, "Okay, so you wouldn't answer me? I feel to
give you a good slap." He grabbed Charlie King's arm. "Okay,

come on to the police station and ah warning you, if you ain't open yuh mouth I'll give you a few good batons and throw you in the cell."

They reached the charge room and Charlie King was so vexed and taken aback he had not said a word yet. He was almost panting with rage. As the two lanterns on the counter lit up his face, Acting Corporal Gilroy Price stiffened. He had bent down to reach for the charge book, and when, in rising, he saw the face he said, "Wait, nuh!"

It was only then that the lance-corporal looked, and when he, too, saw the face his mind was thrown into all sorts of confusion. He seemed to panic and freeze up.

Corporal Charlie King was looking at them fiercely.

Lance-Corporal John said, "In the dark ah didn't make you out, Corporal King. Sorry for me words, Sah. Ah mean if ah didn't respect you ah wouldn't ah get the rig man uniform for you, but in the dark ah didn't know it was you. Beg pardon, Sah."

Corporal King stared at Lance-Corporal John for minutes, and he said not a word. He breathed out loudly. Then he swung round and left.

28

Pa Jakes and Chee Fong were chatting quite brightly when they suddenly stopped. Chee Fong had been leaning over the counter towards Pa Jakes, getting the latest news of what was going on, when Ma Chee Fong, who was on the side, half hidden by the glass case, said something in Chinese. Chee Fong suddenly straightened up and of course Pa Jakes knew that meant 'Shut up!'

After a few moments Jonas walked into the shop.

As he entered he said, "Chee, how you going?" Then he looked on the side. "Pa Jakesey."

Chee grinned and stretched out his hand. "You win in the boxing. Velly good. Me happy."

"Oh yes. Thank you, Chee. And I was suffering afterwards. Ah come to say thanks for the poultice. Pa Jakes, how you going?"

The old man said, "Oh, me boy. Hm. Ah don't know how ah really going, believe me. How you do – you know how long I ain't see you? How things, Jonas? I hear this feller in town – well I ain't hear, ah see. Ah mean, Charlie King. Charlie King in town."

Jonas forced a smile. He did not want to talk. He had come to say thanks, and he had come for just a few things because Elsie was busy and he had to rush with Butler to San Fernando. Swithin Paul had come with a message that Rienzi wanted to see Uriah urgently. Jonas beckoned to Chee Fong, for it was only Chee Fong behind the counter now.

Pa Jakes said, "I hear the boys stocking up?"

Jonas said, "Stocking up what, Pa Jakes?"

"Well, they say food. Somebody bring a pamphlet saying so. Saying 'workers beware'. You know. 'Little more oil in yuh lamp'. Look as if the fellers will come out on strike, boy."

"Well, I don't know. And I ain't even know who stocking up. And we ain't have no oil in the lamp," he said, trying to giggle. "If anybody stocking up maybe Chee Fong would know."

Chee Fong nodded his head approvingly, and Pa Jakes said, "Well, that is what ah telling you, you didn't hear me? Chee Fong could tell you the fellers stocking up. They say Butler calling strike."

"Well, I don't know about that."

"Well, that is what ah telling Chee, that although Butler's always by you, you ain't have to know the man's business. I was saying that since yesterday. Eh, Chee?"

Chee pretended he was looking out into the road.

"Yesterday this feller was here," Pa Jakes went on, "this silly policeman. The lance-corporal nah. John. He say Butler calling strike next week. I don't know where he get that."

Jonas had got what he wanted and was on the point of leaving, but this latest news jolted him. How did this leak out to the police? They probably knew the day as well. He looked at Chee Fong, then he looked at Pa Jakes.

Pa Jakes said, "I tell the silly lance-corporal you and Elsie ain't bound to know nothing even if Butler was by you twice last week. I tell him that flat."

Hothead said, "Well, if Butler was by me that ain't the business of any lance-corporal or anybody."

"And he boasting he give Charlie King a proper ticking off."

As Pa Jakes talked he had his stick in his right hand, and moving it about he almost knocked down a half-full bottle of White Star Rum which was on the bench beside him.

Jonas said, "Ah hear this talk about John ticking off Charlie King. Is true?"

"Sound like a damn lie to me but he talk about how he insult him and rough him up. By the way, you know Charlie King taking over the whole station until the strike?"

"Until which strike?"

"But ah tell you Butler will call the strike? You don't know?"

Jonas just looked at him and said nothing.

"Well, Butler might call the strike next week."

"I didn't know about that. Pa Jakes, ah have to run."

"Well that's what I hear," Pa Jakes said. "Oh, you going? Take yuh time." He laughed.

Jonas hurried out of the shop, smiling, but hurting inside, and as he went he left another peal of laughter behind him.

When that peal of laughter died down Pa Jakes turned to Chee Fong's wife, who was already behind the counter. "He say he ain't know Butler calling strike next week!"

Ma Chee Fong looked at her husband and laughed, "Hee! Hee!".

Pa Jakes said, "Who the hell he think he could fool?"

When Jonas got home Elsie was in the kitchen making the coffee, and when she saw Jonas she said, "I fix you up already. You get the bread and sardine? Bring it, and go and change."

Jonas said, "Look, Elsie, ah don't want to eat this morning."

She just stared at him. She went into the sitting room where he had rested the bread and the tin of sardine on the table. She came back to him. "Why? What happen?"

She said again, "What happen, Jonas? Something happen?"

"Don't worry. Nothing ain't happen. Only that these people so damn – ah don't know what to say. You know they done know Butler calling the strike for Saturday? They ain't say Saturday, but if they know he calling the strike next week they bound to know the day."

Elsie stared at him dumbfounded. She couldn't believe it. Finally she said, "They know he calling strike? Then somebody in the inner circle is a damn traitor. You told the fellers at Forest Reserve and I told my girls. But we thought that was confidential."

"Those people wouldn't talk."

Elsie said, "Well, I don't know."

Both of them were silent, and at length Jonas said, "They call me Hothead. *You* call me that too, sometimes. But I taking it cool. Perhaps if ah wasn't a hothead I woulda give up already. But I ain't giving up. You see, some of us just pretending, but we want to hand over Butler. But I ain't handing over Butler. And I ain't giving up. You hear what Butler said the other day? He going till the final bell. You hear that? They'll have to count him out on the canvas."

She went and threw her arms around his neck. He did not look consoled. He looked her in the eye and said, "And is right there they'll have to count me out too. On the canvas."

There was silence. As he came out to go down the steps, Elsie said to herself, *Is true, some people want to hand up Butler. But it's no and never.* Seeing that Jonas was ready to leave, she said, "Hurry up, boy. We have to see what we could do. Those officers want him by the hook or the crook." As she looked at the skies again she noticed there was a little drizzle.

He said, "We'll win in the end, girl. Aha, you didn't hear Marie Vidale? Marie Vidale said, 'Let not your heart be troubled.' And then she said, 'The power and the glory cometh in the morning.'"

Elsie said, "That's not Marie Vidale. That came from Christ. Christ said that."

"Oh, yes. Is Christ? Oh yes. Yes, girl."

She liked how he said that. She tried to cheer him up to make him forget. She wondered if at this point it really mattered who knew if Butler was calling the strike. She said, "Hear him. Hear that talk! He said, 'Oh yes. Yes, girl.' He trying to be Mr Uriah Butler."

"There's only one Uriah Butler."

She smiled. He looked at the drizzle, then he turned round to her. "Elsie, I'm going now, but if you don't see me come back, please go down to Cola and tell him, and ask him if he could do anything at all. You hear? Because …well, things looking funny."

She looked at him and shook her head ever so faintly. He got so easily affected by indifferent news. She stared through the window.

"Listen, Elsie, you with me?"

"I with you seven years now. Go on. What's it?"

"If something happen – "

"Nothing wouldn't happen, Hothead."

"That's all you could say? Okay, wait. Marie Vidale said, 'Those who have eyes to see let –'"

"That's from the Bible, boy! Not from Mamselle Marie Vidale."

She wondered what was going wrong with him. Maybe he was beginning to believe Marie Vidale was Christ? But she herself, Elsie, could not remember exactly whether it was Christ who said, 'Those who have eyes to see let them see.' Or if it was Paul the Apostle. She could not be sure. Her mind was full of other things.

The truth was that she herself was uneasy. Because *she* had eyes to see. She was trying hard to keep Jonas from getting alarmed but there was a good chance that Charlie King would try something. Just hearing the strike was planned for Saturday Charlie King could trump up any charge and arrest Butler. At least, try to arrest him.

She went and stood up at the window looking out at the green fields and the heavy grey skies and the drizzle and the derricks in the mist, but she was seeing nothing. And of course she did not notice how much the weather was changing, with the wind rising, and the entire sky becoming overcast. She said to herself, *Don't forget Butler have to see Rienzi at eleven a.m. sharp. And Rienzi is a man for time. I only hope they make it quick and safe. I don't know what message from the Governor Rienzi get. It's a pity **he** can't come instead, but ah know Cola busy. And Charlie King in town, oh Jesus.* Then she told herself, *But look how these people in Fyzabad sell us out, eh? It's somebody in the inner circle. Ah wonder who is that traitor?* She went to close the window.

She heard Jonas behind her, and she turned and said, "Look the rain start blowing in. You going in the rain?"

"Yes. Just leave me alone now. Sure Butler in the railway station orready so ah going."

"Okay, boy, okay."

He was going down the steps "It's nearly ten o'clock orready, you can't see?"

"Okay, okay."

She bit her lips. She looked at him and her heart shook as there was a clap of thunder and the rains came down as in a cloudburst. She had to shut in the front door and half-open the window to see him go. She saw him running and then he disappeared in the bend of the track. He was too far for her to call him back, and he would not come back anyway. She said to herself, *He getting wet. No umbrella, no nothing. True, a man down when he poor, yes! We always say that but this is ridiculous, man, because me and Jonas have money from the boxing and I went and put every cent in the bank and we ain't buy a damn thing. Chuts! I put the whole two hundred dollars in the bank and ah umbrella cost two shillings. I mean, when you poor you have to be stupid too? Oh Father! I said I had to save up for a rainy day, and this is the blooming rainy day – the real thing. O God, this ain't really so much, but look how Jonas getting wet. No place to shelter, and he only have that old jacket over the jersey. And then ah have to wonder if Mr Uriah will make it or if he really at the railway station orready. It's ten to ten now and the train leaving at ten. Ah know Jonas will reach there, soaking, but Mr Uriah? We did so much this morning we could do no more. Look at water. Torrential they call that. And look at steam – ah mean, mist. You can't see nothing now, and with this rain I can't even hear when the train coming. Oh Jesus, I only hope they catch that train. Lord, be with us.*

29

T HE rains fell for a long time but when they were over Elsie went pensively looking out of the window. And just as she was wondering how the meeting with Cola Rienzi was going, she put her hands to her mouth in shock. Both Jonas and Butler were coming through the track.

When they reached near enough she cried, "What happened? You miss the train? Oh Jesus!"

Jonas waited until he was near. He said, "You ask what happen?"

"Well, don't tell me you reach San Fernando orreday and come back. In fact, you ain't left here one hour yet. And, oh God, look at you, Jonas! What happen to your jersey – you was fighting?"

He looked down at his jersey. They completely forgot about the old jacket he had used for the rain. The jersey was ripped down the front and the merino showed a part of the skin of his ribs. He looked down at himself and then he looked quickly at Butler. They were walking up the steps now. Butler didn't say anything. Then Jonas mumbled, "We had a little, well a little incident, at the railway station."

"What *incident?*" She looked towards Butler. "Mr Uriah, what was it?"

"Just a little scuffle. Hothead."

"Oh crimson, what I hearing! A scuffle? How come? Somebody interfere with you, Jonas?"

"You could say that."

"But why? You left to go San Fernando. Who was it? And why you didn't go to the police. You went to the police?"

"No."

She looked at Butler and then she looked back at Jonas. "So Jonas all this time and you didn't go to the police?"

Butler said, "Because it was the police who did it."

She opened her eyes in horror.

Butler said, "It's my fault. It's entirely my fault. I was with him. When the train stop and we went in, Charlie King and Lance-Corporal John just slip inside the carriage, and right away

Charlie King asked me where I was going. I said, 'San Fernando'. Charlie King said, 'I have a warrant for you.' Before he even finish saying that both me hands was locked behind me back and before I could turn round Jonas was on him and they was struggling. This time the train already pull out of the station but you should see the crowd ah passengers rushing on Charlie King. And Lance-Corporal John was between two seats with a big heavy feller on top of him."

Elsie cried, "And the train didn't stop?"

"The train stopped right away," Butler said.

Jonas said, "You sure? I don't think the train did stop."

Butler said, "You was fighting. You was scuffling with Charlie King. Somebody, maybe it was the ticket-collector on the platform, he screamed to the engine-driver to stop and he gave three sharp pips on his whistle, and the next thing ah see was that the train stopped and started to go backwards to the station. All this time Charlie King was collaring you by the front of yuh jersey, and you was trying to lock his neck and bruise him against the edge of the seat, and people was trying to pull him away from you to get at him to beat him up."

Elsie said, "Lord what is this! I just had that feeling that Charlie King would try something but I didn't know he was so bold. Right there on the train?"

Butler shrugged, "Well, they desperate. They trying to capture me before the strike."

"Mr Uriah, I told you about that date they done know about but you said it don't make no difference. But what they want is to capture and detain you so it wouldn't have no strike. Tell me, when the train got back in the railway station, what happen?"

Jonas had gone and sat down at the table, propping up his head with his hands.

Butler said, "What happen? Well that was the time the rain was coming full cry. Torrential. The sky dark. The news travel all up the train and people was running down the platform to our carriage. A big crowd, and the rain pelting down. And you know, under the heavy shower Charlie King and the lance-corporal still in the train pushing and struggling to get out, and swinging their baton, and you know they managed to slip outside, and through the rain, they took off. I never see policeman run so."

Elsie said, "A close shave. If it wasn't Fyzabad it woulda be amen for you."

Jonas's voice startled them. Still propping his chin, he said: "Uriah mustn't go out. Let him stay right here until the strike." There was silence.

Elsie said, "We'll definitely have to tell Cola Rienzi what happened. By the way, so Cola in San Fernando waiting for you – "

Butler said, "We sent a message by Swithin Paul. Swithin was there in the crowd and know everything. We sent a message saying what happen and we can't come again."

She said, "You know what caused all this? Giving out the date for the strike. I was expecting them to get desperate, but oh God not *this* desperate. Me heart still beating!"

Butler said, "It still beating? I so glad."

Jonas was still sitting at the table. Butler went on, "Anyway, don't worry about the date for the strike getting on the streets. People have to know, especially now where it's only a few days more. Jonas was saying even Pa Jacobs know. But nothing ain't secret in Fyzabad. Perhaps everybody know. But it's just a few days left. Today is Wednesday. You know what I say? I say, let the battle start. The important thing is for every man to down tools Saturday and leave Apex property. Walk out. Come to Emporium yard. Today is Wednesday 16th; it ain't matter now if Pa Jacobs know or if Charlie King know. The important thing for me now is to watch how ah walking until this strike come off. That's what Mamselle Marie said."

Elsie said, "So Mr Uriah, you didn't know that until Mamselle Marie said so? Well I'll tell you this, if you don't watch how you walking me heart will really start beating – then stop." Then after a brief moment she said, "Come, come now, Jonas. Get up and come. Let's see if we could prepare something in the little back room for Mr Uriah to stay. He mustn't leave here. Then I have to hurry up and cook something. It must be nearly twelve o'clock."

It must have been around three in the afternoon when they heard a knock on the door. Elsie went to open it, and on opening it she shrank back. A well-groomed man with thick eyelashes, sleek black hair, a blue suit with waistcoat, and holding a briefcase stood before her. He was smiling broadly.

"Good afternoon, Ma'am."

"Good afternoon, Sir. Who you looking for? Sir, I think this is the wrong house."

"Oh, I hope not." The man looked uneasy and apologetic. Butler was in the back room with Jonas. He couldn't hear well, but just thinking he recognised the voice, he came out to see. Then he said, "Oh my goodness. Man, I knew I heard yuh voice." Then he said to Elsie, "This is Cola Rienzi."

Her heart thumped. She said, "Oh, hello Mr Cola."

Butler said, "Come right in, Cola." Then he called to Jonas. When Jonas came Butler asked, "You remember Cola Rienzi?"

"Oh yes. Mr Rienzi. I saw him a few times." He turned to Rienzi, "The name is Jonas, Sir. Hello. Thanks for all you doing for Uriah. And for us."

Rienzi was smiling. He said, "Hello again, and I thank you. It is good to be here. I hope everybody is well. Can I sit here?"

Elsie said, "Come to the table, Mr Rienzi." She passed him through the living room door, and there he saw a dark-stained mahogany table and a few chairs. On the other side of the room, through the window, there were a few drenched-looking coconut trees, their green fronds against a slate-grey sky. To the right, far in the distance, was an oil derrick.

Rienzi drew the chair to sit down and he was still smiling. He shook hands all over again. Then he said, "If it is all right, may we all sit down for a little while?" He placed his briefcase on the table. Then, thinking he must have seen Jonas's face before, he said, "Buzz, is this the right-hand man you told me about recently?"

"Yes, yes. Oh, yes."

"Very well." He smiled at Jonas.

He opened his briefcase and perused some papers, and then he said to Butler, "Swithin came, as you of course realise. He told me of the commotion this morning, on the train. The train had just left the station for San Fernando?"

"Oh yes, Cola."

"It must have been traumatic."

"Yes, yes." But none of them knew the meaning of the word.

"But first," Rienzi said, "let me tell you this. This morning it rained buckets of drops in San Fernando, and the mist was so thick you couldn't see the San Fernando hill. And I actually wondered if you could make it there, Buzz. If you would be able to come. And I did think if the afternoon turned out nice *I'd* try and come. Well, the afternoon did not turn out nicely, but nevertheless I'm here."

Elsie said, "Thank you, Mr Rienzi."

Then he put his left hand to his chin and he said, "Buzz, if you like, we can sue the Crown for the assault of this morning. I can send Charlie King a letter on the issue but we need not take action until after the strike." He looked among the papers in his briefcase. "I have a note saying the strike is Saturday. Is that right?"

"That's right."

"May it be successful."

Elsie said, "Amen." Butler said, "Thanks, Cola, but you know I can't move from here? You know that?"

Rienzi said, "It is unbelievable how even the police are trampling on the rights of the people. I can file a writ you know. I can file for unlawful harassment. But is it worth it at this stage?"

Jonas was thinking in terms of *habeas corpus* but he wasn't sure what that was. He said, "They wanted to kidnap Uriah. Mr Rienzi, you couldn't file a writ for *kidnap*?"

"*Sequestration.* Did they have him in their possession at all?"

Butler said irritatedly, "Cola, what you bothering with all those legalism for? I ain't want no writ and no courthouse. This morning I give Charlie King good with me elbow and me fist. Now all I praying for is a successful strike."

Cola Rienzi said, "Well, that is the really important thing, from which everything else will flow. Which leads me to the reason I asked to see you, and to the reason why I came. Charlie King tried to arrest you. Or as your companion said, he tried to kidnap you. And he would have tried again on Thursday. This morning the people of Fyzabad saved you. In the case of Thursday, tomorrow, nothing would have saved you. Do you know who stood between you and detention?"

All three were dumbstruck.

Butler said, "What about Thursday? I don't know about Thursday. Somebody saved me?"

"Your friend – Friend Fletcher."

Butler said irritatedly, "Good heavens, Cola, if you telling me something, tell me!" He got up from his chair, then sat down again.

"Okay, it is this." He turned to Jonas and Elsie. "Now this is extremely confidential and it was meant only for Butler's ears. Can I speak? Yes? Promise me it will remain right here. All right, I shall tell you.

Mavrogordato, Hickling, and Charlie King had an audience with the Governor and suggested that since they need to stop the strike and since apprehending you in Fyzabad will lead to riots it would be better to invite you to a conference, at Government House – with just the four of them – and detain you there.

"At first Fletcher said absolutely no, and that the solution was for Apex to pay more money. But afterwards, scared of the pressure they were putting on him, and suspecting they would suggest to the British Government that he, Fletcher, is clearly on your side, Buzz, he pretended to agree. But as soon as the meeting was over he called me on the telephone and told me they would seek my approval to invite you to the conference but on no account must you turn up.

"I did not mention it to you because I knew you wouldn't hear about it and therefore couldn't go. I wrote to them saying you said you were too busy organising your party – or something like that – and that you begged to decline their kindness. But I thought I'd get you aware of all that was happening around you, and now that the strike is due for Saturday I felt I'd tell you this, so you would be careful and watch out. That's why I sent to call you."

All three stared at each other. Butler said, "Thank you, Cola. And I thank Friend Fletcher, too."

Rienzi, getting up, said, "Fletcher is a real friend to you. Anyway, I wish us good luck for Saturday. And to all of you, I thank you for your kind audience. Buzz, I hope to see you soon."

And Cola Rienzi was soon walking out of the muddy track.

30

THE more Lieutenant-Colonel Hickling thought of the woman in mauve it was the more he thought he should speak with her. At least to have some idea of her powers – if indeed she had any powers at all – and if she did, whether she was likely to retaliate when they held Butler. In fact, he was in haste to act because the Chief of Constabulary, Colonel Mavrogordato, had already written to Cola Rienzi inviting Butler for talks, and the talks were scheduled for Thursday. It was the Tuesday, and although the lieutenant-colonel had not rested after a hectic weekend, his thoughts were busy with finding ways and means of getting a message to Marie Vidale.

But he did not want to involve Lance-Corporal John, for he wanted to meet with her in absolute secrecy.

He sat in his office looking at the calendar on the wall with the red circle showing what the date was. He began to think of how best to get in touch with the woman in mauve. He bowed over his desk. He thought of several things but the one he settled on was sending a letter to her by his yardboy, Kissoon.

He pulled open the drawer with the letterheads, and took up his pen from the holder. He wanted to write a brief letter, not over respectful, and yet not curt and impolite, because he wanted her to come. He did not know how to put what he had to tell her, and he wasn't even sure whether he knew what he wanted to tell her. He did not even know if she had due respect for the foreigners as the rest of the natives did, but he was expecting she would be hostile because the lance-corporal had already seen her talking with Butler.

It was a long time since he had such trouble in beginning a letter. The printed letter heading simply said: *Apex Trinidad Oilfields, Fyzabad, Trinidad*, and below that he put the date: June 15th, 1937. He did not know if she was Miss or Mrs Marie Vidale, but since the natives called every woman 'Miss', he simply began: *To Miss Mamselle Marie Vidale.*

Under that he wrote: *Lieutenant-Colonel H.J.H. Hickling of the above oilfield, at Fyzabad, requests that Marie Vidale calls at his office to see him this afternoon at four p.m. As this is rather important I look forward to the interview.*

He read it a few times and it was just brief enough and stern enough without being hostile.

He signed it *H.J.H Hickling.* He addressed an envelope, put both letter and envelope into the drawer, and sent to call the messenger. When the messenger came he sent him to his home on the camp in order to get Kissoon.

As soon as Kissoon arrived the lieutenant-colonel said, "Kissoon, you know of Marie Vidale?"

"Yes, Sir."

"Where does she live?"

"Siparee, they saying."

"But you don't know exactly where."

"But I could find out."

"Are you afraid of her, Kissoon?"

"No, Bass."

The lieutenant-colonel did not want to say any more. He did not want to say too much. He put the letter in the envelope and handed it to Kissoon. "Go and give this to her."

Kissoon looked at the envelope and he looked at the floor and was puzzled. The lieutenant-colonel noticed but he did not want to say anything, for the simple reason that there was nothing to say. Kissoon waited a little bit because he wanted to know if the boss expected him to walk to Siparia. After a few moments Hickling said, "What is the matter?" And then he himself said, "Oh, yes, oh, here is your bus fare." As he pushed his hands into his pockets he said, "How much?" Then giving him the money, he said, "Kissoon, the time is already half past nine. Make sure you are back by noon."

"Yes, Bass."

In Siparia, when Marie Vidale opened the letter that Kissoon brought she said to herself, *But look at my crosses!* Then she said, talking to Kissoon, "We was talking about him just yesterday. *Yesterday,* you know!" Then she looked at the boy directly and said, "He's your boss?"

"Yes, I is the yardboy."

"But what he want me for?"

Kissoon didn't know.

Marie Vidale had the impulse to throw the letter into the rubbish bin. She said, "If Hickling want to talk to me he can't call me like that. Today for today. I ain't working with him!" She paused then added, "And the first thing he have to do is to tell me what he want to see me for, then ask me if I will have time."

Then on reflection she said, "I'll go, you know, but not today. No, it can't be. Those people always take you for granted. They expect you to jump at their beck and call. You bet it's some stupid thing about Butler, because he probably saw Butler and me walking in Fyzabad. But I'll go, for Butler's sake. Let me hear what they want."

The boy was still there. She went to the window and looked out. Then she suddenly turned round, "Oh good. All right. You still there. You better wait. I think I'll scribble some sorta answer for him. He asked you to bring back a message?"

"No, he didn't say nothing."

"You said you are the yardboy."

"Yes, Madam."

"Well this is not yardboy work, eh! Let me tell you."

She brought a penholder and a relief nib and when she pushed the nib in the holder she went for an ink-well and put the two things on the table, and after a little bit of searching she found a writing pad. The boy looked at what was going on and then he looked around. There was a strong smell of sweet-broom and wild senna and khus khus grass, and the faint smell of chandelier and rosemary seemed to be wafted somewhere on the wind. The unmistakeable scent of mammie sepote, and bay leaf, and cinnamon came freshly to him as he moved to the window, and these leaves were plainly before him on the table to his left, but he did not know them. As the Mamselle sat down to write she saw the boy looking at the long blades of khus khus grass, thick in a joint of dried bamboo. Then she saw him lean his nose towards it.

"You know that grass? You know what they call it?"

"Yes, Madam."

"Just call me 'Marie Vidale'. Or just 'Mamselle Marie'."

He was surprised. It was the first time he had seen a lady who did not want a handle to her name. People always demanded Mr, or

Miss, or Mrs. He felt good about Mamselle Marie. He could not guess what his boss wanted of her. He looked at her as she was taking her time to write, and she was making her letters beautifully. She was making her letters extremely beautifully for an obeah woman.

"Okay!" Marie Vidale suddenly said, getting up from the chair. It was a short letter and after writing it Marie Vidale looked over it well. She had written the date on top: *15–6–1937*, and her words were: *Dear Lieutenant-Colonel H.J.H. Hickling,*

I received your letter. I will come to see you but not today, as I am too busy. Maybe I will come tomorrow at four p.m.

With regards,
Marie Vidale.

She could not find an envelope and as the boy watched, she took a plain sheet of paper and folded it, pressing the flaps neatly, folding and turning, and presto! There was an envelope. Kissoon looked shocked. She looked up and saw his face. She said, "What happen?"

He said, "Ah never see nobody make that!"

"That's why they calling me obeah woman."

The boy laughed.

Promptly at four the next day, the woman in mauve was at the Apex Administration Office. Hickling was right in front of the door and quickly invited her into his office. In fact, he was anxious that she should not stay in sight too long lest people thought he was involved in witchcraft.

In his office he sat in his accustomed seat and had put a chair in front of his desk for her. When she sat down he said, "I am glad you came, Marie Vidale, they tell me you know a lot of what is going on round here and I thought I would have a discussion with you."

"Yes. Okay. Tell me."

He was taken aback. She did not seem in awe. He was distracted by it and then he said, "The workers of Apex feel we are being unjust, and I would like to have your opinion of it."

"My opinion of what?"

He looked at her. He was not often spoken to like that.

"Your opinion as to whether we are unjust, and afterwards I want to show you some figures to prove that we are not."

"You don't want my opinion if you have figures to prove Apex is not unjust."

"Because I want to convince you."

"But why me?"

"Because they say you are a woman of influence."

"That's news to me. I thought you were going to say, 'Because they say you are an obeah woman'."

Hickling was so surprised that he laughed. He said, "Marie Vidale, you are very singular. I have not laughed all day. First of all let me ask you this, because this has struck me very forcibly. Where did you learn your English?"

"I don't know what you mean."

"Well, that question is straightforward enough."

"Which means I really don't know English."

He laughed again. "I would have to call you the extraordinary lady. Have you lived abroad?"

"No."

"Well, I must say this is surprising and I must say I hope you don't feel offended but, generally, people in Trinidad don't speak English. They murder it. I have great difficulty in understanding them. Most times. Have you always been here?"

"Yes. And I agree with what you say. The crimes against English. People know English of course, especially the ones who go to school. At this time, 1937, almost every child goes to school. At least, leaves home for school. Whether they end up in school I do not know. Because education means little in their lives; because with all the education they are refused jobs – except as labourers. And so life is so full of pressure that people don't take time to speak correctly. It is a constant battle. And people are worried and frustrated. They want fair play and fair pay. That is why when you asked my opinion as to whether Apex is unjust I did not care to answer. Because you *must* know that Apex is unjust."

Hickling felt as if he was given a stinging slap across the face. He said now, seriously, "Marie Vidale, have you discussed this matter with people who are in conflict with Apex?"

"Everyone in Fyzabad is in conflict with Apex. I discussed this with most people. I discussed it with my friend, Uriah Butler. I expect everybody in Fyzabad knows he is my great friend. But perhaps you do not know."

"I did not say I did not know."

"Glad to hear that."

"Well, you heard Butler's viewpoint. Do you want to hear mine? Or the oil company's, rather."

"No, because you will bring figures to show your point and only an expert will understand them. I have no experience in this sort of thing. I have experience in living. And I don't know how Butler himself can live from what he is earning. And Apex is always declaring high dividends on the newspapers. And anyone can see that there are people rolling in luxury at Apex, and those are not the people of Fyzabad. It wouldn't even be necessary to see your figures. Because if the figures don't add up to the fact that Apex is doing well while its workers are catching hell, the figures will be lying."

Hickling's attitude changed altogether. He saw there was no point in talking to this lady in mauve. What he thought of dealing with now was what he had wanted to handle in the first place, and he should have done this without asking if Apex was good or bad.

He said, "You know we have been dealing with Butler?"

"Well, if you put it that way – yes. I have to say yes."

"You know about the strike Butler is planning to call."

"I thought he might have called the strike already. But it will take place later."

"On what date?"

The woman in mauve smiled. "My name is Marie Vidale not Uriah Butler."

Hickling looked at his desk. He felt furious. No native had ever dared to trifle with him like this, or had shown this general self-assurance. No native had ever insulted him.

He said to her, "Could you explain to me what witchcraft is? Is it a real thing?"

"It's real all right. But I can't explain it. Perhaps the people who say 'Marie Vidale's working obeah' can explain. I don't know."

Hickling was so confused that he came out with the plan made between Mavrogordato, Charlie King, and himself. He said, "To avoid such a strike, which might cause civil unrest and loss of life, to avert such an event we might have to detain Butler. I take it you might counsel the forces of law and – "

She said, "I can tell you for a certainty that if Uriah Butler is detained the forces of resistance as well as the forces of obeah will be let loose."

"You are probably trying to frighten me. I don't quite believe in obeah."

"And why do you think I'm wearing mauve?"

He looked at her and she looked at him with her large black eyes. He was trembling.

31

COLONEL Mavrogordato pulled into his garage in his little Ford car. He could not stay long today. He had come only because Olga was getting on so nervous and excitable it was as if she did not know he was the chief of all the policemen and that he had a job to do. He had planned staying only two hours. On his way back down he had to go to Pointe-a-Pierre first to see the General Manager of the oil refinery. He mustn't forget that. He got out of the car and at the same time he pulled out his pocket dial to see the time. As he put it back into his pocket he heard a slight scream and Olga was upon him.

She just held him and squeezed him but she did not say anything. He put his hand on her head and ruffled her hair. Not that he was in a playful mood. He just felt sorry he had been so harsh to her on the telephone.

When they got into the house she just stopped, held him still, and said, "Stephen, I'm so glad you've come. Thanks. Okay?"

He said nothing.

She said, "You ain't still vexed. I just wanted to see you."

She looked up into his face. She had given him some good hot words when he was reluctant to come. Now she, too, was sorry.

Before she took him to the second floor, to the study-room where they usually relaxed, she called the maid.

"Bernice, get a drink for Colonel Mavrogordato, please."

"Yes, Ma'am."

She did not have to tell Bernice what sort of drink to get nor where to bring it. The maid was well used to their routine.

They went up the flight of stairs and got into their study-room. The room was very ample, with the chairs soft and comfortable, the upholstery light, with restful-looking frilly cushions, and fluttering curtains. Everything else was creamish. Just to look at the room she felt rested. She hardly sat here. She was too busy in this big house. But she always liked Stephen to come here and relax and talk to her.

No sooner had they entered the room and sat down than the maid brought the colonel a large tumbler full of vermouth, cold, with a little beaten ice and nutmeg, over which she had sprinkled some Angostura bitters.

Bernice said, "Anything for you, Ma'am?"

"No. Not really."

When the maid left, Olga said, "Stephen, you so quiet. What's the matter?" And then she thought, *If you wouldn't talk to me it's better you didn't come.*

Stephen Mavrogordato was silent for a little while and then his face softened. He said, "I had to be harsh with you, Ga-ga. And it's because of all this strain. I have to be up here and down there almost at the same time. It's a strain, Olga. But it's my duty. And if it's one person who should make things easier for me it's you. But you make things more difficult." He put his hand on her head and ruffled her hair again. She felt good. She knew he wasn't vexed.

But she herself was getting nervous. She didn't like to hear him say, 'It's a strain', because she already knew it, and this kept her being mad at the authorities. And then he had said, 'It's my duty.' *To hell with duty*, she thought. She was already getting tense.

Now she said, "I'll tell you this, as I always tell you. You talking about duty, but when they kill you for me I ain't want to hear about duty you know. They can't put all that strain on you when some of the others just posing and making style and doing nothing. I mean it's ridiculous you have to be looking after Port of Spain and looking after San Fernando, and then having to look after this damn guerrilla."

He couldn't help laughing. Then he said, "Ga, you know what is a good solution to this? Let them put somebody to do half the duties of the Chief of Constabulary and let me do the other half."

She looked at him. He continued, "I'm sure they could get someone, they don't even have to send to England. They could find someone here. What you say? I could approach Fletcher tomorrow to – "

"Look, Stephen, don't talk nonsense."

"But how do you mean? I sincerely think they can split the job."

"Look, Stephen!"

"But I can't understand you. You feel I'm working too hard, well – "

"You crazy! Look how far you come to get up to be the head of the constabulary, now you will be content for somebody to just come and cut down your job? They should cut your pay too! Give you half and give the other person half! Look, your head needs examining. This is outright nonsense. There is only one Chief of the Constabulary. Nobody must share that job with you."

He had expected that reaction of course, and in any case he did not intend to share the job with anyone. In a way he was just trying to tease Olga as she was always blaming the authorities for working him too hard, saying they had him rushing pell-mell, like a madman, to San Fernando and back, and sometimes to Princes Town.

He said now, "You know I could only spare two hours."

"Well, you said so already."

"In fact, I said I couldn't stay long. Listen, I reached here at ten to eleven and now it's five past eleven. Which means we have – let me see – an hour and forty-five minutes. Okay? Let me tell you what's happening. Things are really getting tense."

She sat back to listen. Her large eyes were staring at him.

"The first thing I have to tell you is that I went to Fyzabad yesterday and Charlie King's in town."

"Oh, good. Then why *you* have to go down there? Let Charlie King hold Butler. He has the knack. In fact Corporal King is the man for them."

"Yes, it's fine to say that but Corporal King will hold Butler where? In Fyzabad? Do you know what surprises me? Not even Corporal King realises this. From what I've heard from Hickling it's more than 95 per cent certain the people will riot and probably burn down Fyzabad if Corporal King was to be so rash."

"But how does Hickling know that? He's probably a damn coward."

"He might be and he might not be, Olga. Well, let's put it this way: he might be right or he might be wrong. But do you think I'm willing to risk having Butler arrested in Fyzabad to find out if Hickling's right? That's why we had that plan."

She was irritated and she said impatiently, "But didn't Butler turn it down? Why talk about that now? You all will have to do better than that. You think Butler is a damn fool?"

"I'm not so sure Butler himself turned it down. Well we only heard so."

"Well, you all approached him through Rienzi? I'm talking about the lawyer."

"Of course. You know what's happening now? I didn't tell you this, did I? Did I tell you of an obeah woman called Marie Vidale?"

"What's up now? What's she doing? Oh you believe in obeah now – it's not superstition again!"

He really felt silly to carry on with this theme, but he just wanted to tell her what Inspector Power told him that Hickling had said, and he went on, nevertheless: "I don't know anything about it but Edmund was saying that Lance-Corporal John saw Marie Vidale with Butler on two occasions. Twice for this week. And you could say what you want but there must be something in it. Good heavens, Ga-ga, I'm not saying that I am a believer in this evil but – "

She looked as though she wanted to laugh.

"This thing called obeah, I can't subscribe to any belief, Ga-ga – "

"And why you mentioned it?"

"It's Edmund Power. Hickling called him for reinforcements at Coronation. Some imagined riot. Remember? Then talk of strike – "

"And Butler'll call it too. Simply because Fletcher and Nankivell are nincompoops. Look, Stephen, the case is simple. I meself don't know about obeah, or any black magic. I don't know if it works, but these illiterate people will believe in anything. I don't know a single thing about obeah. But I have an open mind, I ain't going to cry 'superstition'. But I'm quite sure that the obeah required now – and this is the obeah I believe in – the obeah required now is to send in the blasted troops to arrest Butler."

He looked at her, furious. "How could you expect us to do that? Are you forgetting what we are? Do you think we are like the Assyrians in Trans-Jordan, or like Mussolini in Abyssinia? What is the matter with you, Ga-ga? We are British!"

"Oh, yes? You are British. Naturalised. And you go by the law. So it was the law when you and Hickling and Charlie King went to beg Fletcher for the four of you to kidnap Butler. Yes, I really believe that is British law. British colonial law. You hypocrites – "

"Kidnap, Ga-ga?"

"I'm going by what you told me."

"I never said 'kidnap'. I never used that word."

Olga looked at him straight in the eye and said, "You didn't say 'kidnap'? I remember as clear as day that – "

"I never used that word. I said 'detain'."

She broke out laughing. She said, "Oh. Yes. That's right. The word you used was 'detain'. And that doesn't have anything to do with kidnap!"

"Of course not. Kidnap is taking away somebody illegally and against his will. When it comes to the word 'detain', only the police have the right to detain."

She was sure he was wrong but she didn't see any point in arguing with him. She simply said, "And what happening again? The strike still on? I mean are they still planning?"

"Right now it's just silence. We have the date but as of now we are hearing nothing. Oh, I forgot to tell you – Hickling had a meeting with this sorcerer, I won't say 'obeah woman'. She was wearing mauve, Ga-ga, and with her dress down to her ankles. That's what Hickling said. And her head was tied with a mauve head-tie and – "

"And you all got frightened!"

The colonel turned to her. "Olga, what's wrong with you this morning? Will the police be scared because a woman is in mauve? But anyway, I'll tell you something. She tried to get Hickling scared because when he told her the police might have to detain Butler she said if Butler was detained the forces of resistance and obeah would be let loose, or something like that."

"And the coward got even more scared."

The colonel could not help laughing, and as he moved, his hands touched something hard in his pocket, and he suddenly remembered his watch. He stood up and anxiously pulled the watch from his pocket. It was only half past eleven. He was relieved. He had fifteen more minutes.

When she saw him look at his watch she immediately became soft towards him and fearful he was going to leave right away.

She asked, "Time for you to go, me darling?"

"I have ten minutes more. And after that, I just have to go. So you wouldn't try to detain me, please."

"No. But I might try to kidnap you."

He laughed.

"Boy, I hope things don't worsen down there."

"I hope so, too. But today is already Wednesday 16th. On Tuesday when I reached Fyzabad remember I told you how things were quiet?"

She nodded.

"And remember what you said: 'The calm before the storm'?"

"That's how I still feel."

"And that's how I feel too." He got up.

She got up and embraced him. "Darling, I'm so scared. You'll take your time, eh? You'll take a lot of care for me, won't you? I don't know why you all didn't carry out that plan to invite him to Government House and kidnap him."

"Detain, Ga-ga."

"Oh yes, detain, that's what I mean. Why didn't you all detain him? If you had detained him, all now we would have had nothing to worry about."

"Well, it was for tomorrow. I told you Rienzi wrote to Governor Fletcher saying Butler was too busy organising his men in the oilfield and could not come to Port of Spain. And that is another part of the reason why we are so worried. What is he organising? The strike? As you realise, the crucial date is Saturday 19th. We don't know what will happen, if anything at all will happen." And pulling out the watch again he said, "Look, Ga, I'd better leave now. It's three minutes to twelve." Then, as he took down his constabulary helmet from the rack, he said irritatedly, "For heaven's sake, Ga-ga, stop that nonsense. A big woman like you will cry?"

32

KID Felix did not run to Siparia this morning because of the tension that had suddenly taken over the oil belt. Or maybe 'suddenly' only so far as Kid Felix was concerned. From the eastern outskirts of Fyzabad he merely ran to Pluck Village, which was only two-and-a-half to three miles away, and he came back home. Hardly sweating or blowing he went to have a bath, and when he was about to leave the bathroom, there was his mother with the towel.

She said, "You took it light this morning."

At first he did not answer. He just went into the small bedroom to change and he saw his little brother, Rennie, sitting on the bed.

Then after about two minutes the mother came into the room. She said, "Any sign of anything like strike, Felix?"

"Oh, it's strike you want?" was all he said. The little brother rolled with laughter.

Both Felix and his mother knew that all he was thinking about was his Discovery boxing bout.

The brother looked at him and said, "Ma, Hothead, who is the champ – "

Felix snapped, "He wouldn't be champ for much longer."

The brother continued, "Ma, you know Hothead is close close with Butler. Well, yesterday Felix asked Hothead if they having a strike and Hothead said he don't know nothing about that."

The mother said, "Well, that's funny. Yesterday in the market everybody was shoo-shooing. Tension, boy. Soldiers down here. No strike talk but they say Butler want to see what he could do."

Kid Felix said, "Yes, to see what he could do for Butler."

Rennie laughed till he rolled off the bed.

The mother was shocked to hear him talk that way. She stared at him. Rennie said, "It's because Hothead giving him a chance at the title. He feeling like a champ already."

Kid Felix was now dressed in a brown shirt with grey trousers and he was sitting on the bed, bending over to lace up his sneakers. He said, "Rennie, I wouldn't bother to answer. Discovery night you'll see. Not long again. First Monday in August. You'll see who'll be champ. Take it easy."

"So you ain't respect what Hothead did with Kid Tiger?"

"Take it easy. Discovery night you'll make yuh own discovery."

The brother said, "Ma, Felix just going crazy. He so glad Hothead give him the bout yet he saying Hothead knocked out Tiger with a lucky punch. He don't like Butler because that's Hothead pal."

The mother watched him as he was ready to go out. He looked good. She said to him, "Going to look for a job?" Then she decided to stop wasting her time. But she could not help saying to Rennie, "I wish he could get in a lucky punch somewhere and bring home some money."

Rennie shrieked out with laughter.

33

IT was the early morning of Thursday, June 17ᵗʰ. Day had not dawned completely and there was a moon still in the sky when Charlie King saw the door of the house open and someone walk down the steps. The person's shadow was big against the house. Then there was another behind. The light of a torch was moving to each step, showing the way, as the first shadow came down. Charlie King stood in the dark beneath the coconut tree. He watched the figure walk down to the bottom of the stairs and he heard a voice at the top of the steps say, "You all right? Safe journey, eh. Thanks for coming. You sure you don't want me to take you to the train?"

"No, no, no. Continue what we started. You'll see me at six. Be of good cheer."

Suddenly Charlie King blew his whistle. The person who had walked down the steps stopped. Out on the main road there was a figure hurrying through the track but in the grey of morning this person could hardly be seen. Not far behind there were figures running into the track, for the whistle had been very loud and shrill.

Charlie King was advancing to the steps and the figure hurrying through the track had all but reached the yard of the house. By the time Charlie King reached the person at the bottom of the steps, the one who had been showing the light of the torch saw and rushed down the steps. When he saw who the policeman was he became even more furious. He said, "What you want here, Constable?"

"This is not a constable. It have three stripes on me shoulder."

"It could have – " He stopped to look at the figure running down. He said, "Go back, Uriah." Butler came down and tried to pull back Hothead. Hothead said to the officer, "It could have ten stripes. What you doing in me yard so early in the morning?"

"You talking to me so?" the policeman glanced around. There were already about a dozen people who had come because of the shrill police whistle.

"Yes, I talking to you so. I know you is Charlie King but this is my house. We having a prayer meeting here, and you come spying in me yard."

Charlie King said, "Who is this lady? And you see this man behind you? I know him good and I want to find out why you have this agitator in your house."

"That is against the law? This man isn't charged with a damn thing. He is my friend, Tubal Uriah Buzz Butler. You want to hear the name again? Tubal Uriah Buzz Butler. The police saying they have a sedition warrant for him. Tell them to serve it!"

"Have no fear. I will serve it."

Butler mumbled something, trying to calm down Hothead. There was a little buzz around. A few people were trying to restrain Hothead but he wrung himself free and said, "Let me see you serve it. Serve it here and now."

With the day clearing up everybody could see that the figure who had walked through the track was another policeman. As Butler held on to Hothead, Hothead cried again, "You could serve the warrant here and arrest Butler. Go on. Arrest Butler."

The crowd had become bigger now, and Charlie King, glancing back quickly and seeing the hostile faces, looked at the ground and said, "This is no time of morning to serve a warrant. But I came to see what happening."

"Oh God, Corporal King, Look the man here. While ago you said you know the man. I still give you his name. You is the great Charlie King. Take him nah. Do what you did on the train last week. You remember how you and John run through the rain? We'll make you run so fast you'll break yuh own record."

Charlie King was enraged. He looked at the threatening crowd, with some people having lengths of wood, and he knew he would have to back out without delay. When he saw a few men stripping off their shirts and cursing wildly he realised he had to move.

At the same time Mamselle Marie Vidale whispered nervously but sternly to Jonas, and Jonas said, "Mamselle Marie, I know 'Blessed is the peacemaker', but these people don't want peace, they want war. Charlie King come quite in me yard." Then he turned to Butler. "Uriah, the Mamselle want you to go upstairs, and I meself begging you to go upstairs."

As Butler slowly walked up the flight of steps, the eyes of both policemen gave him a vicious look. Marie Vidale said, "Corporal Charlie King, let peace reign. I don't know you personally, but I know this other policeman, Lance-Corporal John. Let peace reign. I want you to know that I am a woman of God and a woman of prayer. I have nothing against policemen. They are necessary to keep the peace and to keep law and order. But we are holding this prayer meeting here tonight, the 16th. Well, it's the 17th already, Thursday. We are holding this prayer meeting here and Corporal King is under the coconut tree. Spying on what, only God knows."

Charlie King cried, "The police have to know what going on."

She went on as if he hadn't spoken. "Should this sort of thing happen? Is this provocation right? You will never go on the expatriate camp and spy. Why spy on this house?"

Lance-Corporal John said, "We don't know what happening upstairs – if any obeah working."

Marie Vidale looked shocked and then she regained her composure. She smiled and looked towards Hothead who had already flared up. She barred him, and Elsie held him.

Mamselle Marie said to the little crowd, "Thanks for coming, because if you weren't here, you know what would have happened?"

Lance-Corporal John said, "What woulda happen?"

Marie Vidale said to the crowd, "If you all were not here they would have gone with Butler."

The crowd was roused and Hothead was jostling with three bare-backed men to get at Lance-Corporal John. They held him away, and Mamselle Marie Vidale stepped between the little group and she cried, "Corporal King – you and the lance-corporal – please leave. Please. Not for my sake but for God's sake."

Big, strapping La Brea Charles threw his shirt behind his head. He was one of those who had restrained Jonas but now he released him and was going out to Lance-Corporal John himself. But the lady in mauve just stepped in front of Charles and said, "Peace! Peace!" Then she said, "Swithin, hold back Hothead." Then she cried impatiently and loudly, "Hothead, go up the stairs, please! Please do that for me."

Elsie and Swithin Paul were holding Hothead but now he wasn't struggling. Mamselle Marie said, "Jonas, you was praying with me this morning. You said you believe in Christ. Well, Christ is the Prince of Peace."

"But it's the same Christ who said, 'I come not to bring peace but the sword'. Mamselle, if you want peace tell these officers to leave me yard. They can't stay there without a warrant. They have to go now. And ah mean *now*." But he restrained himself out of respect for her.

Yet more people had come into the yard and the crowd seemed on the point of lynching the two policemen. People had surrounded them, but Mamselle Marie stepped into the mêlée. Lance-Corporal John had already taken a step back, and maybe some chucks too. Mamselle Marie almost screamed, "Let him pass for heaven's sake!" Then she turned to Charlie King. "Corporal, hurry up and get out."

Charlie King immediately withdrew, and as a few men followed the two policemen they both ran out of the track. Some of the women in the yard laughed scandalously.

The woman in mauve now went up the steps, leaving hefty La Brea Charles downstairs.

When Mamselle Marie got upstairs she met Butler in discussion with both Hothead and Elsie. The morning being Thursday morning the principal thing now was the success of the strike.

Mamselle Marie said, "Jonas, you too is a marked man. You and Butler have to stay in hiding all day today and I suggest you don't stay in this house."

Jonas cried, "Mamselle Marie, if we 'fraid to stay where we living – "

She said, "You ever hear the saying, 'Take in front before in front take you'? Well, please take in front. Because the next thing that would happen is that you two would be detained. And no strike. That's what they want. Because, I didn't think about it, but the two policemen came to capture Uriah Butler. They are desperate. Now with the two policemen gone, the next thing is they might send soldiers here. Hickling will get soldiers down. A lot of people will be around to defend you but they can't fight guns. The soldiers will capture Uriah."

Elsie was afraid. She said, "You two could slip out now? Jonas, you could find a safe place for yourself and Uriah? But come back tonight, you know. Let's see, who outside?" She looked, then said, "Those are friends. Oh Lord, be with Butler and Jonas."

Elsie went to one of the windows and Hothead joined her. Hothead looked outside towards the road and he looked the other way towards the Godineau track. There were a lot of people about. People ready to fight for them. He came back and said, "Uriah, what you think about going somewhere else? Leaving the house. If we have to go we have to move now."

Butler said, "The Mamselle is right. They'll raid this house, and the friends we have downstairs can't fight guns." And although he did not say it, he was thinking most of all of the two women they would be putting in danger. He said, "Come, let's get down the steps quick and vanish." In his haste he stopped and looked back, "But we coming back here tonight. Okay, Elsie, okay, Mamselle Marie. We going."

34

COLONEL Stephen Mavrogordato turned into Stanmore Avenue from Tragarete Road and drove right into the yard. Then, opening the pantry door from the garage, he walked into the kitchen where Bernice was. She was surprised to see him. She had a quick look at the clock and it was not quite eleven. She said, "Colonel, the Missis gone down town, I ain't sure where. She wasn't expecting you. You might only have to wait, let me see, she said she was – "

The colonel did not wait until the housemaid finished talking. He stepped out and looked into the stables and saw that both the victoria coach and the horse were gone. He came back inside and said, "The Madam said when she was coming back?"

"Somebody came here early early with a message and she went out and she said she'd be back round about half past eleven. So Colonel, if you could wait – "

"Blazes! I can't. When she comes back tell her I can't come home this afternoon. Tell her I just had news from Hickling that not a soul in the morning shift turned out to work. But we have to wait on the evening shift and the night shift, and I'll certainly have to get Fletcher to put the army on alert and then I may have to go down meself to Apex to see what's going on. Tell her she'll probably see me tomorrow."

The maid looked at him. She was thinking there'd be an outcry by the lady of the house if he did not come home this afternoon, and how if the Madam had only known that he was going to be here at this time wild horses would not have got her away from the house this morning. Bernice also knew that if at all she mentioned the question of Hickling and strike and calling out the army to the Madam, the Madam was going to launch into a wild tirade against Butler and no doubt against his supporters too, and upset her for the whole day. So she would try her best to forget all about that. But she'd keep her own ears open to hear if Butler was getting through.

She went on preparing lunch and she only remembered the hour when she heard Simon outside bringing in the victoria coach. She looked out of the window and saw Simon scolding the horse for taking the driveway too awkwardly and she heard the Madam laughing and saying the horse should not be called 'Victor' but 'Butler'. That made her wonder if the Madam had heard something.

Bernice went back to the kitchen and in a short while the pantry door was pushed open and the lady of the house came inside. Bernice hastened to see if any help was needed and as soon as Olga Mavrogordato saw her she said, "Bernice, it's all right. I saw him. The colonel. He came right over there and he told me."

"Oh, yes. You need any help, Madam? Anything to bring in?"

"No, Bernice, thank you. The only help you could give us is to rid us of the madman, Buzz Butler."

"Madam, I mean anything from the coach. Anything to bring in?"

"Anything to bring in at all is to bring in Mr Butler to justice."

Bernice affected surprise. "He did something?"

"Is there a time when Mr Butler isn't doing something? Didn't my husband tell you to tell me there was a strike at Apex? Well, who did it? Did it happen for itself or did Butler do it?"

As the maid watched her, Olga said, "Anyway that strike is finally going to be his undoing. The colonel said they are going to hold him on the warrant – the old warrant, for sedition – they will arrest him tomorrow morning after the night shift."

Bernice did not say anything. "That's right, Bern. Saturday. So Sunday will be a day of peace."

Bernice looked at her, and the lady of the house continued, "Oh, yes, they've finally come round to it. And what will happen? The men will have to go back to work. They are hungry, and without their agitator. So this is something to the good. Eh, Bernice?"

Bernice had already turned to take some of the shining pots from the shelves and to tie the curtains. She just said, "Yes, Madam."

"That will set our minds at rest. The best news for the day."

Bernice said to herself, *But the day isn't finished yet, Madam.*

Olga still stood in the kitchen. She felt relieved and she was in a good mood She wanted to talk to someone and as there was no one else to talk to she stood trying to make conversation with Bernice.

She said, "At last those gentlemen have grown up. I thought they never would!" She laughed, and it was as if a bird had chirped. "They didn't want to take Butler in Fyzabad. What nonsense, Bern!"

Bernice peeped into the pot, then went to the pantry for a touch of brown sugar, and after sprinkling it into the pot and putting in the veal she went upstairs and came down with the cobweb broom.

"Oh, yes, Bernice, and you see – " Then Olga stopped short when she saw what Bernice was going to do. She said, "Holy heavens! That's jeps up there. Jack spaniards, wasps. Bernice! Bernice you can't remove that little nest. I'm in the kitchen! When I'm gone call Simon to smoke them out."

"To smoke them out, Madam? You want to burn down the house? These jeps only came here yesterday, I don't know why. They looking for a place to build something, but not over *my* head!" She put down the broom in the corner.

Mrs Mavrogordato laughed. She was looking up at the ceiling where about five or six jack spaniards clustered round one another. She giggled nervously. She was thinking there was another jack spaniard who was soon to be smoked out.

Bernice looked up, then took the cobweb broom again to get rid of the little nest, and before she could look round Olga Mavrogordato had fled up the stairs.

35

T̲H̲E̲ crowing of the cocks woke up Jonas. He was sleeping downstairs in his storeroom, in front of the big open space he called the gym. He stretched and pushed open the door of the storeroom. Outside, the night was black. He could see nothing. He got up from the plank upon which Elsie had spread some old clothes to make a mattress for him and which had made his back a little stiff. His heart was thumping as he looked out into the blackness, and he was wondering what sort of day this day would turn out to be.

After a few moments he heard stirring on the other plank beside his, and he looked back and said, "Uriah?"

There was a little grunt and then the voice said, "Oh, is you. You up?"

"Aha."

"I wonder what the time is now?"

"Well, the cocks done crow. At least first cock done gone. It look like something like half past four."

Butler lay on his plank, and his heart started to thump too. He said, "Ah was dreaming and in me dream I forget completely today is Saturday. You could beat that?"

"You was dreaming? What you dream?"

Butler chuckled. He said, "I ain't Mamselle Marie, you know."

"I only hope the night shift didn't go on. This is the great test. Oh God, Uriah, if they let us down, no amount of water will wash us. We'll be so shame. Hickling and Power, and this Mavro what-you-call-it. And even this Lance-Corporal John, they'll laugh till they drop. You with me? What you thinking?"

"I ain't thinking nothing. This is the morning of mornings and I have faith. Help us, Lord! I hope every man jack on the night shift stayed away from Apex last night. As planned. And I hope when they down tools every man coming to Emporium yard. Hundreds of them. And they'll see us. Let them see us. Let them – "

"You'll be talking to them, Uriah? You addressing them?"

"But of course. I have to give them pep. I have to give them courage. Men with families on strike? Men not working and mouths to feed? I have to congratulate them and comfort them."

"We going over to Emporium at about six – you still saying that?"

"Yes, because from about six they beginning to come out. The morning shift. What I told them was, instead of going to work they coming to Emporium yard. So they gathering from six, and so around seven so when work start almost everybody in Emporium yard. And we want to keep them there until about ten o'clock. I'll be telling them the sacrifice is not for Uriah Butler. No, Sir!" He rolled over on the plank and looked at Jonas. "No, Sir, not for Uriah alone. The sacrifice is for themselves and for their children and for generations to come. And we'll be talking about the just cause. But wait, look how outside clearing up! Thank you, Jesus. The morning's here, Jonas."

Jonas looked and his heart thumped. The night was no longer black, but grey. His first thought was to run up the steps and wake up the two ladies. But he did not want to get too excited. He looked at Uriah. "What you think I should do now?"

"Well, we have to get ready. It must be at least half past five. Perhaps we can't even get strong coffee now. I ain't hearing anything upstairs so perhaps they still sleeping." He rose and sat up. "You better go up and rouse them quick. Then if we could prepare and get dressed then go over to Emporium yard." He looked at the other wall and thought a little. He thought about something that was disturbing him. He nodded his head slowly. Then he rolled over again. When he noticed Jonas getting up but still holding on to the door of the storeroom, he said, "You still here? What's the matter, boy? Why you don't go and wake up the ladies?"

Jonas was so overcome he could hardly move. There was no response from him. When Butler realised what was happening he got up and went to him.

Butler said, "Heroes don't cry. This is *our* day. We waited for it so long. Come on, man, Hothead, let's cry tomorrow. Go and wake up the girls, man."

He went to the back of the storeroom where there was a little window, and he looked out. The morning was already light grey and there were many stars in the sky. Silently he sang in his mind,

Morning star begin to rise
Rising till the break of day,
Children awake, awake, awake,
Children awake, awake, awake.

He turned back to encourage Jonas again, but Jonas had gone upstairs. He said to himself, *Buzz don't lie down again. Get up. Let Elsie and the Mamselle see you. Come on. Go upstairs.*

The two ladies were not only awake but had made coffee and were already dressed and preparing to come downstairs. Butler was surprised and pleased. Jonas was still so overcome with emotion that tears were still running down his cheeks.

Elsie said, "What's wrong with you, boy? You didn't want today to come or what?"

Butler winked and she stopped. Butler said, "I smelling coffee."

The lady in mauve tried to pour a cup. Butler watched her well. She was trying to appear normal but her heart, too, was full. And he thought to himself, although he never knew it before, that although Jonas was a hothead, he was really soft, and it was Elsie who was tough like a rock. And that although Mamselle Marie Vidale was so impressive, and could appear so forceful, almost arrogant, that was only a front.

He had already sat at the table, having the coffee, and he said to them, "It's nearly six, you know. Let's try and make it to Emporium."

Elsie put on what she called her 'crêpe soles' and she gulped down her coffee. She was wearing a red dress with a white band. She said, "Jonas, you was telling me about the colours you saw in Butler's place once. These is my colours: red for victory, white for purity, and black for strength. Dress red, belt white, skin black. That's it. Okay, I ready. Drink up your coffee, boy, and let's go. Mr Uriah, you and the Mamselle could start going down the steps. Me and me hothead right behind. Let me lock up, eh, and let's go. Look, hear that police siren. We better move fast. Things happening already. Come, come, let's go!"

36

THINGS were certainly happening when Elsie, Marie Vidale, Jonas and Uriah Butler reached Emporium Hall. It was just after six but already there was a crowd in the yard. The great majority were the workmen on strike, and these were in militant mood. So much so that Mamselle Marie said, "Uriah, wait. The fellers too excited."

"I'll have to go in at some time."

Elsie did not say anything. They moved off again and Jonas said, "Come on, let's get in."

When they walked in, and when the crowd noticed Butler, there was wild commotion. Elsie held on to Jonas and Jonas to Marie Vidale, and what with the jostling and jamming and pushing, the three of them managed to free themselves and to move on to a less crowded part of the Emporium yard. The chant had risen all round the ground, "Hail to the Lord's annointed", and not too far from where the three were standing there were women in white singing in a calm and serene way: "Bread of Heaven, Bread of Heaven, feed me till I want no more."

When Elsie saw them, she cried, "Oh God, these are my girls. The Women's Branch. This morning I was wondering where I'd see them or if I'd see them. But now I feel to stand up right here. But the crowd so big we have to keep together. Else somebody will get lost."

Marie Vidale was holding on to both Jonas and Elsie. She joined in the singing for a while, then she said, "Mr Uriah will be safe?" When the crowd had moved on Butler there was nothing they could do. Jonas barely heard her. He said, "This is his place. This is his day. They love him. He bound to be safe." She did not hear.

There was too much of a buzz. Elsie tried to listen without saying anything. She heard nothing distinctly.

In any case, the crowd was much bigger than she had expected and was growing by the moment. Near Emporium gate she had spotted police vans, the blue-green of army uniforms and the cold white steel of rifles. She was not afraid. And she did not mention it.

As the singing pervaded the place Mamselle Marie had both her arms around Jonas and Elsie, and was still singing 'Bread of Heaven'.

The voices of the ladies in white pervaded the place. As the crowd kept growing none of the three could see anything ahead except Emporium Hall. Jonas was uneasy. A big roar went up and the singing ceased.

"Look," Elsie said.

Although the three were swallowed by the crowd, looking slightly upwards they could see Butler climbing the steps of Emporium Hall. In the thunderous applause nobody could hear anything. What was happening was that the crowd who had been surrounding and embracing Butler were now taking him up the steps of Emporium Hall for him to address them.

Jonas's heart thumped. He did not like that. He did not feel it was very safe in this bewildering, excitable crowd. But he was too far from Butler. His head felt hot. He could not even speak to Elsie and Mamselle Marie because in the noise they could not hear. He shook them both and by sign he asked them to remain right there. He disappeared in the crowd, pushing people aside.

The two women held on to each other but could say nothing. Mamselle Marie tried to talk to Elsie, but it was quite impossible. Then both women looked towards Butler who seemed ready to speak.

And it was then Elsie remembered the dream. It was a scene just like this picture before her eyes. A big, sprawling, pinkish high house like Emporium Hall, a man with a loud-speaker being taken up the steps, the man on the verandah … . It was exactly the same picture, and the only thing that remained to complete that picture was, yes, fire.

Her mind came back to the moment as Butler walked to the banister to start speaking. The crowd fell silent.

Butler's booming voice cried, "Brothers and sisters, friends and comrades, thank you for coming out in such large numbers. This is the great day of all days. Yes. Thank you my brothers and sisters. Because the enemy did not think us capable of this. Look at this crowd. They did not think us capable of unity and caring, and love for each other, but we are showing them this today. Yes, friends. Congratulations."

Amidst a constant roar of cheering he continued, "This is the great day, the day we are saying 'no' to the Apex slave-master. Let the police listen. Let the police write. Today we are saying 'no' to Hickling and 'no' to Apex, and we are saying 'no' to all the other oil companies because from today we are not going to be bullied and badgered and enslaved in our own land."

The thunderous applause from the strikers did not die down as Butler continued. "Yes, my brothers and sisters, Hickling doesn't want you to strike. But you think he'll give you a little more on your pay? No, not at all. Hickling mean to hell with you. When I was coming in here this morning, you know what I saw. Just there on La Brea Road? Yes, friends, La Brea Road. You know what I saw? I saw the place dark with soldiers and guns. So you ask for bread and they want to give you steel. You ask for bread and they say, 'Here, take bullets.' Yes, brothers and sisters. But I thank you for being strong.

"Friends, let us all thank the Lord for this morning, 19th June, 1937. Because this is the morning of deliverance. Because this is the day of glory. Yes, brothers and sisters. Because they don't want you to strike, but you showing them. They say you hungry. They say you'll crawl back begging."

He raised his voice, "But Butler say you are as strong as the steel they have for you. You'll sacrifice to death in your own land." A roar like thunder went up. He paused. Then he said, "Yes, my friends, the police cannot force you to work. You are not slaves. Butler, the Black British, say this is a British country and you have a right, under British law, to work when you want to, and if the work is oppressive and conditions are not right, to strike if you want to."

There was commotion in the crowd as two police caps came into view near the Hall.

Butler said, "I see the police come up near to listen. I'll speak louder for them to hear. Lance-Corporal John just over there – he could hear me. Look Charlie King right here. What a huge turnout, my friends. Let the police watch. And let the other oil companies take note. It ain't have no workers at Apex this morning. Let Hickling take note. What a huge crowd, my brothers and sisters. And did you hear the beautiful voices singing 'Bread of Heaven'? How beautiful. Brothers and sisters, I come this morning to congratulate you. I asked you to strike as one man, and it's like one man. I'm overjoyed. No morning shift. No afternoon shift. No night shift. This morning Apex is empty. No oil drilling this morning and what Apex will lose today, just a small part of that would have kept you on the job. Their fortunes would have multiplied. But they prefer war." He spoke through a constant roar, and his voice rose hoarsely, "Brethren, he who loveth his treasures will lose them. They brought soldiers with guns and bullets and bayonets. They have soldiers and police like ants here. But we'll never surrender. We want Charlie King to know, and Hickling and Inspector Power, we want them to know, and we want Colonel Mavro – "

"Stop!" The loud harsh voice sounded. It was Charlie King's voice. He pushed his way through the crowd, with Lance-Corporal John and another policeman behind. And behind them was Inspector Edmund Power with a loudspeaker. When they reached up to the steps of Emporium Hall Inspector Power passed a sheet of blue paper to Charlie King, together with the loudspeaker. Charlie King went up the stairs to Butler and asked in a thundering voice, "Are you Tubal Uriah Buzz Butler?" Butler turned to him and with a surprised look said, "Yes, of course." Then Charlie King, with loudspeaker to his lips, turned to the crowd and began to read out the warrant for Butler's arrest. The old warrant. Everyone was stupefied.

Elsie saw this and felt inflamed. She said, "What they want to do, arrest Mr Uriah?" Even Mamselle Marie could not hear her, but they both made a move to push their way towards Emporium Hall.

Hothead, who had long slipped into the crowd, was now right there behind the policemen. Charlie King had already read the sheet of blue paper – the warrant – and he had already arrested Butler and was now going down the steps gripping Butler's arm. Inspector Power was on the other side and Lance-Corporal John was clearing the way in front, followed by Gilroy Price. The silence which had seized the crowd had broken into an angry hum, and the crowd was surging and getting more and more hostile. And now there was the shrill-sounding siren of the army trucks coming to escort Butler to prison. Inspector Power stopped, pushed his hands into his pocket and brought out a pair of bright, glistening handcuffs. He handed them to Charlie King, but as Charlie King made to slip them on Butler's hand, Butler turned and cried to the crowd, "Brothers, you would let them take me away?"

As if from nowhere a man sprang on Charlie King and with a flying butt knocked him down flat. In fact, King did not know what happened even when he was on the ground. In the scuffle and confusion King got back up and tried to use his baton, but getting so many kicks and other blows, he had to break away and disappear in the crowd. Lance-Corporal John fled straight into a battalion of soldiers but Inspector Power was being kicked and beaten on the ground. Soldiers rushed into the Emporium yard. The whole place broke out in riots and the atmosphere was blue with rifle smoke.

The soldiers did not notice Charlie King running to take refuge in Chee Fong's shop just a few doors away. Hothead, who had floored him with a butt to the head, was in hot pursuit, pushing aside people in order to get at Charlie King. Then, breaking out into the road, he spotted him running desperately towards Chee Fong's shop. He chased after Charlie King, hoping to corner him in the shop. He was closing fast on him but as Charlie King, frantic, tried to jump a drain, he slipped and fell into it. Hothead jumped the drain and rushed into the shop. The first thing he noticed was the four-gallon tin in the corner. In the shop were Pa Jakes, Chee Fong and Chee Fong's wife. Jonas was feeling crazed and like a madman. He remembered that it was on Fridays that Chee Fong got the four-gallon tin of gasoline to use in his gaslamp and now he said, "Morning Pa Jakes, Morning Chee, Morning Mrs Chee. Mr Chee I want this tin of gasoline urgently, I could borrow it?"

Before Chee could answer, Hothead grabbed the tin and rushed out of the shop. He poured the whole gallon of gasoline on Charlie King lying in the drain, and then he lit a match. By the time billows of flame burst from the drain Jonas had already disappeared from the scene hotly pursued by soldiers.

It was not until ten o'clock in the morning that Colonel Stephen Mavrogordato arrived from Port of Spain. Lieutenant-Colonel Hickling, who had been notified as soon as the riots broke out, reached Emporium Hall accompanied by soldiers. There were still scuffles, and occasional shots from the police, but the grey smoke from the rifles was obscuring everything. When the lieutenant-colonel met Lance-Corporal John he said, "No need to ask if they held that ruffian. He should now be – "

"We didn't hold him, Sir. He escaped and we looking for him."

"My God," Hickling said, "King let him escape? Where's Corporal King?"

"Charlie King?" the lance-corporal said nervously, "I didn't tell you, Sir?"

"What happened to him?"

"Come, Colonel, Sir."

He walked a little distance with the lieutenant-colonel and showed him Charlie King's charred body in the drain.

"My God!" Hickling said, and buried his face in his hands.

"And I didn't tell you about the Inspector?"

"What happened? They killed him too?"

"Nearly. The soldiers from the frigate had to save him. They had to pick him up from the ground."

"The officers did not contact Colonel Mavrogordato?"

"Yes, but he wasn't in the station and he wasn't home, but they told his wife Olga that he was to – "

"Lance-Corporal you are too bloody long-winded. Does Colonel Mavrogordato know?"

"Yes. The police in San Fernando said they made contact and he's on his way."

"Well that's all. That's all I want to know!"

It was a full hour later that Colonel Mavrogordato arrived at Fyzabad. He knew Butler was still at large and he brought down a company of policemen to join in the search. He had a quick conference with the police units and the soldiers, and he made arrangements for their deployment, for he knew the strike was spreading. He went to the hospital to see Inspector Edmund Power and he was so shocked to see the injuries that he immediately made arrangements for the inspector's transport to England.

In the afternoon he was in Fyzabad again and got the bad news that Butler was not seen. There he heard from Hickling that Apex had come to a complete stop.

When he got together with Hickling and got the police report of what had taken place, he said, "Lieutenant-Colonel, I told you – I warned you that you were not to take Butler in Fyzabad. It was not prudent – "

"But it was Charlie King. He boasted – "

"Yes, but you see what has become of Charlie King. He boasted, yes, he boasted he had taken Dalgo, Bango, and Castillo, all single-handed. But they were not Butler. They did not command the support of the people. They had no just cause – I mean, they had no cause. They were just thieves!"

"And Butler is a crook and a criminal." Hickling's face hardened. But he looked shattered and powerless. Just a single day of the strike seemed to have finished him.

As Colonel Mavrogordato took his leave he said, "I guess by to-morrow they'll find Butler. Keep me informed by the moment. We'll have to deploy police and troops throughout the oilfields because we have to put an immediate stop to this rut. We'll have to see what will happen tomorrow. I want to have a quick meeting with the commanders of those frigates. In other words, Lieutenant-Colonel, and as you yourself told me, Butler always said he was going until the final bell. We are going up to the final bell, too.

37
Epilogue

IT was after midnight, and a tense night of anxiety and pain for Elsie and Marie Vidale. They were not hurt in the riots, but had searched for Uriah Butler and for Jonas in vain. No one, except policemen, was on the streets of Fyzabad, and every time Elsie and Mamselle Marie made the mistake of enquiring for Butler they were put under such rigid interrogation that they soon gave that up. At length, tired and depressed, Elsie and Marie Vidale retired to the house.

They sat up until the late hours of the night. Where could Butler be? What could have happened to Hothead?

At one time during their search their hopes had been suddenly raised when they met Kid Felix. It had been quite early still, and although there was rioting, the shooting had not begun yet. And there had still been plenty of people about. When she had called out to Kid Felix he had run over to her and told her he had just seen Jonas in the crowd. Elsie had said excitedly, "You sure it was he? We looking and we can't find him. You sure sure it was Jonas you saw?"

And Felix had said, "How you mean sure? I have a bout with the man to come in August. In fact I interested in nothing happening to him. But I saw him running, and I hope he was running home. Because I train hard hard and I want to fight for the championship. So when I saw him running and those soldiers behind – "

"What!" Elsie had screamed.

Felix jumped and quickly came to his senses. He had known very well what had happened when soldiers with bayonets had moved upon Jonas. He had even seen when Jonas fell. But it would have made no sense to talk about that.

He had added, "I didn't even see Mr Uriah. But I know Hickling was vexed because I hear him shouting at the lance-corporal. He said Lance-Corporal John had no blinking right to let Butler escape and go into hiding."

But the women had not believed that.

They sat there bewildered and jaded but Elsie managed to get up and she staggered to her bed. Mamselle Marie was going to get up too, but she was so tired that in trying to rise, she swayed back onto the armchair near the door and she remained right there and fell asleep.

It could have been about three o'clock in the morning when Mamselle Marie heard what sounded like a light knock and she jumped up and rushed to the door. She cried, "Mr Uriah? Is you and Jonas?" There were tears of joy.

She was so nervous and fidgety that on the other side of the door Butler whispered, "Do quick, nah. Oh Christ, man. Don't put on the light. Just open – just open the door quick."

Marie Vidale said, "What happen? You alone? Jonas there? You safe?" When she succeeded in opening the door, she cried: "Mr Uriah!" She all but broke down. She said, "Thank you, Lord. Mr Uriah, where's Jonas? He safe?"

"No we ain't – we ain't safe." He was panting. "Jonas didn't come? I saw him running – soldiers – I come to say if Jonas come – don't let him stay – don't let him – stay here because those soldiers – those soldiers will come. Look, I have to vanish. I just wanted to tell – to tell you. Tell Elsie – where's Elsie?"

Mamselle Marie turned round giddily. "I'll call her. Oh Saviour. You have to go? And we ain't see Jonas yet. You want to run? Wait one second. Where you'll go, Mr Uriah – where you'll hide?"

As she turned to go and wake up Elsie, he was already gone.